Mad Eye

Mad Eye

Book Two
Xenofreak Nation

By Melissa Conway

Chapter One

Scott Harding kicked the covers aside and jackknifed up in bed, every hair standing on end, claws fully extended. He didn't have to look at the clock to know it was the middle of the night. This was the third time it had happened this week, but he'd planned ahead, and tonight he wasn't going to let her take control.

He rolled off the mattress and, sweating profusely and bent nearly double, stumbled to the bathroom. The mere act of sliding the shower stall door aside and turning the knob took a monumental effort. Stepping under the cold spray was painful, but thankfully, it provided enough of a physical distraction to take the edge off the intense pleasure flooding his body. The nanoneurons embedded in his cerebellum were doing a number on him, and Padme was the only one who could be behind it.

As the needle-sharp water rained down over his head, Scott began to shake from the cold, his teeth chattering so violently he briefly worried he might chip a tooth. But he wasn't capable of more than fleeting thought as waves of ecstasy flowed through his nervous system. Just when he thought she was never going to let up, never going to release him from this exquisite torture, the pleasure abruptly stopped. It had been years since he'd cried, but as he cranked the water to hot, he felt tears of relief start in his eyes. He stripped off his soaked boxer shorts and rested his forehead against the tile.

This could not continue, and yet the XIA had no idea how to find her, much less stop her.

He stayed in the shower until the small bathroom was filled with steam. When he finally stepped out, he heard the faint musical tone of his holophone. He grabbed a towel from the rack and hurried through his bedroom, snatching the phone off the nightstand.

With a flash of grim hope that it might be Padme herself, he glanced at the ID. It was a holo of a little white mouse.

Carla.

He tapped the holo control to set it to voice, since he couldn't very well project himself naked.

"Hello."

"Scott? Is that you? Something's wrong with Bryn. She's all freaked out! Seriously, she's acting like she's on drugs or something, but she would never take drugs!"

"Slow down. Does she seem, uh, happy or scared?" With his free hand, Scott rubbed the towel through his hair and down his body.

"She's terrified. Ranting and raving. It's-" a screech from the background drowned out Carla's words. Scott didn't recognize the noise as coming from Bryn, but he knew it had. Padme wasn't done meddling this evening, but while Scott had gotten a dose of pleasure, Bryn was being flooded with fear.

"How long has it been going on?" he asked.

"God...about five minutes. I asked her what's wrong, but she's not making any sense. My neighbors are gonna call the cops if this keeps up. Should I call an ambulance?"

He tucked his holophone between his cheek and shoulder and pulled on the jeans he'd discarded on the floor earlier. "No. They won't know what to do. I'll be there as soon as I can. Tell her it's her nanoneurons. Tell her...they're malfunctioning, and she should distract herself."

"I can't tell her *anything*! She's too far gone. I'm so worried, Scott. Please hurry."

He disconnected and quickly finished dressing before tucking his gun into its holster. He grabbed his leather jacket and left the apartment, taking the stairs two at a time to the parking garage. The temperature was typical for January; a not-so-balmy thirty degrees Fahrenheit, but his motorcycle cooperated for once and started on the first try. The trip to Carla's apartment building in Brooklyn took almost twenty minutes, even with him speeding through the nearly empty streets.

When he knocked, Carla yanked the door open as if she'd been hovering over the doorknob. She wore a tattered black silk kimono and was smoking a cigarette. She pointed. "Over there."

He didn't see Bryn at first, but as he got closer, he spotted her huddled on the floor in the corner of the room. Her arms were wrapped around her legs, knees pulled tightly to her chest. The quills on her head were puffed up defensively.

He squatted down and said gently, "Hey."

He halfway expected her to explode, but her voice came soft and weak, "Hey."

"Is it over?" he asked.

"I think so." She looked up. Her green eyes were huge and bleak. "What *was* that?"

He wanted to tell her. He wanted to wipe that look of devastated confusion from her face. But the XIA had been specific about what he could and could not reveal to her. As long as she still had access to visit her father in prison, she might inadvertently pass along information that could cripple the investigation.

But he wasn't going to lie. "I can't say."

Her voice shook. "You told Carla it was my nanoneurons. They malfunctioned?"

Harsh light shining down on her quills from the nearby floor lamp sent jagged black shadows slanting down the wall behind her. Sometimes, and not just because the quills gave her the illusion of toughness, he forgot how vulnerable she was. She'd not only proven to be resourceful under extreme duress but had somehow retained her sweetness when other girls might have turned bitter and defensive. This, though...this attack from what would appear to be her own psyche - as if she were suddenly struck with a violent mental illness - this she couldn't fend off with cleverness.

He held out his hand and said, "Come on. Get up."

Her fingers were ice cold. He led her to the couch and the pullout bed she'd been sleeping on when Padme attacked. Bryn collapsed face down onto a tangle of blankets and burst into tears. Scott gently rubbed her back, sliding his cougar pads up and down the patterned flannel of her pajamas. He glanced over at Carla, who was standing nearby with a freshly lit cigarette. The older woman blew out a stream of smoke, placed a fist on her hip and demanded, "How you gonna fix *this*, hero?"

Chapter Two

Normally, Bryn loved to ride on the back of Scott's motorcycle; it gave her an opportunity to put her arms around him. But this morning she was too on edge to enjoy much of anything. She simply could not stop thinking about last night. It had started in her sleep, when a perfectly pleasant dream about swimming with Scott in a warm, iridescent pool had gone horribly awry. In the dream, he'd suddenly changed into a cougar and begun mauling her until the water was scarlet with blood. She woke under an unrelenting spell of pure fear, as if the imminent danger inspired by the nightmare was unable to switch itself off. In her eighteen years, she'd never felt anything like it - not when she'd been kidnapped, not when she'd faced torture, not when Fournier's underground facility was burning all around her and she had no way out. Even under those dire circumstances she'd retained enough sanity to fight back. Last night, not even the smallest corner of her mind had been spared from the bombardment of terror; there'd been no place for her to take refuge.

It had been the single most horrific experience of her life to date. A twenty-minute trip through several circles of Dante's inferno, all without leaving Carla's modest apartment.

She'd gotten very little sleep despite the fact that Scott had bunked out on the floor next to the pullout bed. He'd made a call to his handler not long after sunrise and now they pulled up to the gate of XIA headquarters, where Scott waved to the guard and held his palm under a holoscanner. When the gate didn't automatically open, the guard approached. He had a light blue surgical mask over the lower half of his face.

"I'm sorry, sir," he said. "Security's been upped. I'll need to I.D. your guest, too."

Bryn handed the guard her driver's license and unfastened the chinstrap of the helmet covering her quills. When she removed it, the guard's eyebrows rose in alarm and he stepped back, saying hastily, "Oh! Wait here."

He went back to his booth. Bryn saw through the reinforced glass that he was calling someone. A few minutes later he was back. He handed her driver's license back and said, "Sorry about that. How are you this morning, Miss Vega?"

"Fine, thank you." It was a lie, of course. Even now, while casually exchanging pleasantries with the guard, she felt twinges of last night's fear pinging along her nervous system.

When she and Scott entered the building, she went to the left to wait in line for the full-body scanner, while he went to the right, pulling a gun she didn't know he'd been carrying from the holster at the small of his back and setting it into a plastic bin. All the employees seemed to be wearing the same blue surgical masks as the gate guard.

She and Scott met on the other side of the security barrier. He holstered his gun and asked one of the guards, "What's with the masks?"

"Just a precaution. There was an incident at the downtown courthouse a few days ago."

Bryn exchanged a concerned look with Scott. She'd known it would only be a matter of time before Dr. Fournier's handiwork began to surface again. Her frank discussion with the doctor when he thought he was dying had confirmed for the XIA what they already suspected: Fournier had branched out from bioengineering and cloning into experimentation with a deadly bio-agent. His main facility may have been destroyed, but he and his staff had gotten away and a madman like him would surely set up shop elsewhere.

They took the elevator to the ninth floor and walked down a long, deserted hallway. There were no pictures to break up the monotony of the white walls. Even the carpet was boring; grey and unpatterned. Bryn had been here before just the once, after the fire, for a 'debriefing.' It was still a cold, impersonal place, just what you'd expect from the headquarters of an elite branch of the government. The Xenofreak Intelligence Agency wasn't a secret organization, but hardly anyone knew it existed nonetheless, and Bryn supposed that was the way they preferred it.

The end of the corridor opened onto a reception area. A lone woman sat at a counter behind a square of the ubiquitous reinforced glass. This woman, too, had a mask over the lower half of her face, but Bryn saw her eyes crinkle in a welcoming smile.

"Well, good morning, Agent Harding. Ms. Fox is expecting you."

A buzz and a click heralded the unlocking of a heavy security door to the left. Scott led the way into the interior, an open space crowded with cubicles colored a slightly lighter shade of grey than the carpet. The office was bustling with personnel going about their business. To the casual observer, this might be any other place of business, but to Bryn, the professionally dressed men and women all seemed uncommonly fit and she suspected that like Scott, most of them were packing concealed weapons.

Over the last several months, ever since Bryn had been forced to undergo the surgical xenografting of a porcupine pelt where her hair used to be, she'd amassed a collection of headwear designed to hide her quills. She'd been in such a state of upset when she left this morning that she hadn't brought a hat or scarf with her. She caught several sidelong glances from the XIA personnel. A few stared openly.

The story of Bryn's kidnapping and mutilation had been broadcast all over the world, so it was unlikely the gawkers didn't recognize her, even if they didn't know the details of Scott's undercover operation. Still, she worried they would judge her. She couldn't have the graft removed altogether because the doctors had warned her they didn't know what her nanoneurons would do if they weren't able to perform their intended function. She did have the option of clipping the quills short, but in the end, she'd felt a strange kinship with her donor porcupine. The poor animal had been bioengineered by Dr. Fournier to be compatible with humans for the express purpose of harvesting its body parts as decorative grafts. Bryn knew it was irrational, but she didn't want the little guy's sacrifice to have been in vain. Besides the fact that twice now her quills had actually protected her.

She lifted her chin a little higher as they walked to one of the doors set along the perimeter of the office space. Scott knocked, the fur on his knuckles muffling the sound.

"Come in."

Inside the office, Shasta Fox sat behind a wooden desk, tapping rapidly at the holo keyboard displayed in front of her. She glanced up as they entered and swept a hand over her work, dimming it from their view.

"Sit," she said.

Scott's eyebrows shot up. "You on an op?"

As Bryn perched on the edge of one of two chairs in front of the desk, she flashed on the first time she'd seen Shasta; right after the older woman had rescued them from the blocked escape tunnel. Bryn had been too sick from smoke inhalation to register much about Shasta's appearance other than that she was a thin black woman with very short, greying hair.

Today Shasta looked completely different. She'd gotten hair extensions that hung to her shoulders. The dark brown strands curled gracefully around a face that, unlike the few times Bryn had seen her since that first meeting, was expertly made up. Her features were too austere for her to be called pretty, but she was attractive - like an uncut diamond in a fancy new setting.

Shasta's red lips pursed. "You know I don't go into the field. If you're referring to my appearance, that's not what's relevant here, is it?"

Scott sat in the other chair and replied, "No, ma'am."

"Tell me again what happened," Shasta said.

Scott leaned back in his chair. "Remember that, uh, malfunction of my nanoneurons we talked about earlier this week?"

"Quit dancing around it," Shasta interjected. "If Padme Lango is attacking Bryn, the agency can no longer justify leaving her on her own. She needs to be taken to a secure facility."

"What?" Bryn looked from Shasta to Scott. "*Padme* did that to me?"

As Scott avoided her gaze, she suddenly remembered what he'd said last night. She'd asked him what had caused her nanoneurons to malfunction and he'd muttered, "I can't say." He hadn't meant that he didn't know; he meant he couldn't tell her.

A slow fury began burning in her stomach. She'd been kept in the dark for the last four months, never knowing what the XIA was doing to find Fournier, terrified that at any moment he'd send his goons after her. Scott had supposedly been pulled from the investigation to teach new recruits how to fight, but now it seemed that wasn't all he'd been up to.

"She can *control* my nanoneurons? When were you going to tell me this?"

"I wanted to," he said, shooting Shasta a dark look.

Shasta pressed her lips together. "It wasn't an issue until now. Padme's equipment and files were destroyed in the fire. There was no evidence she had a backup system, but now it's obvious she either did, or she was able to recreate the program. Regardless, we know from the number of xenos who've died of apparently natural causes from inside our prison system that she has the ability to literally scare anyone implanted with Fournier's nanoneurons to death."

A sickening chill travelled from the base of Bryn's brain to her ankles. "My God," she murmured. She looked at Scott. He'd asked Shasta if she remembered discussing his nanoneuron 'malfunction' last week. "She did it to you, too?"

Scott blanched and avoided her eyes again. "Yeah, kind of."

Bryn didn't have a chance to ask what he meant, because Shasta tapped a holokey and said, "Send Agent Alton in, please."

A disembodied female voice responded, "Right away."

Scott leaned forward. "*Is* there a secure facility? Where Padme can't reach her?"

Shasta nodded. "It's not ours, but the FBI has agreed to accommodate us on this one. The facility is crude, and it hasn't been used in years, but it was constructed in an old Atlas Missile silo two hundred feet underground so signals from nearby cell towers are blocked."

"Cell towers?" Bryn asked.

"That's how Padme activates the pleasure or fear," Shasta replied.

Pleasure? Bryn blinked and looked at Scott. An uncharacteristic flush stained the tops of his cheekbones.

A knock sounded on the door and Shasta barked, "Come."

A man entered, shut the door and moved to the side of Shasta's desk, standing with his hands shoved in the pockets of his ragged, dirty jeans. He had a full beard and his shaggy brown hair was matted and greasy. Bryn's nostrils flared in disgust as a pungent combination of body odor and sour beer followed in his wake.

Shasta sighed. "No time to shower and change, Agent Alton?"

"Two hours ago I was deep under cover. Had me a cozy crib under the Yakaburra underpass. Six months of work and I get yanked to babysit your girl." He jerked his head towards Bryn, who detected more than a trace of resentment in the brown eyes that flickered briefly over her face.

"Is your cover story in place?" Shasta asked.

He nodded. "Local cops arrested me in front of my crew, and as far as any of them know, I'll be extradited to Utah for murder."

"Hey," Scott said. "I recognize you. You're a Mad Eye."

Agent Alton sent Scott a jaunty salute. "No flies on you."

Bryn knew about the Mad Eye gang - everyone did. They were the chief rivals of the XBestia, the xenofreak gang Scott had infiltrated to get to Dr. Fournier.

"Agent Alton will escort Bryn to the facility," Shasta said, "and guard her twenty-four seven."

"Why not me?" Scott asked at the same time Bryn burst out with, "For how long?"

Shasta pointed at Scott. "Because Padme is clearly trying to contact you. When you didn't go looking for her, she started in on Bryn to more effectively get your attention. Agent Alton's xenograft wasn't done by

Fournier and it's not functional - he doesn't have nanoneurons so she can't get to him."

Shasta turned to Bryn. "In answer to *your* question: for as long as it takes. You don't really want it to happen again, do you?"

Bryn felt her stomach clench at the very thought. "No."

Shasta placed her hands on the desk and pushed her chair back. "This is the only way to protect you."

She stood, and Scott and Bryn followed suit.

"Agent Alton," Shasta said, "You have your orders. Agent Harding, I'm not done with you."

Agent Alton went to the door and opened it, looking at Bryn expectantly. She leaned towards Scott and reached out for his hand. He clasped her fingers briefly, turning what she'd intended as a goodbye gesture into an impersonal handshake.

He'd been distant these last few weeks, just when she'd thought they were getting closer. She'd attributed it to the stress of work - and she'd probably been right - except it now seemed the nature of his work wasn't what she'd thought it was.

As she walked out the door, she wondered if she would ever really know Scott Harding.

Chapter Three

Scott watched them leave, frustrated that he couldn't properly say goodbye. Bryn had looked at him like he'd suddenly become a stranger. He wanted to reassure her, but even if he could honestly tell her everything would be alright, he wasn't about to get sentimental in front of Shasta and Alton.

When the door clicked closed, Shasta sat back down in her chair, but Scott was too wired. He barely stopped himself from pacing back and forth in the little office.

"The incident in the courthouse the other day," he said. "From the masks, I assume it had something to do with the typhoid?"

Before answering, Shasta tapped a holokey again and said, "Send in Dr. Padilla."

Then she reactivated her holo monitor. "Do you recognize this man?"

The hologram had been taken from a downward angle, but the subject's face was turned upward directly facing the camera. His head was shaved completely bald, but from the slight shadow of regrown stubble around his ears, Scott could tell the man would have been mostly bald anyway. The subject had a large, doughy nose and a low brow.

"Never seen him before."

"This is a still from a security camera at the courthouse, taken three days ago. As we speak, four civilians and six county employees are in quarantine at Middleborough Hospital, every one of them apparently in the last stages of this damned super typhoid. We can verify this man, identified as Robert Cruise, had contact with seven of them. Witnesses said he had a xenograft on his forearm."

Scott wished the holo was clear enough to see the subject's eyes better. Did the guy know he was a living, breathing bioweapon?

Shasta unwittingly answered Scott's unvoiced question. "Witnesses also said he was coughing - a lot - without covering his mouth. Not genuine coughing, though. More than one witness said he seemed to be faking it. It looks like he deliberately took every opportunity to spread this thing."

Someone rapped on the door and Scott opened it, stepping aside as a petite woman with black hair pulled back into a loose bun entered. She was Asian, seemed to be in her mid-to-late twenties, and quite beautiful. From her flawless skin to her bee-stung lips, she reminded Scott of the antique porcelain figurines lining his grandmother's shelves.

She looked at him and did what most people did when they first saw his face: her dark eyes followed the line of the scar that sliced through his eyebrow, broke off at his eye socket and started again on his cheek, ending in a pucker on his upper lip. From the question in her eyes, he figured she was wondering why he'd kept such a disfigurement when it was so easy in this day and age to erase scars. She then took in the fact that his brown hair was pulled back into a short ponytail, all but the hair from the top of his ears down, which had been shaved. He knew her impression would be that he was a punk - that's what she was supposed to think.

Shasta stood. "Dr. Padilla, thank you for coming. This is Agent Scott Harding. He'll be working with your team."

Scott held his hand out, but Dr. Padilla only looked at it, her doll-like face frozen in a look of wary fascination. Scott curled his fingers into a loose fist and dropped his hand. Shasta cleared her throat, effectively disrupting the awkward moment. "Dr. Padilla is with the CDC. She's an expert on infectious bacteria."

Dr. Padilla's slight smile looked forced. "It's ironic, given my profession, but I'm a bit of a germophobe. Nothing personal."

Scott shrugged. This wouldn't be the first time he'd been snubbed. He'd long since stopped trying to explain why he'd gotten his xenoalteration. It didn't matter that his motivation had been selfless; some people simply could not understand why he'd chosen to essentially mutilate himself.

Shasta sat back down. "Alright. To bring you up to speed, Doctor, the man in this holo is the suspected carrier. He's been identified as Robert Cruise, a xeno with a few arrests on his record, but nothing more serious than a misdemeanor. Agent Harding will be going out to Cruise's last known address this morning to bring him in for questioning."

"I'd like to come along," Dr. Padilla said. "If this man is sick, we'll need to get him isolated as soon as possible."

"I'm afraid that would be too dangerous for you. From what we know, Cruise is deliberately infecting people. Agent Harding's xenograft protects him from exposure."

Dr. Padilla's arched eyebrows rose. "The CDC has found no evidence to support the hypothesis that xenografts boost human immunity."

"Have they looked? For evidence?" Scott asked. "Because I haven't been sick a day since I got these." He held his hands up.

"While it's true the bacterium that causes typhoid doesn't produce symptoms in animals," her eyes slid to Scott's hands, "just because you've been hale and hearty, and just because the XIA has identified one xeno who *might* be a healthy carrier of this disease, doesn't guarantee anything."

"Actually, not only have we identified two carriers now, both xeno, but not one of the *victims* has been a xeno." Shasta smiled like a person who'd made a chess move and declared, "Check."

Dr. Padilla shook her head impatiently. "Which could easily be attributed to statistics; the xeno population makes up only a small percentage of people worldwide. The odds of one of the forty-four identified victims thus far being a xeno are unlikely. What's more relevant to this investigation is how the typhoid is being transmitted."

"It's airborne," Shasta said decisively.

"That's beyond unlikely. The disease is transmitted through contact with infected feces or urine. These particular bacteria reside in the human intestinal tract, not the respiratory system. We've done cultures on every single victim and haven't found a thing to support an airborne mode of transmission."

Shasta threw her hands in the air. "Because it doesn't spread through the victims!"

"That I *will* concede to," Dr. Padilla responded. "As far as we can tell, none of the victims have infected anyone they've been in contact with. Which is unusual but given the rapid onset and severity of the disease, could be explained by the patients not having had *time* to spread it before it immobilized them."

"I understand the CDC has also conceded that the bacteria have mutated?" Scott recognized Shasta's 'patient' voice when he heard it.

Dr. Padilla sighed. "Bacterial mutation is more common than people think. It's a survival adaptation. We've sequenced the genome of this sample and, yes, it's different from the known varieties, but not significantly so. In fact, it closely resembles one particular multi-drug-resistant strain that many undeveloped nations have been dealing with for the last twenty years."

"Resembles how?" Scott asked. "Under the microscope or from the symptoms?"

Dr. Padilla licked her lips, a nervous gesture that told Scott she was headed into territory she was less sure of. "Not the symptoms. Normally, secondary infection arising from typhoid is rare, but in one hundred percent of the patients thus far, it's developed into a deadly form of bacterial meningitis. This strain multiplies explosively, much more quickly than has ever been documented before."

"What about immunization?" Shasta asked. "Four of the victims have a history of travel outside the U.S. and their medical records show they were inoculated against typhoid."

Dr. Padilla slowly nodded. "Vaccination may help. We'll have to see if those patients do better than the others. Otherwise, the vaccine may not be effective against this strain."

Shasta cleared her throat again. "I don't agree with this, but for the time being, our respective directors have decided against warning the public and causing a potential panic. When and if another incident occurs, Agent Harding will accompany your team to the site. I'm sure I don't need to remind either of you of the sensitive nature of this assignment."

Scott nodded, but Dr. Padilla just stared at Shasta.

"I want you to know," Shasta said, staring back, "that regardless of the CDC's stance on it, we have solid intel indicating that xenos *are* immune. Intel from the source; the man who first identified the pathogen: Dr. Fournier."

Dr. Padilla's eyes widened. "I'd heard a rumor he was behind this. What I don't understand is why he would send his people out to deliberately infect the public."

"There's been some educated speculation as to why," Shasta said, "but that's need-to-know. The important thing is to contain this thing before anyone else dies."

"And before word gets out," Scott said.

"Exactly." Shasta dimmed her monitor again. "It will be impossible to suppress it for much longer as it is, and once John Q. Public hears about it, there will be panic, not to mention demands for retribution from a lot of innocent xenos, and we all know what that means."

Scott flexed his claws, ignoring the badly disguised look of revulsion that crossed Dr. Padilla's face.

"Bloodbath time," he said.

Chapter Four

Bryn cracked the window and held her hand to her face, but even though she surreptitiously blocked her nostrils and breathed out of her mouth, Agent Alton's pungent body odor was overwhelming. It was patently clear from his brusque attitude that he didn't want this assignment and resented being pulled from his last one. She wondered if he'd deliberately not taken a shower in order to punish her.

She watched him out of the corner of her eyes as he drove in what she could only interpret as a brooding silence. Under the grime, he had a surprisingly nice profile. His nose was straight and his jawline firm - what she could see of it under the scruffy beard. He'd taken off his filthy pea coat, revealing an equally filthy t-shirt. His lean, muscular arms were covered with scrolling black tats that extended up his wrists and disappeared under his sleeves. She didn't see a xenograft, but assumed he had one somewhere.

When they'd first gotten into the beat-up old truck, she'd asked him where they were going and he'd responded curtly, "Were you listening to Agent Fox?"

After about ten minutes, she'd asked what she was supposed to wear, and he'd told her there was a bag for her in the back of the truck.

She almost asked what was in the bag. Had they sent someone over to Carla's to get her own things while she'd waited for him to take care of some unfinished XIA business, or was she stuck wearing generic XIA clothing for the next who-knows-how-long? But it was clear Agent Alton didn't want to talk. She continued watching him as he drove, noting the occasional slight movement of his lips, as if he was arguing with someone internally.

The answers to her questions could wait. As much as she didn't want to walk away from her life and go into hiding, she was grateful the XIA had finally decided to protect her. Two days ago she would have been outraged at the suddenness, but not after last night.

She pulled her holophone from her purse and popped the earbugs out of their compartment. She'd just put them in her ears and accessed her playlist when Agent Alton reached over and snatched the phone out of her hand. To her astonishment, he tossed it out the window onto the freeway.

She turned to him, her mouth open wide in indignation. "What the?"

"It can be traced. Do you have any other electronics in there?" He gestured to the purse.

Bryn sighed and handed him the earbugs. He tossed them, too, and continued driving without further comment.

Every time they went uphill, the truck engine growled and sputtered and filled the cab with a noxious combination of exhaust and gasoline that competed with Agent Alton's funk. It reminded her of the Warehouse, with its strange, overpowering chemical smell. She doubted the truck was up to EPA standards. On the dash, none of the gauges seemed to be working. There was no clock, so she was forced to estimate how long they'd been travelling. About an hour out of the city, they exited near the Come and Shop outlet mall. From there, Agent Alton drove into the hills through an upscale housing development and beyond that to a country road that wound on and on. He turned several times, each road getting narrower and bumpier. He finally drove down a dirt path, where a low concrete building squatted in the center of an overgrown field.

He shut off the engine, which turned over a few more times as if gasping in protest. Dust from the road hung around them in the stillness of the morning.

"Home, sweet home," he said.

Shasta had said it was a converted missile silo, but somehow Bryn had expected the 'house' part of 'safe house' to apply. This place was as rundown and scary as the Warehouse had been.

Agent Alton took a long, narrow bag out from behind the seats and got out. He reached into the bed of the truck and slung two more bags over his shoulder, then leaned into the cab and asked, "What are you waiting for? I'm not the bellboy. You carry your own."

Bryn scrambled out of the truck. She recognized the battered gym bag he handed her as coming from the back of Carla's bedroom closet and sighed in relief. Having her own stuff would help.

"What about those?" She pointed to several cardboard boxes.

"Food. Supplies. I'll bring that in later."

There was no sign of a path, so they forged ahead through the underbrush around to the back of the building. Mounted on the wall next to a large green-painted steel door was a standard holoscanner. Agent Alton held his palm under it and a moment later there was a dull clang from somewhere inside. He leaned on the door handle, which gave under his weight, but not easily. The entire structure had been built generations ago - built to withstand a nuclear attack. Bryn hoped it was strong enough to withstand an attack from Padme.

It was pitch black inside. Agent Alton stopped a few feet in and said, "Hold the door."

Bryn placed her foot against the bottom of the heavy door, but found she had to lean her whole body into it to keep it from closing. He went in, trailing a hand along the wall. Seconds later, a line of bare bulbs running down the center of the low concrete ceiling lit up, revealing a long tunnel. She'd never been claustrophobic, but as the door closed on the brightness of the day, she felt as if she'd been entombed.

Halfway down the tunnel, there was a deep booming sound that she felt as a pressure change in her ears more than heard. "That's the ventilation system kicking in," he said. "We triggered it when we entered, so it should get warmer in here."

At the end of the tunnel, a studded metal door led to a stairwell that was also lit with bare bulbs, one per level. The spiral staircase had white-painted mesh steps that were worn down to the metal along the path countless feet had trod over the last half century. Shasta had said the facility was two hundred feet deep, and as Bryn leaned over the rail to look down, she felt a wave of vertigo that prompted her to pull back and focus on Agent Alton's back. It was cold in the stairwell and got colder with every clanging step of their descent. A faint breeze blew upward.

At the first level, there was a metal platform with a door set in the concrete. Agent Alton stopped, but instead of opening it right away, he lifted his chin and his nostrils flared. "You smell that?"

Bryn had a hard time keeping her face neutral. "I smell you."

He laughed. "Yeah, alright."

He opened the door and flipped another switch. Light bloomed from a modest chandelier hanging over a dining room table. He went further in and switched on two floor lamps and a table lamp next to a large beige sectional couch. To Bryn's surprise, the interior did indeed look like a house; albeit a sterile one. There were walls and doors and furniture. No windows, of course, but several paintings hung on the walls; bright landscapes that seemed to have been picked deliberately to offset the lack of

16

a real view. Other than the paintings, the decor was utilitarian, just like the XIA safe house she'd stayed in with Scott.

She didn't want to think of Scott and the night he'd held her in his arms. The night she'd been willing to give him anything he wanted. He hadn't felt the same way then, and it looked like he still didn't. She wondered what she was to him - a friend? A responsibility?

Agent Alton pointed to one of four doors, the one furthest to the left. "That's your room."

He put his hand on the knob of the next door down from hers and she said, "Um...sir?"

He stopped and looked almost offended. "The name's Jason."

"Oh, okay... Jason. Are we far enough down?"

He took his holophone out of his pocket, and she rolled her eyes. *Her* phone could be traced, but not his?

He must have seen her reaction, because he said, "My phone's secure. And it looks like we do get a weak signal, but there are something like ten more levels to this facility. If this Padme chick activates your nanoneurons, we'll go down until it stops."

Bryn wasn't okay with that. "I'd rather just go where the signal can't get through at all." She didn't want to experience one additional second of the fear that Padme could begin dishing out at any moment.

He shrugged. "Fine by me, but I'm staying here. The other levels are unfinished."

He opened the door and she caught a glimpse of bathroom fixtures. After he'd disappeared, she stood there for a moment, trying to summon the courage to explore the other levels. Ultimately, she decided against it, thinking that maybe the weakened cell tower signal meant Padme's attack would also be weakened.

She shook off a feeling of premonition and entered her designated bedroom. It was small, about ten-foot square, lit with a plain dome light in the center of the ceiling. There was nothing whatsoever on the white walls aside from a vent that began to blow warm air into the room. The mattress on its steel frame was bare. The only other piece of furniture was a narrow standing cupboard in the corner made of white laminate. She opened it and found sheets, two blankets and a pillow all sealed in plastic.

After she'd made up the bed, she went through the bag from Carla's house. It was clear from the contents that Carla herself had packed it. Besides the undergarments and clothes Bryn was most likely to need, Carla had made up a smaller bag of Bryn's favorite cosmetics, the special veterinary shampoo she had to use on her quills, and her toothbrush and toothpaste. Plus, at the bottom of the bag was the stuffed panda Scott had bought her at the zoo the day they'd gone to see the real panda they'd rescued from Dr. Fournier.

Bryn buried her face in its fur, inhaling the faint, familiar odor of cigarette smoke. She'd nagged her godmother to quit smoking and for the most part, it had worked. Carla only smoked now when she was under duress. Like last night. Bryn felt tears sting her eyes.

Her psyche had finally begun to heal from her father's betrayal, and she'd accepted the new direction her life was going. She would never be the innocent girl she'd been before Dr. Fournier got his hands on her, but she'd come to terms with the limitations of her future. She'd gotten to know Carla during the months she'd stayed with her, and through Carla, had gotten a better idea of who her mother had been.

But all of that had been an illusion. She'd never been safe with Carla, not while Padme was out there. The xenofreak girl had already tried to kill Bryn once, and now she had a weapon that Bryn could only run and hide from.

Chapter Five

Scott held the door for Dr. Padilla as she exited Shasta's office, but when he made a move to leave as well, Shasta said, "Just a moment, Agent Harding."

He let the door close once more.

Shasta opened the top drawer of her desk and removed what looked to Scott to be an old-fashioned pencil box with a tiny bow on top. She handed it to him.

"Happy Birthday."

Scott was twenty years old today, but he felt much older, especially after the last week. He used his forefinger claw to open the hinged lid of the box. Inside was a tube with a medical label on it, like he'd seen on prescription pill bottles.

"Um...thanks."

"It's an auto-injector. Tranquillizer." Shasta made a stabbing motion towards her leg. "In the outer thigh, right through your jeans. It'll take less than a minute to work. You know, in case Padme switches you over to the dark side."

The dark side. If Padme activated his nanoneurons to produce fear instead of pleasure. "This is my birthday present?"

Shasta's red-lipsticked mouth curved in a rare smile. "I thought you'd appreciate it more than flowers."

He chuckled and reached for the door handle. "Well, it's just lovely. Thanks again."

"Scott."

He turned. Shasta's smile had given way to her usual dead serious expression.

"Under no circumstances," she said, "are you to die from a heart attack because you didn't use that tranquillizer on yourself. Do you understand?"

"Yes, ma'am." He put the box in the pocket of his leather jacket.
"That'll be all."

After leaving Shasta's office, he wove his way through the cubicles to the one he shared with another agent. Technically, that agent was Scott's partner, but they'd both been assigned solo duties and almost never crossed paths.

Someone had been watering the plant he and his partner had inherited from the previous occupant of the cubicle. It was some sort of hardy ivy with tendrils that clung to the fabric of the cubicle walls. He wondered idly how an aggressive plant like that would do out from under the halogen lights and into the sunlight. Probably take over the world.

He unlocked his desk drawer. As he was reaching for the keys to his assigned vehicle, someone behind him said, "Agent Harding?"

He twisted his torso around. Dr. Padilla was standing there, an uncertain look on her face.

"I thought you left," he said.

"I'm sure I was supposed to, but I couldn't fight this feeling that I should accompany you when you go see Mr. Cruise."

"No offense, Doc, but next time you should fight a little harder. Even if I thought it was safe, I'd rather jump off the Brooklyn Bridge than go against Shasta's direct order."

Dr. Padilla offered him a wan smile. "She seems...competent."

Scott suspected she'd been about to use a different descriptive word but changed her mind out of politeness.

"Right," he said. "Is there anything else I can help you with?"

"I guess I'm just trying to understand the big picture here. This supposedly rock-solid intel," she made quotation marks with her fingers, "that xenos are immune and Fournier is deliberately infecting them - and then sending them out to further infect the public. How is he finding the carriers? The odds are five percent. Out of a hundred people, only five can potentially spread typhoid."

"Have you ever been to Coney Island? They got more xenos than the sewer has rats."

"So how does he test them all?"

Scott looked away as something occurred to him. "What kind of tests would he need?"

"A blood or stool culture."

He sat down in his office chair and activated his holo keyboard. After accessing the Fournier case files, he scrolled down until he located the transcripts of Bryn's debriefing.

After countless XIA agents had tried and failed, Bryn had single-handedly identified the company Dr. Fournier had been using as a front for his illegal enterprises. Shasta's boss, Deputy Director Mark Unger, had decided against shutting Best Medical Services, Corp down because Fournier was still out there - unaware that the XIA had a bead on his business dealings. Fournier had used his own secretly owned company as the supplier for his bioengineering lab, and to launder the money he made providing illegal xenografts.

XIA analysts hadn't been able to pinpoint any suspicious activity since Fournier's facility had been destroyed, but they were watching Best Medical closely, hoping it would lead them to him when and if he began providing xenoaugmentation services again.

Scott pulled up all the businesses run by Best Medical. As he expected, most of them sold medical supplies. He knew from the smell of her perfume that Dr. Padilla had moved to look over his shoulder, and he was just about to tell her to back off when her arm shot out and she pointed. "There!"

BMS Blood Donation Center.

"Yeah, but the FDA prohibits xenos from giving blood," he said.

"So? Would Fournier let that stop him?"

She had a point. Scott dragged the address for BMS Blood Donation Center to his holophone icon before shutting his computer down and standing.

"I'll walk you out," he said.

"That's it?"

He made a pained face at her. "For you it is. Go do what you do and let me do what I do. Hopefully, we won't have to meet again. No offense."

He stuck with her until the parking garage, when she got off the elevator on the visitor's floor. Something about the way she said, "See you later," made him nervous. In all likelihood, she simply expected them to meet the next time the super typhoid struck, but she didn't have to sound so cheerful about it.

He got into his assigned car, a dark sedan identical to all the other XIA cars, and for that matter, identical to the cars supplied to the FBI and who knows how many other government entities. He knew the agency didn't have the funds to purchase a variety of cars that would better serve an undercover who didn't want to be outed by the very vehicle he drove. At least the sedans were comfortable, reliable, and fast, although he personally hadn't had the opportunity to take it over eighty miles-per-hour. As he drove out of the parking garage, he thought about Bryn and wondered if she was right now riding in a car just like this one.

She'd looked so tired after a restless night where she'd startled awake at every little sound. Since she got up, there'd been smudgy blue half-circles under her eyes and a desperate cast to her every glance, as if she was pleading with him to promise it would never happen again.

God, he wished he could.

Instead, he'd stood by helplessly as she left with Alton, whose xeno name was Dragila, after his infamous xenograft, a dragon that he'd supposedly designed himself out of the skin of a Gila monster. Alton had a nasty reputation as an agent who would do anything to close a case. Some would call it dedication; and Scott was no stranger to that mindset. But he'd heard Alton had been given the same immunity with the Mad Eyes that Scott had been given when he'd been under cover with the XBestia. While Scott had done some things that would forever weigh on his conscience, it was rumored Alton had done much worse - and bragged about it.

Scott drove onto the freeway. The suspect lived in the Bronx, in a neighborhood composed of primarily of low-income xenos - but not as low as the average xenofreak.

It was eleven a.m. when he found a parking spot half a block away from Cruise's apartment building. The people going about their business were xenos of all ethnicities, and most of them openly eyed his sedan. He got out and made sure his claws were easily seen. Leaning against a lamp post nearby was a woman with a frizzy red wig and a short, very tight black dress. She called out to him as he passed, "You wanna date, handsome?"

"Next time," he replied.

Double-parked in front of Cruise's building was a white van. Scott thought at first it was a delivery van until he saw the letters OCME emblazoned on the side.

The medical examiner.

With a feeling of trepidation, he took the front steps to the building's open double doors. The walls of the small foyer were painted various shades of green in layered rectangles that obviously covered graffiti. On the left was a bank of mailboxes. Scott located Cruise's and started up to the third floor. He only got halfway up the first set of narrow stairs when two medics hauling a stretcher made him go back down again. He backed up against the mailboxes to let them pass. Strapped to the stretcher was a black body bag.

"Hey," Scott said to the medics. He nodded to the body bag. "That wasn't apartment 315, was it?"

"318," one of them replied.

"What'd he die of?"

"Do I look like they pay me to know that?"

"Was he a xeno?"

"What are you, a reporter?"

Scott stepped closer and lifted his shirt to display the badge on his belt. "I'm a cop. Now answer my freakin' questions."

If he thought the medic would stop with the sarcasm, he forgot he was in New York City. "They let xenos be cops? What'll they think of next?"

"You wanna stand here over this dead body and debate the subject or you wanna answer me?"

"Come on, man," the other medic said. "I'd like to get to lunch on time for once."

The first medic pushed on the inside of his cheek with his tongue for a second, but he said, "Guy wasn't a xeno. Lived in the building for thirty years. Not popular from what the manager said, but it looks like he croaked from natural causes."

"Thanks." Scott started back up the stairs. On the third floor, he knocked on Robert Cruise's door. No answer. He kept knocking until the next door down, number 321, was yanked open.

"Take a hint already!" The speaker was an elderly black woman in a thin cotton housecoat. "When they don't answer, it means they *ain't home*!"

Before he could ask if she knew where Cruise was, she slammed her door. Scott sighed and went back downstairs. Outside, the van was gone. He walked to his car and found the frizzy-wigged woman leaning against it.

"Sure you don't wanna date?" she asked. "You look like you could use a friend." She lifted her already short skirt up until it was almost indecent. Wrapped around her upper thigh was a snakeskin xenograft in the shape of a snake.

"Nice," he muttered, getting in the car and waving her off. She huffed away and he pulled into traffic, activating his holophone.

"Shasta Fox," she said by way of greeting. "Are you driving, Agent Harding?"

"Yes, ma'am. But I promise I won't look away from the road."

"Did you pick up Cruise?"

"Wasn't home. But one of his neighbors, a non-xeno, was just taken away in a black plastic suit."

"I'll have Dr. Padilla check into it. Did you find a place of work for Cruise?"

"He's on disability, so he could be anywhere. I have a lead on something else, though." Driving through traffic, he told her of his conversation with Dr. Padilla. "I'm headed out to the BMS Blood Donation Center right now."

"Keep me apprised," Shasta said, and disconnected.

Scott fed a parking meter two blocks up from BMS and walked. The air was still cold, but the sun came out from behind the drifting clouds briefly and warmed his back. He decided to stop for lunch at the Holo House Cafe, which was across the street from the center, where he could eat and scope the place out at the same time.

There weren't any empty tables on the terrace, but he spotted a lone woman reading a holo tablet and drinking a cup of coffee. Even before he got close enough to see her face, her pulled-back black hair gave her away.

"Dr. Padilla," he said.

She looked to the right and to the left before leaning towards him and saying quietly, "It's Mia. And since you probably don't want to advertise why you're here, I should call you something other than Agent Harding, don't you think?"

She was trying, but he wasn't charmed. "My name is Scott, and you can't be here."

Chapter Six

Bryn opened her eyes. For a disoriented moment, she didn't recognize her surroundings, but then she remembered laying her head down on the pillow; she must have dozed off. Voices and music came through the wall from the main room.

She sat up, set the panda bear she was clutching aside, and stood, smoothing her hands down her clothes. She was still wearing the jacket she'd arrived in, but even though the room was warmer, she kept it on because the heavy fabric with its high collar protected her neck from her quills. In the living area, she found Jason lounging on the couch. A holovision she hadn't noticed before was blaring some kind of action movie.

He glanced over at her and turned the volume down. "Have a nice nap?"

She nodded, but the truth was, she rarely napped because she hated the groggy feeling it gave her.

"There's no cable," he said. "But we got a huge library of movies."

He'd showered and shaved, and was wearing grey sweatpants, a black t-shirt and white tube socks. Bryn was astonished at the change. Not only did his comment make him seem far more pleasant, but the malodorous man who'd driven her here was gone. She tried not to stare, but the hints she'd gotten from looking at his profile in the truck hadn't prepared her for the face hidden under the beard and hair and grime. He was strikingly handsome.

He noticed her hesitation and paused the movie. "What's wrong?"

"Nothing." She shook her head and looked at the frozen holo of a scantily dressed woman holding a shotgun. "I doubt you and I have the same taste in movies, is all."

"I'm sure we can agree on something. Not much else to do."

She went to the opposite side of the curved sectional and sat, leaning against one of the oversized throw pillows. "Do you like romantic comedies?"

He snorted. "No. Do you like horror flicks?"

Now it was her turn to snort. "Not so much."

They whittled down the acceptable categories and settled on their first movie, a thriller.

Before he queued it up, he said, "You know what? We need popcorn."

He got off the couch, but instead of heading for the little kitchenette, he shoved his feet into a pair of unlaced tennis shoes, opened the door to the stairwell and disappeared. Bryn waited all of two seconds before springing up and following him. She didn't want to be left alone here; the whole place seemed so strange and unnatural, like a dollhouse or an alien habitat for humans meant to fool them into thinking they were home.

She ran up the stairs after Agent Alton - *Jason* - and caught up with him halfway down the tunnel to the entrance.

"What are you doing?" he asked.

"Coming with you. To help carry the boxes."

He shook his head. "Sorry. Too dangerous."

She ignored him and kept pace with his long strides. When they reached the exterior door, he said, "I'm serious. You stay here."

She let out a *tsk* of disappointment, crossed her arms and leaned against the wall.

"Pout all you want," he said, stabbing a finger at the keypad mounted on the wall by the door handle. Four beeps and the little red light turned green. Bryn strained to see but didn't catch the numbers he punched. He leaned on the handle, depressing it downward, and she realized once the door closed behind him, she'd be locked in.

The same feeling she'd gotten earlier, as if something bad was going to happen, swept over her. "What if you trip and fall and hit your head and I'm stuck in here?" She looked pointedly at the laces trailing from his shoes.

He looked back at her like she'd spoken Chinese. Slowly, as if he was talking to a child, he said, "I'll be careful."

He opened the heavy door and gave her a warning look that clearly said, "Don't even think about it," before slipping outside. The door swung closed, but before it could fully shut, she grabbed the handle and leaned back with all her strength. The ventilation system had created a wind tunnel that effectively sucked the door closed even faster than it normally would. Her heart began hammering in her chest, and even as she acknowledged that her reaction was probably unreasonable, she lifted her leg and placed her foot against the wall for leverage, desperate to prevent the closing of that door.

Sunlight slanted in through the two inches of space between the edge of the door and the wall. She clearly heard Jason's voice. "I'm XIA! Reaching for my badge."

Bryn's entire body jerked at the report of what could only be a gunshot, followed by another. She had no idea who shot at whom, but she straightened her knee and heaved against the door. It opened a couple of feet and she looked out. Jason was in the dirt on his hands and knees. As she watched, he surged to his feet and lunged for the door. Behind him, a big man in a black leather jacket and sunglasses advanced, raising his gun. He fired another round just as Jason dove under her leg and yelled, "Shut it!"

Bryn didn't have to be told twice. She let go of the handle and fell back. The door clanged closed.

Jason got to his feet and tucked his gun into its holster at the small of his back. His face grim, he reached into his pocket and pulled out his holophone. After a moment, he muttered, "Damn, *now* the signal's gone."

He looked at Bryn. "We're safe in here-" but he was cut off by a small but ominous beep. They turned to the door, where the light on the keypad had inexplicably turned green again. The door handle turned downward.

Jason hurled himself against it as Bryn cried, "Who *is* that?"

Even with the extra help from the wind tunnel, Jason's full weight against the door didn't stop it from inexorably opening. The barrel of the intruder's gun poked through and Bryn squealed and leaped out of the way just before it went off. The sound of the shot echoing through the tunnel was deafening.

Jason sank down with one leg extended, bracing his shoulder against the door like a football player. Bryn heard the intruder grunting with effort. Whoever it was didn't dare stick his gun in any further in case Jason managed to shut the door on his arm. He must have decided he needed both hands to push, because the gun disappeared and the crack in the door gained a few more inches.

Bryn was terrified but wasn't going to stand around doing nothing while the bigger man overpowered Jason and came in shooting. She pulled Jason's gun from its holster, ignoring his, "Hey!"

Crouching down, she gripped the pistol with both arms extended and locked at the elbow like she'd seen in the movies. She gritted her teeth and moved into the light from the opening, blindly firing. The recoil knocked her onto her backside, but she instantly rolled away.

The door slammed shut. Jason straightened up, took a step back and kicked at the keypad, shoelaces flying wildly, until the device broke away from the wall and hung there from its wiring.

Bryn got to her feet. Jason shook his head at her, breathing hard from exertion. "That was just *stupid*."

He held his hand out. She meekly passed him the gun and waited while he put it back in its holster.

"Don't ever touch my gun again. Let's go." He shoved her ahead of him and they began running up the tunnel.

She'd hoped he was done chastising her, but he was still angry enough to practically shout, "Have you ever even *shot* a gun?"

"Yes." It was a lie. She'd pointed a gun - once - at that crazy Coney Island vampire wanna-be, Nosferatu. Now was not the time to admit that she hadn't known enough to take the safety off.

"You didn't grip it properly. And next time, keep both eyes open."

"I had the sun in them," she snapped. "And it worked, didn't it?"

He didn't answer. They ran down the spiral stairs and entered the safe house. Bryn didn't know why they were running if the intruder couldn't get in, but Jason went straight for the back wall to the furthest door. He opened it, and she saw a closet-like space with a set of steep stairs going up.

"This is the escape hatch. I'm going out to see if our guy is wounded or what. Do you think you could stay the hell here this time?"

She wanted to point out that not only had she not left the building before, but the fact that she'd kept the door open may very well have saved his life. But she noticed something odd about the tattoo on his left arm. The scrolling design she'd secretly admired in the truck was now crisscrossed with smeared lines of... "Is that blood? Are you *shot*?"

Chapter Seven

Scott hadn't been able to oust Dr. Padilla from her self-appointed surveillance of the blood donation center. Before he'd even had a chance to argue with her, she'd played her trump card by saying, "You can drag me out of here kicking and screaming, or you can avoid making a scene and join me at this perfectly situated table."

The table *was* in a good spot. Scott plunked himself ungraciously in the plastic chair next to her, where he had full view of the building across the street.

A waitress came by and he ordered lunch. Once she'd left, he asked, "Did Shasta call about the dead guy?"

"Cruise's neighbor? Yes. I sent my team to pick up the body."

"Shouldn't you wait for the autopsy? What if he died of something else?"

"We need to contain this thing, remember? Assuming the medical examiner finds something suspicious, how long do you think before word gets out?"

A few minutes later, the waitress brought him his sandwich, which he wolfed down, deliberately forgetting his manners.

Dr. Padilla avoided looking at him, especially after he shoved the half-eaten pastrami on rye under her nose and asked, "Want a bite, *Mia*?" She'd shrunk away from him so violently he thought she was going to fall off her chair.

Now he took a long drink of his soda, belched loudly, and licked the cougar pads on his fingers in satisfaction. Mostly, the satisfaction came from seeing the supposedly germophobic Dr. Padilla's discomfort.

All the while, he watched the foot traffic in front of the blood donation center. Most people walked on by, but occasionally someone went in or came out of the center. None of them thus far were obviously xenos. They might be, but Scott couldn't tell. Since xenos were prohibited from

29

donating blood, if they were going in there, they'd be smart to hide their alterations.

Dr. Padilla, or Mia as she'd asked him to call her, although he was having a hard time thinking of her informally, continued reading her holo tablet. He found himself glancing at her again and again, trying to determine how old she was. He'd originally pegged her in her twenties, but it was unlikely someone that young would be in charge of her own team.

She must have noticed, because without looking up, she said, "My father was Filipino and my mother Korean."

"Okay," he said, making it sound like he couldn't fathom why she'd offered the information.

"Well, you were wondering, weren't you?"

He kept his face averted, catching sight of a man three blocks up the street whose walk seemed familiar. "I wasn't, actually."

"Oh. Because most people I meet want to know why I have an Hispanic last name when I look Asian."

"I was wondering what you were reading," Scott said. The man he was watching had stopped at a crosswalk, still too far away for him to see his face.

Mia set the holo reader down on the table. "Just scanning through some research abstracts. Not finding anything to corroborate the whole 'xenos are immune' thing."

"Nothing *official*. You should check the internet." Scott kept a close eye on the man as the light changed and he began crossing the street.

"What, for testimonials? Come on."

Scott shrugged. "Well, you're not going to find the proof you need looking at research studies funded by pharmaceutical companies."

"And why's that?"

"You think Big Pharma wants to actually cure anything? No, they want patients to take a pill every day for the rest of their lives. And then of course they'll need more pills to combat the side effects of the first pill, and so on. Keep them alive, but sick. An entire populace of cash-cows."

"That's mighty paranoid of you, Agent Harding."

"Is it?"

"Not to mention the majority of modern-day illnesses are the result of poor eating habits and lack of exercise. Is the junk food industry in collaboration with Big Pharma?"

"How many studies on xenos has the government funded?"

"Medical research funding isn't allocated on a whim. What reason would the government have to study xenos?"

"Huh." Scott heard her, but the man across the street was now close enough for him to identify: *The Viscount.*

He stood, tossed a twenty-dollar bill on the table and hopped the low wrought-iron fence surrounding the terrace. He jaywalked across the street and intercepted The Viscount before the older man could reach the door to the blood center. As soon as The Viscount saw Scott, his battered face creased in a smile, and Scott relaxed a bit. He'd had no idea whether word had gotten out that he was a cop. Only one person within the XBestia gang knew four months ago, and that was Padme. Scott had been pulled back from the investigation, but not pulled off of it entirely because it was unknown whether Padme intended to reveal his true identity to Dr. Fournier. If in the intervening time she had, it didn't look like the information had trickled down through the organization far enough to reach a low-level thug like The Viscount.

"Hey, Cougar! Long time no fight," The Viscount said. "Where ya been? Thought mebbe ya got caught in the fire."

"Nah, I been around. What you been up to?"

"Just goin' in for my inoculation. You get yours yet?"

"No, man, what's an inoculation?" Scott asked.

The Viscount thumped him on the back, forcing him to take a step forward. "You kiddin' me? I thought everyone knew. You go in, get a shot, then come back in a week to donate blood and they give you a hunnerd bucks. Easy cash."

"Sounds sweet, but I got a gig. Later," Scott started to walk off, but just as he was about to step back into the street, a wave of pleasure overcame him. It was only a short burst this time, but it was enough to stop him cold. Across the street, Mia was standing with her holophone held out in front of her, but she was looking past the holo of whoever she was talking to, staring at him. He glanced around, expecting to see Padme, see her with wire wrapped around her fingers like a puppeteer. She wasn't there, but he spotted a security camera mounted under the roof overhang at the corner of the blood bank building. Of course she'd be watching; he'd been stupid not to expect it.

He choked down an unexpected rise of bile and put a happy expression on his face before lifting a hand to his lips and then extending that hand towards the camera. It was essential that Padme think he still cared, even though he never had.

31

Chapter Eight

Bryn hadn't noticed Jason's injury before because his t-shirt was black. Now she saw a tear in the fabric of his sleeve, a horizontal slice about two inches long. She pinched the seam at the top of his shoulder and attempted to lift the fabric, but it was stuck from partially dried-on blood.

He slapped her hand away. "Yeah, he clipped me. It's no big deal. Stay here."

Before he even crossed the threshold into the escape hatch, a bright light appeared from somewhere at the top of the steeply rising steps. At first, Bryn thought he'd activated an automatic light, but then a dark, ovoid object the size of a softball clattered down the steps.

Jason slammed the door and yelled, "Get down!"

He pushed her violently into the little kitchenette to the left of the door and she dove onto the linoleum floor. A heavy weight fell on her just as a concussive blast shook the safe house. She lay there for a moment before trying to get up. The weight was Jason's body; he'd thrown himself on her to shield her, and now he wasn't moving. She heaved him onto his side and got to her knees. Her head hurt, her ears were ringing, and her eyes felt like they were filled with grit from the thick dust now filling the air. Coughing, she put her fingertips against his throat and was reassured when a pulse beat strongly there. Before she could check him for injuries, the ominous sound of heavy footsteps coming from the escape hatch alerted her.

The door had been blown inward, clearing the way for the man who'd shot at Jason and tried to force his way in through the front entrance. From this angle, she couldn't see into the escape hatch, but the blast must have damaged the lower steps, because he landed in the room heavily, as if he'd had to jump.

She was still on her knees and had to crane her aching neck to look up at him. He had short, black hair, and the sunglasses she'd seen earlier

32

were resting on his head. He was very tall, at least six-foot-five, with a heavy build. No wonder Jason couldn't close the door on him.

The barrel of the big gun she'd seen earlier was pointed right in her face, but she was encouraged that he hadn't shot her the instant he appeared. She struggled to her feet and said, "You killed him," pleased that the words came out sounding sincere. She'd been a bad liar her whole life, but in this situation, it wasn't hard putting the right amount of outrage and fear into her voice.

He squinted at Jason with cold blue eyes. "Excellent. That just leaves you, doesn't it?"

She flinched when he moved his gun hand, but it was only to gesture her out of the kitchenette. She obeyed, terrified he was going to ensure that Jason was really dead by shooting him a few times.

"Go on," he said, tilting his head toward the door leading to the spiral staircase. She didn't want to turn her back on him but didn't have a choice. She went past him, wondering why he hadn't killed her. Did he simply prefer that she walk to the place he planned on disposing of her body so he didn't have to haul it around along with Jason's? Not that Jason was actually dead...yet. But for all she knew, he was gravely injured. He was tough; all XIA agents were, but was he tough enough to overcome being shot and then blown up?

The important thing was to do what her captor told her, lull him into a false sense of security.

For when Jason gets up and rescues me.

She glanced back, but all she could see were his feet, still wearing the untied shoes. She preceded the intruder through the door into the stairwell. With every step she took, it seemed less and less likely she'd get out of this situation alive. Still, she held onto the irrational hope that Jason would somehow regain consciousness and save the day.

She debated telling the intruder that the keypad on the exterior door had been damaged, but to her surprise he told her to go down the stairs instead of up. A shiver crawled down her spine. Whatever waited for her at the bottom of the old abandoned missile silo, she doubted it was a welcoming party.

Her head still throbbed from the explosion, and as she descended the steps that went down and around in a seemingly endless spiral, she fought the urge to vomit. It didn't help that there was an odd smell to the place that got stronger the lower they went.

The levels below the safe house were unfinished, as Jason had said. The dim light from the stairwell didn't reach far, but she saw that each level was bare concrete around the perimeter of the circular structure - all but the center of each floor, which was open. She imagined a huge missile squatting at the bottom of the silo, ready to be launched straight up and out through the holes in the floors.

By the time they reached the lowest level, she was winded and dizzy. He grasped her arm and hauled her along with him towards the center of the floor until the gloom got too heavy to see ahead of them.

"I'm going to put my gun away," her captor said. "I don't recommend trying anything."

Despite his advice, she frantically thought up and rejected several escape plans. She heard more than saw him put his gun away, and then heard a metallic jingle that could only be from a set of keys.

"I've had this on my keychain for years and never used it before," he said in an absurdly conversational tone. Light flared from his hand. It was a small flashlight with a weak, unfocused beam, but it was enough to illuminate the floor directly ahead of them.

"You're probably wondering why I left you alive."

He pushed her ahead of him until the flashlight revealed a dark form on the ground. Bryn gasped and stepped back. It was the body of a man, dressed in jeans and a red leather jacket. Bryn froze in place and stared down at the dead man's feet, clad in black socks, no shoes.

"Stinks, huh? But it would be a lot worse if it weren't so cold down here." He walked around the body and stopped by the head. "You take his feet."

He lifted the flashlight to his mouth and bit down on it to keep it lit, keys dangling against his chin. He squatted down and slid his hands under the dead man's shoulders. It was obvious now that Bryn was only alive to help him move the body. A body that he had likely dumped here thinking no one would find it since the safe house hadn't been used in years. But then Bryn came along and needed a place underground, and someone within the FBI had offered the silo safe house to the XIA.

It stood to reason that the man in front of her was an FBI agent. How else had he known they would be here, and how else had he gained entrance past the holoscanner?

She didn't move, but not just because she didn't want to touch the corpse. A tiny red laser light had appeared at the top of her captor's head on one side. It took all of her self-control not to glance upward, through the holes in the floor to the person at the other end of that laser.

Her captor looked up at her and the light in his mouth made her squint. He spoke around it, "Get his legs, *now*, or I'll-"

34

He didn't finish his sentence, couldn't because the shot from above blew half his head away. Thankfully, she didn't see much because the light was blinding her; just an impression of something spattering the ground before his body hit the concrete with a thud. She screamed and fled for the stairs, running up and up until she couldn't run anymore.

Jason found her on her knees, gasping for air. She reached out for him, but he recoiled, going so far as to take a step back up. For a brief, horrified moment, she thought it was because she was covered in blood, but she glanced down and saw that she wasn't - she'd been standing the full length of the dead man's body and then some, too far away and at the wrong angle to get hit with the spatter.

"Is he dead?" Jason asked.

"Yes." Tears formed in her eyes and spilled over.

"Get up to the safe house-"

"No! Don't leave me."

He shook his head. "I gotta go down."

"I'm telling you, he's definitely d-dead."

He started past her, and she noticed he had a flashlight in one hand. "I need to I.D. the bodies."

She collapsed on the step and waited, shaking from cold and shock. Jason must have done what he needed to do without dawdling, because he was back within minutes.

"Alright, come on."

Dazed, she stood. He didn't try to comfort her, just took her elbow and steered her up the stairs. She wiped a hand under her nose and tried not to replay the horrible images of what had just happened in her mind. It had been a kill or be killed situation. She had no doubt that Jason had saved her life. Twice.

At the second level, he stopped and retrieved his rifle, shoving it and the flashlight back into the long case he'd taken from behind the seats in the cab of his truck when they'd first arrived. Had that only been a couple of hours ago?

The safe house was a disaster zone. There was a big, jagged hole where the door to the escape hatch used to be, and every surface was covered in white dust.

"Go get your stuff," Jason said. "We can't stay here."

He disappeared into the bathroom while Bryn went to get her bag. Luckily, she hadn't unpacked. She slung it over her shoulder and winced when a sharp pain lanced down her neck. She was definitely sore from the grenade blast.

35

When she went back into the main room, she heard him call out, "A little help here?"

She opened the bathroom door and her bag slipped to the floor as she stared in slack-jawed surprise at Jason's naked back. He'd pulled his t-shirt over his head, but it appeared to be stuck in several places around his shoulders. Blood was smeared everywhere. What surprised her, though, was his xenograft. She couldn't see the whole thing, but it was clearly a dragon, its 'scales' the pebbled black and orange skin of a Gila monster.

"Are you there?" he asked.

"Yes."

"I can't get my shirt off. I got hit with some flak when the grenade exploded. Lucky the door blocked most of it."

She came closer and said, "Yeah, oh, that looks bad. Um, hold on, I think Carla packed my tweezers."

He laughed a little. "Why would she pack tweezers?"

"I'm a girl. We pluck," Bryn replied, nonplussed at the turn the conversation had taken. She never would have imagined she'd need to use the same tweezers she groomed her eyebrows with to remove shrapnel from someone's body.

The tweezers in question were, indeed, in the bag, along with a mini sewing kit with a small pair of scissors and a mini first aid kit. Carla always did like to be prepared.

Bryn started by cutting away Jason's shirt from around the three largest bits of shrapnel protruding from his back. He pulled the tattered remains off while she found a washcloth and wet it in the sink.

"This is gonna hurt."

"Just do it."

He held still while she wet the remaining fabric and peeled it away, and then picked the shrapnel from his skin, gently dabbing at the blood.

Two of the splinters were about an inch long and had entered his skin shallowly, but the third was more of a chunk, half an inch in width and deeply embedded in his trapezius. She dug away at it and could see from his face reflected in the mirror over the vanity that it hurt, but the only sound he made was a hiss or two of pain.

"Is my xenograft okay?" he asked.

When he'd taken off the rest of his shirt, she saw the entire dragon. The Gila monster graft was in the center of his back in the shape of the dragon's body. The rest of the dragon, head, tail and wings, were tats. The wings extended across his back, up over his shoulders and down his arms.

"There's a nick on one edge, but it's not bad." She ran her fingers lightly down the pebbled surface of the Gila monster skin, noticing that his own skin responded by sprouting goosebumps. In the mirror, she saw his eyes close.

"Don't," he said in a hoarse voice, pulling slightly away.

"Why not?"

She wanted to say, 'It's beautiful,' but didn't because as always, she was torn by her feelings of sorrow for the donor animal.

He said, "It's...sensitive. Are you almost done?"

"Yeah, let me clean this gouge from the bullet on your shoulder and bandage you up. You really need stitches."

He just grunted and said, "Hurry up."

When she'd finished, he pulled a clean t-shirt from his bag and she helped him ease it over the bandages.

He'd come straight into the bathroom when they'd first arrived at the safe house and had left his bags here after he took his shower. He gathered them up and said, "Ready?"

"How are we supposed to get out?"

He shrugged and then flinched. "Ow. Remind me not to do that. We go out the escape hatch."

She recalled that the lowest steps had been blown away and thought it was easier said than done, but asked, "Are you taking me back to XIA headquarters?"

He shook his head. "Not if you want to live, I'm not."

Chapter Nine

Scott crossed the street, planning to let Mia know he was leaving, but she said, "My team just called. There's a problem at the morgue."

"Medical Examiner won't release the body?" He started walking and she fell into step beside him.

"Yeah, how'd you guess?"

"Met him. He's a character."

She sighed. "Awesome. Your car or mine?"

"Both."

"That's not very environmentally friendly."

"Maybe not, but I'm on the job and if I have to leave suddenly, you're walking no matter whose car we take."

"Fine. Did you learn anything from that man you talked to?"

He told her what The Viscount said. She didn't ask any more questions until they'd almost reached Scott's sedan.

"So what happened after you talked to him? When you were about to step into the street. You got this, um, look on your face like, well, I don't know how to describe it. Then you blew a kiss to the building?"

Scott felt his face go hot in a combination of embarrassment and anger. He'd been taken unaware when Padme hit him with the burst of pleasure - not that he would have been able to control his reaction had she warned him. The expression that must have been on his face was definitely something he wouldn't have chosen to share with everyone on the street who happened to be looking his way.

"You don't miss much, do you?" he asked, hoping to deflect her questions.

"Nope. So are you going to tell me?"

"Nope. Here's my car. I'll meet you there."

He got caught in lunch hour traffic, and when he finally arrived at the morgue, he was told Mia was already there. He was sent down to the basement, to Autopsy. The long room had seven stainless steel tables all lined up in a row, but only one was occupied, the body still zipped up in black plastic. Mia stood at the foot of the table, talking with Rex Harrison, Chief Medical Examiner. Scott had met him after the fire at the Warehouse, when Scott had been called in to help identify the bodies of the xenofreaks who'd been killed during the fight between ARA soldiers.

Harrison was an older black man whose hair was completely white. He stood only about an inch taller than the petite Mia, but he more than made up for his lack of stature with his overpowering personality. Although as Scott walked up, he didn't sound as if he was giving her a hard time.

"Call me Rex," he was saying. He lifted a hand to Mia's shoulder and kept it there even though she tried to duck out from under it. Scott smiled to himself, noting that Rex seemed oblivious to Mia's uneasiness.

"Oh, Scott, you're here," she said, a little too loudly. She stepped in his direction, just far enough away from the medical examiner to escape his hand.

"Yeah," Scott drawled, and on a perverse impulse, he placed his hand on her shoulder in the same spot the medical examiner's hand had just vacated. When the fur from his fingers brushed against her neck, she jerked her head away and moved several steps back from both men. Scott expected her to give him a dirty look, but she just pasted a pleasant look on her face as if nothing had happened.

"Um, Rex, this is Scott Harding, special agent with the XIA."

"Yes, we've met," Rex said. "Youngest ever XIA agent, as I recall."

"Yes, sir, I am young." Scott wasn't about to try to explain why the XIA had recruited him. They weren't here to chit-chat. "Has Dr. Padilla spoken to you about the typhoid?"

"She has indeed. And although typhoid is not unheard of in New York City, it's rarely fatal, and certainly nothing that would warrant calling in the CDC. Unless there's something you're not telling me?" He directed rheumy brown eyes Mia's way.

"We have nothing official to tell," Mia replied. "We just need the body, and we'd appreciate some interagency cooperation."

"I see," Rex said. "Would this have anything to do with the incident at the courthouse the other day?"

"What have you heard?" Scott asked.

"Rumors. Of course, your visit is only going to fuel the speculation."

"What kind of rumors?" Mia's voice was soft.

Rex took a breath and sighed. "The kind of rumors you'd expect to come out of a hospital that had to quarantine an entire ward. There's talk of a pandemic, talk of a bioweapon attack." He nodded down at the body bag. "That's not really typhoid, is it?"

"It is, actually. And we'd appreciate it if you'd keep a lid on our 'visit.' Wouldn't want to cause an unnecessary panic."

Mia smiled, and Scott watched in disbelief as the crotchety old Chief Medical Examiner's protests melted under her gaze.

"Alright." Rex sounded resigned. He picked up a clipboard that was resting on top of the body. "Call in your boys. This is highly irregular, but who am I to gainsay the CDC?"

Mia thanked him and they left soon after. Scott was glad to get into the elevator away from the cold basement with its strange odors. He had barely pushed the button for the main floor when Mia demanded, "Exactly how old *are* you?"

He shrugged. "Does it matter?"

"As long as you continue to act like a child it does. Do you think I didn't notice your immature little gesture in there? And sticking your sandwich in my face? I told you I'm a germophobe. Would you please respect that and stop messing with me?"

The elevator doors parted, and Scott walked out, muttering, "Yeah, whatever."

She came after him and grabbed his arm in the lobby.

He looked down at her hand. "I can't touch you, but you can touch me?"

She let go and shook her head. "What *is* your problem?"

He laughed. "You really want to know? Fine. You say it's my germs that freak you out, but it's pretty obvious it's these." He held up his hands.

She swallowed. "To be perfectly frank, it's both, but I really can't help it. And despite my phobias, at least I maintain a professional attitude."

"Well, I'm a xenofreak, lady." He started for the door. "We don't do professional."

Chapter Ten

Bryn sat in a patch of afternoon sunshine coming through the dirty window of Jason's old truck, but she was cold to the bone. She crossed her arms and shivered, waiting while he searched through the black sedan the intruder had arrived in. When he got into the cab and started the engine, she asked, "Was he FBI?"

He shot her a surprised look. "Yeah. He tell you that?"

"No. I guessed. He wanted me to help him move the body." She shut her eyes tightly. Patchy flashes of memory assailed her; the trip down the spiral steps, the blinding light in her eyes, the rifle shot followed instantly by the sound of spatter. Each flash was in black and white except for the color of the dead man's jacket. "Did you figure out who it was? The-the body?"

Jason shifted into reverse and backed the truck onto the dirt lane. "The less you know about that the better."

After they got onto the main road, she asked, "Where are we going?"

"Where the cell signals can't reach you."

She thought about it for a minute. "Underground?"

He nodded.

"Can I call Scott?"

"No," he snapped. Then he closed his eyes briefly, shaking his head. "This is bad...this is real bad."

She'd wondered how he felt, and even though his words weren't expressing regret, she took them that way. "You *had* to kill him. He shot you and blew us both up. He not only thought he'd killed you but was happy about it. He was going to kill me, too, after I helped him. All we have to do is tell them what happened."

"It's not that simple."

"*Why not?*" She heard the plaintive note in her own voice.

Through gritted teeth, he said, "I can't tell you."

"What, you think someone's going to torture it out of me if you do?"

His sidelong glance confirmed it.

She looked out the window. They were headed back the way they came. "Underground. So...a cave? Your mother's basement?"

He didn't respond, so she said darkly, "It's the sewer, isn't it?"

"Close. We need to disappear until I can figure out who else is involved."

"Okay, I get it. Trust no one. But we can trust Scott."

"*You* can trust Scott. I worked really hard creating a persona for myself within the XIA, and I guarantee your precious Scott thinks I'm scum."

"Alright, then drop me off at his place!"

Jason stomped on the brakes and the truck skidded over to the side of the road. The face that he turned to her was livid. "Do you have a death wish?"

She cringed back against the door but responded with spirit. "You want me to cooperate? Give me a good reason."

He slammed the flat of his hand against the steering wheel, making her jump. After a moment: "Did you see the dead guy's face?"

"What?"

"*His face.* Did you see it?"

"No. Just his jacket. It was red leather."

"Damn," he muttered. "I don't suppose there's any chance you could wipe that little detail from your memory banks?"

"Who was he?"

After a long pause he said quietly, "Mad Eye royalty."

He started the truck and pulled back onto the road. She sat with her hands folded in her lap, hoping he would elaborate.

"You know all about undercover agents, right?" he finally asked.

She thought about Scott, how he'd had her completely fooled at first. "I guess."

"Well, it goes both ways. Sometimes cops turn dirty; sometimes they join the force already dirty."

"So...the guy in the red jacket was working for the Mad Eye gang? Killed by a dirty cop who was also willing to kill us to hide his crime?"

"Something like that."

"You're leaving something out."

He rolled his eyes briefly at the ceiling of the truck before staring back at the road. "Are you always this annoying?"

"Only when I'm scared."

He let out a little 'heh,' and said, "Somehow I doubt that."

She knew he was attempting to change the subject again; attempting to distract her from digging any deeper into his reasons for running instead of going to the XIA. She was tired suddenly and wanted more than ever to go home but decided to ease up on him. Jason had begun drumming his fingers on the steering wheel to some rapid, internal beat, and he seemed to be stretched as thin as a wire.

She took a breath. "So am I dressed properly for sewer night life?"

He glanced over. "You got any tats?"

"No."

"Piercings? Anything?"

"I got a porcupine on my head. What more do you want?"

"Jeez, you really were innocent, weren't you?"

She looked away. "That was a lifetime ago."

"Are you a virgin?"

Her head snapped back around. "None of your business!"

"That's a yes," he said under his breath.

"How could that possibly matter?"

"It matters because you don't strike me as a very good actress, and where we're going, you need to look, and act, like someone whose legs aren't clamped together."

It was a deliberately crude thing for him to say. He seemed to be waiting for a response and she realized he was testing her. She'd played Dorothy from The Wizard of Oz in her junior high school play, but that wouldn't help make her case. She thought about Sheila Gottfried, the girl her ex-boyfriend had dumped her for. Sheila's trampy reputation may or may not have been deserved, but she *had* gotten pregnant immediately after graduating. Bryn stuck her chest out and lifted her leg, resting her shoe on the dash, trying to channel Sheila's brash attitude.

"I can take care of myself."

He laughed. "You got any makeup in that bag?"

The bag Carla had packed was at her feet. She bent down, unzipped it and took out the smaller bag. Inside, she found a tube of sparkly pink lip gloss. She held it up.

"That's it?" he asked. "Even I wear more makeup than that."

She thought he was joking, but he leaned over, opened the glove compartment, and rummaged around inside it, all the while keeping his eyes on the road. He pulled his hand out, dropped a narrow pencil in her lap and said, "Here."

It was jet-black eyeliner, the twist-up kind. She almost asked, "What am I supposed to do with this?" but stopped herself. Instead, she flipped down the visor and peered into the small, corroded mirror mounted there. With delicate strokes, she attempted to line her eyes, but the shocks on the truck were so bad every bump in the road sent the liner tip off on a tangent. Even so, by the time they drove past the outlet mall, she thought her efforts would pass muster.

"How's this?" She batted her eyelashes at him.

They were stopped at a light, so he gave her the once over. Without a word, he took the liner out of her hand and began drawing on her face. He was pressing so hard she thought he was going to poke her eye out, so she protested, "Ow!"

"It doesn't hurt," he said, but he eased up on the pressure. He was so close she felt his breath on her chin. After a couple of minutes he said, "There. Now do the other eye like that."

As he started driving again, she looked at his handiwork in the little mirror.

"I look like a..." *Zombie hooker.*

"Tough xenofreak chick?" he asked. "Yeah, that's the point."

"Do you really think it's smart for me to advertise something I'm not selling?"

"You're with me, no one will touch you."

She didn't doubt him. He'd already killed to protect her.

She started drawing thick lines on her other eye to match the one he'd done. "You do know that makeup isn't going to hide who I am, right?"

"Doesn't matter. Everyone knows you were kidnapped and forced to undergo that xenograft. They'll assume you hate Fournier and the XBestia."

Bryn met her own eyes in the mirror. It wasn't just the eyeliner that made them look hard as marbles.

"They'll assume right," she said.

Chapter Eleven

Scott spent the rest of the day chasing down leads on Robert Cruise's whereabouts. Cruise's former boss suggested Scott check his favorite bar. The chatty bartender there said he hadn't seen him in weeks and suggested Scott try Cruise's girlfriend. He told Scott her name was Candy and she worked at a massage parlor. Scott arrived at the establishment in question but found it had been recently shut down by local cops. He went to the precinct and asked to speak with the detectives on the case, but they were out on surveillance. Finally, after knocking on Cruise's door again with no answer, he decided to do a bit of surveillance himself, getting back in his sedan and hunkering down in his seat.

Early winter twilight had fallen over the city when his holophone rang. It was Shasta.

"Where are you?"

"Watching Cruise's place."

"Come in. Now."

"What's up?"

"We'll discuss it when you get here."

Scott knew better than to press her. He drove through town as quickly as rush-hour traffic would allow.

At XIA headquarters, Shasta ushered him into her office and without preamble said, "Alton and Bryn are missing."

A wave of cold dread washed over him. "What do mean 'missing'? Did they make it to the safe house?"

Shasta collapsed into her chair, face ashen. "The FBI says yes. According to the Special Agent in Charge, they were there. One of their field agents hadn't checked in all day, so they followed the transponder signal on his car and found it parked at the silo. There'd been some kind of firefight, and an explosion. I'd send you out there, but the FBI has

45

jurisdiction over the crime scene, and they weren't very happy about finding their agent and another man dead."

"Who was it?"

Shasta glanced over at her holo screen. "An agent Bart Antonovich. They haven't released the identity of the other body."

"But it's not Bryn?"

"No. It's a male, dead for some time. Definitely not Alton."

"Like I give a crap if Alton is dead or alive. He let her get kidnapped...*again*. This is his fault."

"You're upset, Agent Harding." Shasta's voice was firm. "But we don't have all the facts."

"Sounds like we don't have any facts!"

"I've got a call in to Deputy Director Unger, but he's been testifying at a congressional subcommittee all day. He'll get us access to the safe house and we'll see for ourselves what happened."

Scott stood there shaking his head in tiny, frustrated movements.

"Go home, Scott. Get some rest. I'll call you as soon as we know anything."

Scott wanted nothing more than to plant himself outside of Shasta's office until the promised information came in, but even if she'd let him, he was exhausted from a nearly sleepless night and really did need the rest.

He trudged down to the parking garage and started his motorcycle, but when he drove out of the structure, he found himself taking a right instead of his usual left. He wanted to drive fast and far to clear his head, but a thin, low fog limited visibility, and frozen condensation made the roads slick, so he kept to the speed limit.

As he drove with no clear destination in mind, all he could think was: *who took her*?

The XIA had finally placed Bryn in protective custody in response to Padme's attack, but Shasta herself had speculated that Padme had only done it to get Scott's attention. If Padme really had been trying to contact him, she sure hadn't done it to warn him that Bryn was in danger, since she'd already tried once to kill her.

Still, he didn't think she was behind Bryn's disappearance. Padme was Fournier's programmer and hacker - she couldn't have overpowered Alton on her own and didn't have the authority to order someone else to do it.

Scott would be inclined to suspect Fournier himself, but it didn't make sense that he would kidnap her a second time, since the only reason he'd done so in the first place was to help Bryn's father turn her into a

46

martyr of sorts - the anti-xenofreak poster child. It had been a convoluted plan to bring public censure down on the practice of xenoaugmentation, all in an effort to pave the way for his, and Bryn's father's, true agenda: the legalization of human cloning.

While Fournier would certainly be angry with Bryn for her part in destroying his facility, Scott didn't think he was out for revenge, especially since he could have easily gotten to her at Carla's place any time in the last four months. But if revenge was the motive for her disappearance, one person did come to mind.

Dundee.

The psychopathic xenofreak had been blinded by Bryn's quills when she'd fought him off of her. Scott had no idea whether his sight had been permanently damaged, because Dundee had escaped with the rest of Fournier's crew. Just the thought of what that crazy xenofreak might do to Bryn if he got his filthy hands on her made Scott sick.

He revved his engine all the way down the street before noticing where he was: within a half mile of the blood donation center. Had that unconsciously been his destination all along? He didn't pause to think about it but simply headed straight there.

He parked his motorcycle illegally between two cars and stalked to the front of the blood donation center building. Across the road, The Holo House Cafe was bustling with the dinner crowd, but there was no one on his side of the street. He took off his helmet and stood there under the glow of a streetlight, in full view of the security camera he'd noticed earlier that day. There was no fog in this part of town, so if she was on the other end of that camera, she'd see him.

He lifted his hands palm up and spread his arms wide, slowly mouthing the words, "Where are you?"

Then he sat in the middle of the sidewalk and waited.

Chapter Twelve

They'd been driving south for the last couple of hours in the general direction of the Atlantic Ocean but had taken a detour to pick up some fast food after Bryn mentioned she hadn't eaten anything all day. She gave her undivided attention to the cheeseburger Jason bought for her, shoving it in her mouth with gusto until he asked her to open a ketchup packet for him. When she squeezed the red sauce out onto a wrapper, it reminded her of congealed blood and *that* reminded her of the dead men in the silo. Her appetite fled and she stuffed the rest of her burger into the bag.

From past experience, she knew she was in for months of these kinds of random memory associations. She still got uneasy whenever she smelled something that reminded her of the peculiar odor of the Warehouse, and rodents of any kind made her flash on the gruesome sight of Carla's xenograft after it had been cut from her chest.

She looked out the window, catching sight of the ocean glinting through grey winter scrub brush and bare trees along the side of the road. It wasn't until she spotted a sign for the Rockaway Freeway that she realized exactly where they were going.

"Edgemere?" she asked, turning to Jason with lifted eyebrows.

"Yep."

She'd grown up hearing frightening urban legends about the place. A century ago, the beachfront property had been developed as a getaway for townies, an idyllic seaside retreat where whole families stayed in tents or bungalows and strolled along the boardwalk. Like Coney Island, the area eventually attracted a less wholesome crowd, and over the course of time was largely deserted.

Attempts were made to repopulate Edgemere, but all failed. Persistent stories of aggressive packs of wild dogs and homeless camps kept people out. Eventually, the land was purchased by a developer with plans to build a resort, but not long after breaking ground, Hurricane Poppy devastated the east coast - especially Coney Island and the Rockaway Peninsula to the east, where Edgemere was located. Widespread damage to the developer's other properties forced him out of business, and the partially constructed main building was abandoned.

To make matters worse, Poppy uncovered a mass grave near the site, later attributed to a serial killer who'd never been caught. It gave rise to legends that the place was cursed or haunted. Now whenever someone in the city disappeared, it was said they'd been swallowed by Edgemere.

"I heard only the damned were welcome here," Bryn said as they bounced down a road that was peppered with potholes. The tarmac had been partially reclaimed by sand dunes.

"No one's welcome here. It's not a friendly place."

"That's not very reassuring."

"You want me to lie?"

The lowering sun disappeared behind a fog bank rolling in from the water. Jason switched on the headlights and turned right onto another eerily empty street. Ahead, dozens of rusted steel girders thrust unevenly into the sky, like the bloody bones of a beached whale.

This must be the abandoned resort. She remembered reading that the developer hadn't wanted to ruin the skyline, so his plan had been to build an enormous underground shopping mall with only two floors above ground for the hotel, plus several blocks of old-fashioned bungalows.

There were no walls to what was left of the rectangular structure, just mottled grey concrete spanning several acres of ground. Thousands of rebar poles taller than a man were planted in the cement, and strung between them at all angles were sheets of dark fabric. Interspersed at regular intervals in two lines down the center of the slab were dozens of mushroom-shaped aluminum exhaust vents. Smoke or steam rose into the air from the vents. There was only one structure that a person could potentially live in: a crude tent set up on the nearest corner.

As they got closer, a dog of an indeterminate breed came out of nowhere and ran into the pool of the truck's headlights, barking and snarling. It was soon joined by four others and Jason was forced to slow to a crawl. All the dogs were medium-to-large sized, but underfed, if the deep shadows under their ribs were any indication.

A man appeared at the opening of the tent. He stepped out onto the sandy dirt, his long, open black coat swirling behind him like a cape. He yelled at the dogs and they retreated. Jason pulled off the road and shifted into park before cutting off the ignition. In the silence that followed, Bryn

49

nervously watched the man approach. He held something in both hands, and as he got closer, she made out a sawed-off shotgun.

"What's your business here, stranger?" the man shouted. He'd taken care to skirt the headlight beams, but it wasn't quite dark yet, and Bryn saw that despite the cold, he wasn't wearing a shirt under his coat. His skin was very dark and his shoulders so broad it looked as if he was wearing football shoulder pads.

Jason rolled down his window. "Dillo! It's me, Dragila."

She'd never heard Jason's xeno name before. He pronounced it 'Dra-heela,' and she decided it was a combination of Dragon and Gila monster, after his tattoo and xenograft. But it was the man he called Dillo that had her full attention. He came closer, let out a guttural laugh, and kicked the fender of the truck.

"Where'd you get *this* piece of junk?"

It wasn't what he said that made Bryn's mouth drop open. His coat hung partially off one shoulder - which was grafted with the armored plating of an armadillo. He leaned down and peered into the cab of the truck, reaching in past Jason's head and switching on the overhead light in the cab. His black hair was divided into tight cornrows in an intricate pattern. He had widely spaced brown eyes, a broad, flat nose and a thick-lipped mouth tilted up at the corners like he smiled a lot.

Conscious of Jason's advice to look tough, she pulled her chin in and looked up through her quills, sneering ever-so-slightly.

"Hel-*lo*," Dillo drawled. "Who have we here?"

"I picked up a stray," Jason said.

Bryn decided her best bet was to keep quiet unless someone asked her something directly.

Dillo eyed her quills. "Is that who I think it is? XBestia handiwork?"

"She's not affiliated with them."

Dillo put on an exaggerated look of surprise. "I suppose *not*." After a moment, he nodded to her. "What's your name again?"

"Porky," she said.

He laughed, revealing crooked and cracked yellow teeth. "For porcupine? You're too skinny to be called Porky."

"We brought supplies," Jason said. "In the back. But I gotta hide this truck."

"Oh, right. I heard you got busted. They let you go?"

"Nah." Jason didn't explain and Dillo didn't ask him to.

Jason switched off the overhead light as Dillo grabbed the edge of the driver's side door and jumped onto the running board. He pointed his shotgun toward a copse of stunted evergreen trees, saying, "Park 'er in there."

Jason started the truck and drove, heading for an opening in the underbrush. Before he reached the trees, Dillo raised his voice over the engine and said, "Stop here and let Porky out. Those are holly trees."

Bryn grabbed her bag and got out, and then helped Dillo remove the five boxes from the bed of the truck and set them on the ground. She stood next to him while the truck disappeared into the thick growth. He should have frightened her, but he didn't. She'd met some rough characters in the last several months, but under their xenografts, they were still people. Besides, it was a thoughtful thing for him to have done; pointing out that the bushes were holly trees. Bryn didn't envy Jason having to wade through them on the way back out. She wanted to thank Dillo but felt it would be out of character.

"How long you been with Dragila?" he asked.

She inhaled the cold sea air, trying not to panic. Jason hadn't discussed their supposed history. If she said the wrong thing, it could blow his cover.

"Not long," she finally said.

"You had to really think about that."

She let out a breath, halfway between a laugh and a protest. "I'm just not sure of anything at the moment."

Dillo's head and linebacker shoulders were silhouetted against the darkening sky. "Well, you'll figure it out. People tend to get their priorities straight around here; survival will do that to a person."

"Assuming I do survive."

He laughed. "You got that right, but the company you're keeping should up the odds."

Jason batted his way out of the bushes with his bags, swearing profusely.

"Ah, quit your bitchin'," Dillo said loudly. "You're lucky it's dark, or you'd know the real reason no one goes in those trees." He leaned down to Bryn and whispered, "Big-ass spiders."

"I hope he rolled up the windows," she replied, deadpan.

Dillo raised his voice again so Jason could hear. "Alright, we better present your guest to the queen. I'm sure she can't wait to see *you* again." He strode off back the way they came.

Bryn wondered what he meant by that. She hesitated by one of the boxes, but Jason said, "Someone will get that. Come on."

She picked up her bag and they went after Dillo, who veered to the left after he reached the vast slab of concrete. He led them along the perimeter and continued around the corner. The ground sloped downward, and they walked away from the slab. Midway, at least forty feet out, they came upon a circular opening cut into the hill. A faint glow seemed to emanate from within, and as they got closer, she heard what sounded very much like the faint echoes of a crowd of people; voices, music, laughter.

Two armed figures stepped out of the hole, but Dillo called out, "It's good."

When they reached the edge, she saw that the ground had been sliced away from around a huge drainage pipe. The two men guarding the entrance moved out of Dillo's way in an almost deferential manner.

Dillo waved for her to precede him.

"Welcome to Edgemere, Porky."

Chapter Thirteen

Scott had been waiting for an hour and darkness had fully fallen. He'd sat on the frozen sidewalk until his backside had gone numb, and then he'd gotten up and stomped around until circulation returned. Even with insulated gloves and boots, his hands and feet ached from the cold.

He thought about going across the street and getting a warm beverage but didn't want to miss Padme.

It had been four months since he'd last seen her. The xenofreak girl had just declared her love for him, or whatever passed for love in her devious mind. Then she'd ducked into the escape tunnel, leaving the rest of them to fight their way out of the conflagration she'd deliberately started in order to destroy Dr. Fournier's secret bioengineering facility.

Scott looked around for the hundredth time, trying to shove his hands deeper into his jacket pockets. The box Shasta had given him with the auto-injector took up too much room for his right hand to be comfortable. He wrapped his fingers around it with the intention of putting it in the back pocket of his jeans but caught a slight movement out of the corner of his eye. He straightened up, staring into the gloom beyond the front wall of the blood donation center.

"I'm alone," he said.

A dark-clothed figure disengaged from the shadows but didn't move into the light - or within view of the camera. Scott cautiously walked towards the small, shrouded form. When he was a few feet away, she lifted her hands and pushed her customary scarf off her hair, revealing a pale, serious face. The dim lighting emphasized the dark circles under her eyes.

"Padme," Scott said.

"I knew you'd figure it out." Her voice was low, as if she feared being overheard.

"How are you?" Scott, too, spoke quietly, but only because he wanted to foster a false sense of intimacy.

53

Her voice cracked on the one word she uttered, "Lonely," before she slipped her arms around him and pressed her cheek against his chest. He pulled the glove off his right hand and slid his furred fingers into her hair, thinking how many times he'd wished he could do the same with Bryn.

She lifted her head and the locks of hair framing her face fell back, revealing her xenograft, the upside-down cow's ears her uncle had forced on her. Her slightly parted lips begged to be kissed, but he couldn't make himself do it. Instead, he pulled away slightly and asked, "Is this safe?"

She shook her head. "Doubtful. Lupus has been much more...attentive since the fire. He's kept me in isolation this whole time. He finally released me a few weeks ago after I got the nanoneuron program running again. If he finds out I snuck out tonight, I don't know what he'll do."

Scott grasped her shoulder, surprised at how frail she'd become. "Come with me. I can protect you."

He felt more than saw her reaction as her shoulders slumped and she seemed to curl in on herself. "I can't."

"You said you wanted to turn yourself in. To make a deal with the XIA."

"That was then. Things have...changed."

"Okay, then, you don't have to turn yourself in, just come stay with me. I'll keep you safe."

It was a bold statement meant to disarm and further convince her of his sincerity.

"I will never be safe from Lupus."

"What can I do to convince you?"

"There's nothing anyone can do."

The finality of the statement made him wonder briefly why she felt she had no way out, but he didn't ponder it. He'd been hoping she'd mention Bryn, but it looked as if he would be forced to baldly ask about her. He knew he should attempt to manipulate the conversation around to the typhoid, but Bryn was his priority - even if he risked making Padme jealous.

Very gently, he asked, "Where is she?"

"Who?"

"Bryn."

Padme was an accomplished liar, but Scott thought the blinking surprise on her face was genuine. "Is she missing?"

"She and one of our agents were taken from a safe house today. We don't know if they're alive or what."

54

Padme took a step back and let her arms fall to her sides. "You care about her."

"I feel responsible for her." It wasn't a denial, but he hoped she'd take it that way. "You of all people should understand that."

Laughter from a group of diners across the street distracted her and she looked in their direction. "Look how normal they are. They have no idea what's coming."

Scott didn't want the topic to veer away from Bryn, but Padme's cryptic words gave him his other opening. "You mean the typhoid?"

She nodded slowly and took another step back. "You found this place," she glanced at the blood donation center, "so the XIA must have some indication of what's been happening."

Scott sensed she was on the verge of bolting. He had so many questions but needed to ask the most urgent of them. "Fournier. How can we stop him?"

"Give him what he wants," she said dully.

"He hasn't made any demands."

"None that you're aware of."

"What does that mean?" He reached a hand out, but she shook her head.

"I have to go."

She turned and began to move back into the shadows, and he let her go. She was like a skittish horse, and if he tried to stop her, he knew he'd lose the best source of information in his limited arsenal against Dr. Fournier.

"I want to see you again," he said.

"No, you don't."

He struggled to think of the perfect thing to say to convince her and decided to play upon the one emotion she seemed to understand - jealousy. "If you go back to Lupus, I *will* kill him and take you from him."

There was no reply. She was gone.

Chapter Fourteen

The first thing Bryn noticed was the smell. Unlike the Warehouse, which reeked most foully, the odor permeating Edgemere reminded her of slightly moldy coffee. The drainage pipe itself was made out of the eco-friendly building material biopolycrete, and the inside was so wide that even a tall person could walk upright with room to spare. Lining the curved sides were six rows of shelves filled with white plastic sacks the size of a package of flour. Growing from the top of the sacks were mushrooms; thousands upon thousands of them. A clear acrylic tube about six inches in width was mounted to the ceiling. It ran the full length of the pipe and curved back around again at the opening, so it seemed as if there were two tubes instead of one. Inside the tube was a greenish, glowing liquid that provided sufficient ambient light to see where they were going.

As they walked, the end of the tunnel beaconed, lit even more brightly with the same green glow. Bryn stepped out into a truly astonishing world. Construction on the underground mall must have been nearly complete when Poppy hit. She'd expected some kind of cavern, but the vast space confronting her wasn't cave-like in the least. The central area was open to the ceiling far above them, but the long sides of the rectangular area consisted of two levels of what would have been storefronts eventually, but now were merely bare bones steel and concrete. They appeared to be occupied by people using them as living space. The entire place was lit with same glowing tubes of different thicknesses, lining the walls in bright stripes and curves. Along the far wall, huge sections of lightweight biopolycrete drainage pipe were stacked five high in a near pyramid, reminiscent of a chunk of honeycomb Bryn had once eaten as a child. Cinder blocks were laid on the ground to prevent the lowest pipes from rolling away and the entire structure crashing down.

"Trippy, huh?" Dillo said, waving a hand to indicate the lighting. "Our resident bioengineers designed it. It's a complicated system, but basically the light comes from special bioluminescent bacteria that feed on human waste. Not only does it eliminate the need for a sewer, it produces methane as a byproduct, which we then use as a heat and cooking source."

"It's...amazing. Why haven't I heard of this place?" Bryn asked.

Dillo shrugged. "You're not a Mad Eye...yet."

Bryn looked at Jason. In the green glow, his face took on an almost evil cast. She wondered, not for the first time, what he'd gotten her into.

In case Dillo noticed the distrustful look she'd given Jason, she tossed out, "It smells like coffee."

"Well, I doubt you'll find a decent cup anywhere down here," he said with a chuckle. "The smell comes from the discarded coffee grounds we use to grow the mushrooms. Just as an FYI, don't attempt to eat any of them, okay?"

They began walking across the main square, where there were other sources of light besides the bioluminescence. One of the lower level store areas was lit from within with what looked like plain halogen office lights. Another had dozens of camping lanterns hanging from wire strung between the support columns.

"We get some electricity down here from solar fabric," Dillo said. "You may have noticed it up top."

Xenos were everywhere. To Bryn, the atmosphere felt more like a carnival than anything. Like the Warehouse, there were people hawking goods - mostly food, it seemed, but over by one storefront, a woman guarded a rack of clothes, and over by another, a man had laid out garage-sale-type items on the ground. A shirtless man in the center of the square with a crowd of people around him suddenly spewed fire from his mouth in a bright yellow stream. The crowd applauded and encouraged him to do it again. That was when she noticed the children. Unlike the Warehouse, which was largely populated with homeless adults, this place had more of a commune feel to it, with what looked like whole families ensconced within its glowing walls.

They passed a group of four armed men sitting on the cement lip of a circular structure that looked like it was meant to be the pool part of a fountain. The men were playing dice until one of them caught sight of Dillo and said something. Each man straightened up and stood at attention. Dillo made a 'come here' gesture to one of them, a bald man who reminded Bryn of a Neanderthal with his wide nose and heavy brow.

The man started to sputter excuses, but Dillo cut him off. "Save it, Junk. There's some boxes out by the holly trees. Go get a dolly and bring them to the queen."

The man named Junk nodded and trotted off.

Dillo continued on, leading them in the direction of the stacked, beehive-like drainage pipe sections. People seemed to be giving the pipes a wide berth; the area in front of them was deserted. When they were about ten yards away, she saw that all of the pipes were sealed off except the centermost one, and it had heavy black curtains covering the entrance.

Without warning, an old woman with long white braids came from behind them and placed herself in Bryn's path. Her wrinkled face creased in a toothless grin, and with slurred, barely discernible words, she said, "Oh, my Dog, it *is* you!"

Jason grabbed Bryn's arm and tried to steer her past, but the old woman persisted, grasping her other arm with gnarled fingers and declaring loudly, "Look! Esmie knew! It's the Bryn! The girl-girl with the XBestia head!"

"Leave off, ya crazy old hag!" someone yelled.

Bryn looked for the source and spotted a man who could only have come from inside the center pipe. He had very light hair, so light it must have been white blond under the sun, and wore a leather jacket that hung to his hips. He stood there with his legs spread in an aggressive stance, and the rifle in his hands only emphasized that aggression. As soon as the old woman saw him, she let out a squawk of alarm, released Bryn's arm as if it burned her, and scuttled away.

The ambient green lighting made it difficult to make out specific colors, but Bryn thought the blond man's jacket was red. Whatever color it was, the cut was similar to the jacket worn by the dead man in the silo. Were they both part of some paramilitary group within the Mad Eye gang? She met Jason's gaze and understood the warning there. He kept hold of her arm, but instead of offering support, she sensed he was staking a claim over her. She had no argument with *that*.

The blond man just stood there with his head cocked to one side, watching them. Dillo didn't move forward or try to go around; he seemed to be waiting for something. After a minute or so of silence, a hand appeared at the opening of the black curtain shielding the interior of the center pipe. The curtain was swept aside, and a tall woman stepped out. She was dressed all in dark leather that hugged her slim body, and much of her height came from the stiletto-heeled boots that rose up and flared past her knees. Her hair, like the man's, was blindingly blond, but much longer than his, sweeping down to a point that brushed her lower back.

With a slow, regal stride, she came closer. Bryn was considered tall, so the few times she'd had occasion to wear heels, she'd kept them low.

Even so, she'd never gotten the hang of them. This woman had walking in high heels down pat. Her ensemble, and the confident, sinuous way she moved, told Bryn she was in the presence of the 'queen' Dillo had mentioned earlier. Bryn wasn't sure what it was, but something about the woman told her maybe Dillo had left off the 'drag' part.

Again, the green lighting made exact color identification impossible, but Bryn noticed the woman's right eye was different from the left. Not only did the iris seem to have a reddish tint, but the pupil had that strange reflective quality she'd seen in old flash photographs. She'd heard it termed 'red eye.'

"How is it, Dragila," the woman said, "that you were arrested this morning, but are now a free man?"

It was patently obvious that the woman's naturally low voice was deliberately pitched higher to sound female. Her accent gave her country of origin away: India.

"Technically," Jason replied, "I'm a wanted man."

"Yes, well, that's beside the point. Oh, wait, you weren't talking about me, were you?"

Jason laughed in his throat. "If I ever swing 'round to your way of doing things, you'll be the first to know, Maddy."

Bryn kept her chin down and her face blank, but had a hard time not reacting to tough-guy Jason flirting with a transgender woman. He hadn't struck her as a particularly tolerant man, but this insight gave him a boost up in her estimation.

Maddy's glossy lips formed a quick, affectionate moue in Jason's direction, but she turned her attention to Bryn.

"Well, well, well. If it isn't little Miss Bryn Vega, in the flesh."

It seemed as if everyone was waiting for Bryn to respond, so she said, "Hey."

Maddy turned to the blond man and laughed. "'Hey', she says! How quaint."

Her merriment disappeared as swiftly as it had arisen. She laced her fingers together in front of her abdomen and addressed Jason, tone tinged with disappointment. "Why did you bring her here?"

Bryn saw Jason's eyes flicker to the blond man, who'd moved to stand at Maddy's shoulder. The bright hair wasn't the only thing Maddy and her henchman had in common. Although her face was heavily made up and her boots gave her a height advantage, Bryn recognized a distinct resemblance between the two. They were clearly related, and in this light at least, could be mistaken for twins.

"She helped me escape," Jason said. "I owe her."

Bryn wished that Jason had used the time during the drive down to brief her on whatever cover story he'd come up with - unless it hadn't occurred to him to make one up and he was winging it now. All the Mad Eyes had to do was ask them separately what happened, and they were done for.

Maddy regarded Bryn for a long moment. "She doesn't look like she's capable of properly tying her shoes, much less helping you escape, but if you say she's trustworthy..."

Her strange eyes shifted back to Jason. "One bunk or two?"

Bryn was glad the lighting hid her blush as Jason said shortly, "One."

Maddy lifted her chin. "I see. Well, color me jealous."

She spun gracefully on her heel and with a flourishing wave of her hand, indicated they should follow.

Chapter Fifteen

Scott had just started his motorcycle when he felt his holophone vibrate. He took it out of his pocket, looked at the display and sent the call to his helmet. A holo of Shasta appeared to float in front of his visor.

Her head went back, and she looked irritated. On her end, his image would be a night-shot close up of his face. "You're not driving, are you Agent Harding?"

"No, ma'am. I just met with Padme."

"How'd you manage that?"

He told her how he'd lured Padme out.

"Anything to report?"

"She doesn't know where Bryn is. She was a bundle of nerves. She did say something odd, though." He relayed her comments about the typhoid and Scott not being aware of any demands Fournier had made.

"Interesting." Shasta's brow creased as she considered his words, then her face cleared and she said crisply, "We'll talk about it later. Unger got us access to the silo. I'm sending the coordinates. Meet me there."

"Got it."

He called up the map and sent it to the upper right quadrant of his visor. A female voice began gently giving him directions. The silo safe house wasn't close to his current location, but he thought he had enough electrigas to get there and back.

He felt an overpowering sense of urgency but was forced to drive more cautiously on the treacherous roadways than he wanted. All the way there, he ran and reran the facts through his mind, always coming to the same frustrating conclusion: Bryn was missing, but Padme had no knowledge of it.

There were seven vehicles on site, including Shasta's shiny green BMW. Scott parked his motorcycle next to the CSI van. The side door to the van was wide open and a high-res holo camera was just sitting on the nearest seat. Scott looked around, realized he wasn't being observed and picked up the camera. Quickly, he scrolled through dozens of evidence holos until he got to the shots of the bodies. One had been shot in the head, recently, as far as he could tell, but it was the other body he focused on.

Shasta had said that the body found along with Agent Antonovich had been there for some time. The FBI hadn't released the man's name, and the holos gave grim testimony that it might have been because they hadn't been *able* to identify him. A hideous close-up of the dead man's head showed he had no face. There were shots of his hands that indicated some decomposition, but no loss of flesh. Either some animal had very precisely chewed only his face away down to the bone, or it had been surgically removed.

Scott heard someone coming, so he switched off the camera and set it down. He walked around the van and looked for Shasta. Powerful portable lights had been set up, cutting through the drifting fog. He spotted her talking with a group of four FBI agents. She split away to intercept him as he approached. One of the agents, a thin, balding man in an ill-fitting suit, trailed behind her.

"They want us in and out," Shasta told Scott. "This is Agent Kolano. He'll be escorting us." She placed a faint sarcastic emphasis on the word 'escorting.'

Agent Kolano handed Shasta a pair of purple rubber gloves and held some out for Scott, but Scott showed him his hands and said, "Got anything in an extra-large?"

Kolano snorted and tucked the gloves in his own jacket pocket. "Just don't touch anything."

He started walking, but Scott tapped Shasta on the arm and hung back, quickly and quietly telling her about the holos of the faceless corpse. Then they caught up to Kolano, who led them around the low concrete structure to its entrance.

He pointed to the yellow evidence markers and in a monotone began listing what was found. "Three distinct footprints, a handprint in the dirt, bullet was recovered there, plus four casings from two separate firearms."

"All those casings and just one bullet?" Scott asked. That usually meant the bullets were inside a body or two. "Any blood?"

"Two drops."

"Whose?" Shasta asked.

"Your guy. There's a ricochet off the wall, so we're still looking for bullets." He indicated a figure in a CSI jacket running a metal detector over the ground some yards away.

The door to the silo had been propped partially open. A holoscanner was mounted next to the door. They went inside and Scott saw that a keypad locking device had been torn from the wall. He indicated the fluorescent fingerprint powder on the door.

"Whose prints?"

"Agent Antonovich's on the outside, your guy on the inside."

"Do we know what happened here?" Shasta asked.

Kolano shrugged. "We have a basic idea, just not sure exactly who did what yet."

They followed him down a long, dimly lit tunnel to a metal door. A lone evidence marker sat nearby. "Another bullet there," he said, before opening the door and leading them down one level of a spiral staircase.

They entered the safe house and Scott looked around at the debris littering the area. Most of it centered around the far door, which had been blown from its hinges. Holes peppered the walls, ceiling and furnishings.

"Frag grenade," Kolano said. "Probable military issue. Up there is the escape hatch."

"So someone was trying to get in," Scott said. *And didn't care who they hurt in the process.*

Kolano pressed his lips together. "Looks that way."

Scott thought about Bryn, how scared she must have been, and wished for the hundredth time it had been him assigned to watch her. He knew Shasta had pulled him off that duty because she suspected they'd formed a mutual attachment - and she'd been right.

The agent rushed them through the rest of the safe house, pointing out that a bloodstained towel and a bloody, ruined t-shirt had been recovered from the bathroom. Again, when Shasta asked whose blood it was, he said, "Your guy."

Both bedrooms were empty, but in one, the bed had been made up and looked rumpled, as if someone had been lying there. Scott bent close to the pillow. He made out the faint scent of Bryn's special shampoo and saw that the smooth cotton fabric of the case was marred with tiny holes.

He looked at Shasta. "She was definitely here."

Back in the stairwell, Kolano said, "The bodies were found on the bottom level."

They began their descent, but he stopped on the next level down and pointed out another evidence marker resting on the concrete next to a huge round hole in the floor.

"Rifle casing," he said. "Shooter took out our agent from here."

Scott walked over and looked down through the hole. An experienced gunman wouldn't have found it a tough shot from this angle and distance. He thought it odd that the shooter had murdered an FBI agent, but hadn't bothered to retrieve his casing. It suggested the perp was either in a hurry or confident he wouldn't get caught.

They continued down the stairs to the bottom, where someone had set up more of the portable lights. Kolano waited by the entranceway while Scott and Shasta walked a slow circuit around the evidence, but there wasn't much to be learned from a pool of congealed blood with no telltale footprints.

Scott looked up through the holes in the floors to where the rifle casing had been found. With no light source on the lower levels other than that coming from the stairwell, the shooter must have used a night vision scope to see well enough to make the shot.

In a low voice he asked Shasta, "Is Alton a sniper by any chance?"

"He was his squad's marksman in the fourth war," she replied just as quietly. "You think he did it?"

Scott lifted his eyebrows and gave a slight nod. He walked over to Kolano. "Were there fingerprints on the outside of the escape hatch?"

Kolano hesitated but nodded.

"Agent Antonovich's?"

Reluctantly, Kolano said, "Yeah."

Shasta had moved to stand next to Scott. She crossed her arms. "Was the FBI aware they had a rogue agent on their hands, or did Antonovich's actions come as complete surprise?"

Chapter Sixteen

Jason took Bryn's hand, lacing his fingers with hers. It was an intimate action that felt wrong to her, but he must have thought it would be in character. He pulled her along behind him as he followed Maddy to the curtained drainpipe. Bryn glanced back and saw that Dillo wasn't coming. He gave her a thumbs-up and turned to deal with the xeno named Junk, who'd arrived with the dolly loaded with boxes from Jason's truck.

The blond man in the red jacket rushed ahead of Maddy and pulled the curtain aside for her.

"Thank you, Munnu," she murmured, before stepping over the concrete lip. Her hand curled around the railing of a short flight of metal steps and her heels clanged on the diamond plating as she climbed. Jason seemed confident enough, but Bryn didn't particularly want to enter the dark chamber. She imagined Maddy's inner sanctuary as something one might find in the seedier end of some red-light district, with overstuffed pillows on the floor and brocade draperies concealing alcoves with torture devices straight out of some medieval castle.

The reality was far different.

Level flooring had been installed inside the pipe out of the same metal diamond plating as the steps. Like the entrance tunnel to Edgemere, shelves lined the curved walls, only instead of mushrooms, there were guns, grenades and ammunition clips everywhere. The lighting was the same green bioluminescence. The pipe looked to be around twenty feet long, and at the far end was a round table, with two men and a woman sitting equidistant from each other on office chairs. In the middle of the table, a large holo projector displayed a live feed that must have been compiled from thousands of cameras within Edgemere. Each of the three techs also had a smaller holo display directly in front of them. As Bryn watched, the nearest tech zoomed in on two xenos so close she could see their lips moving.

"This is the security center." Maddy grinned at Bryn and opened her eyes wide so the whites showed all around. "I see all, hear all." The grin disappeared. "And don't you forget it."

At the center of the pipe, scaled down doorways had been cut on either side and ramps had been installed across the spaces between neighboring pipes. There was also a round hole cut in the ceiling. A chrome pole mounted in the floor disappeared up through it, just like in a fire station, and hanging from the edge was an aluminum triple extension ladder.

Maddy turned left and ducked through the doorway. The next pipe over was radically different from the security center. The flooring was natural stone tile and the space was furnished; if it weren't for the curving biopolycrete walls, it would resemble a long, narrow Victorian era sitting room. They crossed straight through and entered the next pipe. More stone flooring, but this room was furnished at one end with a couch, chairs and bookshelves with real books on them, and at the other end with a formal dining room table.

"When Munnu notified me of your arrival, Dragila dear, I took the liberty of asking Cook to set another plate," her eyes shifted to Bryn, "two plates, at the table. Are you hungry?"

"Famished," Jason said, although Bryn knew he'd eaten less than an hour ago.

"Very good. Please be seated."

Bryn and Jason set their bags behind their chairs and sat next to each other with Maddy and Munnu facing them.

Within moments of pulling their chairs in, a uniformed servant entered from the next pipe over. She set out bread and butter and poured a dark, foamy liquid in everyone's glasses.

Bryn had been in some strange places under even stranger circumstances in the last year, but Edgemere and its queen topped them all. She almost looked to the far end of the table to see if the Mad Hatter was seated there.

Jason buttered a hunk of bread and set it on Bryn's plate. "Eat," he said softly.

The bread was delicious; soft and warm inside, with a crispy crust. Bryn chewed with enthusiasm, waiting for Maddy to begin the interrogation she knew was coming.

"Word is that your father is responsible for arranging your kidnapping," Maddy said, right on cue.

Bryn inclined her head and swallowed her bite before saying, "That's true."

"Why would he do such a thing?"

Bryn thought about lying, but when Maddy had said she 'saw all, heard all,' Bryn interpreted it to mean that she already knew more than she let on. As the head of the Mad Eyes, the main rival gang to the XBestia, Maddy would know what motivated Dr. Fournier, who had been in league with Bryn's father.

"He was hoping to influence public perception of xenofreaks."

"Fathers are strange creatures, are they not?"

Bryn lifted her eyebrows in agreement and took another bite of the bread.

"My father also had me undergo a xeno transplant," Maddy said. "You may have noticed one of my eyes is different."

Bryn looked into Maddy's face, focusing on the reddish eye. It suddenly occurred to her that the name 'Maddy' was similar to Mad Eye.

Maddy smiled. "No, not that eye. I was born with the red one. If you hadn't noticed, my twin brother and I are albino."

Bryn couldn't help it; she glanced at Munnu. His eyes were both brown.

"Yes," Maddy said. "Munnu's eyes are normal. Even though our DNA is identical, albinism strikes in different ways. Mine was more extensive, affecting my eyes and making them photosensitive. The left one looks more normal because it was from a pig donor, but I can't see out of it. My father had the world's best surgeons attempt to fix me, but optic nerve transection between mammals has never been perfected."

"Is that why you live underground? Because of your eyes?"

"Eye. Only the one I was born with works, and no, I live underground because I like it here. I'm perfectly capable of wearing sunglasses like anyone else who goes into the sun."

Maddy's scornful tone reminded Bryn of her intention not to speak. The queen of Edgemere was obviously touchy and the last thing Bryn wanted to do was to get on her bad side.

"I meant no disrespect," she said.

Maddy made a '*hmph*' sound. "Well, you're polite anyway. Now convince me why I should let you live."

Bryn choked a little on her bread. She coughed a few times, took a sip of what turned out to be beer and looked to Jason for assistance.

"Because she's with me, and I have information," he said.

"Ah." Maddy stretched the word out. "Now we're getting somewhere. What is this information?"

"For your ears only," he replied.

"Munnu is an extension of myself," Maddy declared. "We are practically interchangeable."

In the low light, Jason's face was unreadable. "You sure about that?"

Maddy sat as if immobilized and stared him down. Next to her, Munnu, too, sat unmoving and unblinking. Bryn sensed that Jason had crossed a line and in this moment, they were in more danger than they'd been since they'd entered this bizarre place.

Still without moving, Maddy barked, "Leave us."

Bryn wasn't sure to whom she was speaking, but Munnu shoved his chair back abruptly and departed without a word.

"There," Maddy said in a deceptively mild manner. "Now what is this all-important information?"

"That man?" Jason nodded at the door Munnu had just gone through. "He's not who you think he is."

"You think I don't know that?"

Jason set his fork down and his eyes narrowed. "He killed your brother and took his place, and you just...let him?"

Maddy made a tent with her fingertips. The nails were long and painted with some dark polish. "It's done. Even I can't prevent something that has already happened. As for letting the imposter think he's fooled me? You know the old saying, 'Keep your friends close and your enemies closer.'"

For once, Jason seemed to be at a loss for words.

Maddy laughed. "Don't look so perplexed. I assure you I have the situation well in hand. Is that the extent of your information? And how, pray tell, did you discover it?"

Bryn felt the danger factor ratchet up a notch. Behind Maddy's casually worded question, she sensed a keen, menacing interest. Jason couldn't very well tell her the truth.

He was saved from having to lie, however, when Munnu stepped back through the door and cleared his throat.

"What is it?" Maddy snapped.

"There's a problem." He stepped aside to make room for Dillo, who waited for Maddy to invite him to cross the threshold.

She waved him in. "This had better be good."

"I'm sorry for interrupting your supper," Dillo said. "But the illness I reported yesterday has spread to seven others."

She sighed in exasperation. "I really don't care if a few people get the sniffles. Has Doc Munoz looked at them yet?"

"He's one of the sick ones."

"Well, I'll tell you what. You go now and do your job. If someone *dies*, come back and we'll talk. Okay?"

Dillo didn't leave; in fact, to Bryn, he seemed to deflate a bit as he waited.

Maddy stared at him for a long moment and then asked, "Who?"

"The Fisherman's son."

Maddy leaned forward in disbelief. "He's what, fourteen? Healthy and strong. How could he die?"

Dillo shook his head slowly back and forth. "It's bad, whatever it is. There's two more don't look like they're gonna make it. Both kids."

Maddy stood and tossed her napkin on the table. She looked at Jason. "Stay and finish your dinner. Bunk down in one of the empties. We'll talk more in the morning."

She marched out, all trace of swish gone. Munnu followed, but Dillo hesitated long enough to shoot Jason an enigmatic look before he, too, left.

Bryn opened her mouth to ask him if the real Munnu was the body at the bottom of the silo, but he gave a quick shake of his head that told her not to speak. She thought of the techs in the security center watching everything and everyone at Edgemere on the live holo feed. They most likely had earbugs that fed them anything anyone said, too. Even now, one of them could be zoomed in on Bryn's face, waiting for her to say or do something that would give her away.

Chapter Seventeen

cott had only gotten about four hours of sleep when his holophone rang. He was so groggy he almost rubbed the sleep out of his eyes with his cougar pads, something he hadn't done in a long time, since it was guaranteed to get hair in them.

Shasta's holo showed she was in her office, looking well groomed and refreshed.

"Rise and shine, Agent Harding."

"Any word on Bryn?" he asked, settling on rubbing his eye with the bend of his wrist.

"Still in the wind," she replied. "I need you here in an hour."

He sat up a little straighter. "Yes, ma'am."

"Don't be late."

After she disconnected, Scott forced himself to get out of bed even though he desperately wanted to lie back down.

In the shower, his mind sluggishly began sifting through the facts. Last night, Agent Kolano hadn't been willing to admit that the FBI had a rogue agent in their ranks. He'd blustered about not making assumptions until they had every possible piece of information. Shasta had lost patience right about then and demanded to speak to the Special Agent in Charge, something Kolano didn't have the authority to make happen right then and there.

Now Scott stepped out of the shower, dried off and ran his electric lazor over the stubble on his chin. Bryn had commented once that she liked his face clean-shaven. He looked into his eyes in the partially fogged mirror, but saw her eyes; thinking, *Where are you*?

He dressed in a casual shirt and jeans and grabbed an energy bar from the kitchen.

When he arrived at Shasta's office, she was meeting with Special Agent in Charge Miles Reed. He had thinning brown hair, and his portly physique suggested he'd been out of the field for quite some time.

Shasta introduced them and they shook hands. Not long after Scott's undercover assignment had come to an end, when he was reintegrating into the agency, he'd decided there were two kinds of people - the ones who reacted to his xenograft, and the ones who ignored it. Reed was the latter. It didn't mean he didn't have an opinion; just that he was too professional to express it.

Shasta cut to the chase. "How did Antonovich know Agent Alton would be at the silo safe house?"

"He didn't," Reed replied. "Our agents have access to the safe house system, but it only tracks what units are in use, not who's using them. The silo had been decommissioned for almost two years, but our techs say Antonovich set it up so he'd be pinged if it was ever reactivated."

"So he was trying to retrieve the body," Scott said.

Reed's head dipped in acknowledgement. "We think so."

"Who was it, Miles?"

Scott wasn't surprised she called him by his first name. Shasta Fox knew everyone.

"Munnu Singh," Reed said.

Scott had never heard of the man, but when Shasta asked, "Maddy's Singh's twin brother?" he realized she was referring to the leader of the Mad Eye gang.

"That doesn't make sense," she said. "I was told the second body had been dead for some time."

"Hard to tell how long," Reed replied. "It was near freezing down there."

"Ballpark?"

"M.E. said three to five months."

"Then it couldn't have been Singh. One of our agents reported him alive and well a few days ago."

Scott thought about the grisly holo of the corpse, and asked, "Face transplant?"

"That would tend to explain the missing face on our body," Reed said. "But why?"

"And why dump the body where it could be found instead of destroying it?" Scott asked.

"I'm sure the answers to those questions will be fascinating, but right now, I'd really like to find my agent and our witness. Any idea where they might be?"

Reed frowned and shook his head. "Nothing at the scene indicated whether they walked away on their own steam or were taken by force by an unknown party."

"Let's assume for argument's sake that no one else was there," she said. "Alton realizes he just killed an FBI agent, but the body in the basement makes it pretty obvious that agent was crooked. Forensics says the blood in the bathroom was Alton's, so it's a good bet our witness bandaged him up and he got her out of there."

"Without reporting in," Scott said, unable to keep the contempt out of his voice.

"He panicked," Reed suggested.

Shasta shook her head. "Not Alton. But he would have wondered how Antonovich knew they were in the safe house. I think he came to the conclusion someone within the XIA tipped Antonovich off."

"These days that's not even a paranoid assumption," Reed said.

Scott nodded his agreement. Spies and corrupt employees were rampant within every conceivable government law enforcement agency. Not a week went by that he didn't hear about a terrorist organization or crime syndicate that had infiltrated up to the highest levels. Trust could cost you your life.

"Where would he go?" Shasta said almost to herself.

"You know," Scott said, "he was pretty pissed when you pulled him from his mission."

"What mission?" Reed asked.

She hesitated as if she was debating whether to answer, but finally said, "To get close to Maddy Singh. But she put him out at Yakaburra and he was useless to us there."

She looked at Scott. "What are you suggesting, Agent Harding?"

"Nothing. Just...if it were me, and information that could help me accomplish my mission just dropped in my lap, I might be tempted to run with it. No pun intended."

She looked up at the ceiling for a moment and sighed. "Edgemere *is* underground. You might be on to something. He might have been trying to kill two birds and gain himself some time to think. We've got a semi-reliable informant out there - I'll see if I can find out anything."

She stood. "Thank you, Miles. I know this has been unpleasant. I appreciate that you've been reasonable and haven't turned it into a manhunt."

Reed stood, too; slowly, as if his joints pained him. "Oh, I never said my people weren't out looking for your agent."

She blinked at him a few times. "At this juncture, I'd keep in mind that Alton may very well feel threatened by any FBI agent he encounters."

"We've had a nice conversation, Shasta. But you and I both know a full investigation will be launched. Alton may or may not eventually be cleared, but as long as he refuses to turn himself in, he looks guilty as hell."

Her jaw jutted briefly to one side. "Just a word of advice then, Special Agent. Don't send your people into Edgemere looking for him. It's not a friendly place."

Chapter Eighteen

Bryn woke lying on her side with a heavy weight across her hip. It was Jason's arm, which he'd slipped under her open jacket sometime during the night. Because of her quills, when they'd first climbed onto the thin mattress, he'd had to scootch further down to keep from getting poked. They'd gone to sleep fully dressed and back-to-back, but they'd turned towards each other sometime during the night. She looked down and saw the top of his head. His warm breath penetrated her shirt against her abdomen. It was an intimate position, and yet she didn't feel the slightest stirring of interest. If she'd woken up in Scott's arms, her quills would have reacted by going flat to her head.

Thinking of him made them do just that, and she responded by irritably nudging Jason awake.

He instantly sat up. "What's wrong?"

"Nothing. I think it's morning."

It was impossible to tell. The green lighting remained constant. He reached for his holophone to check the time.

"Do you get a signal?" she asked.

"Very weak. It's six a.m."

Because there were cameras everywhere, she hadn't been able to voice her concern last night that they weren't far enough underground should Padme attack. She'd been scared not just because of what her nanoneurons might do, but because freaking out in this place would be a very bad thing. If she'd lost control like she had at Carla's, it would have gotten her the wrong kind of attention - not that any kind of attention was a good thing here.

Bunking down at Edgemere hadn't been a private affair. Maddy's soldiers filled nearly every one of the fourteen bunks in this, the drainpipe designated for them. When Jason and Bryn had first arrived and he'd chosen a lower bunk at the back of the pipe, she'd rebelled and attempted to climb on the top bunk, but he'd grabbed her arm to prevent her from doing so. It was dark, since only one tube of bioluminescence snaked through this pipe, but she'd seen his warning look: *stay in character*. After hearing the rough banter from the soldiers as they trickled in, she was glad he'd insisted they sleep together, despite the awkwardness.

None of the other occupants stirred when they quietly put on their shoes and hefted their bags.

"Where are we going?" she whispered.

"Breakfast. Maddy's an early riser."

"I need to go to the bathroom."

Outside the pipe, an armed guard was waiting. He said, "Dragila."

When Jason nodded, he said, "Come with me," but Jason responded, "We need to make a pit stop first."

The bunk pipe was on one of the top levels. The guard led them through two doorways until they reached the fireman's pole. He looked at Jason. "You been here before, right?"

"Yeah. Latrine's two floors down."

The guard grabbed the pole, wrapped his legs around it and slid down through the opening in the floor. Jason turned to Bryn. "You got this?"

She nodded. She'd climbed the extension ladders to get up into the higher levels of the lair, but knew she was expected to slide back down.

The opening in the floor was just big enough to accommodate the bags slung over Jason's shoulder. After he disappeared, she quickly followed. She slid down slowly, the soles of her shoes squeaking on the metal. When she arrived at the right level, Jason reached out and grasped her around the waist, helping her traverse the gap.

The 'latrine,' as he'd called it, was all the way back in the furthest pipe on that level. It had two sinks, one long tiled shower facility like they'd had in her high school locker room, and four toilets, none of which were enclosed in a stall. Luckily, it was deserted at this hour.

She walked over and inspected one of the toilets. The water was glowing faintly green. Dillo had mentioned the bioluminescent bacteria produced methane, but it smelled like pine-scented cleaner in the pipe. "Why doesn't it smell bad?"

"I guess there's not a high enough concentration of the bacteria," he said. "If there were, it wouldn't be livable down here - methane's deadly - and besides, now that I think of it, it's odorless. It only smells bad when it's combined with something, uh, stinky."

75

She laughed a little at his use of the word 'stinky.' It seemed too mild a word for him. He must have changed his original phrasing at the last second. It was a small thing, but she thought it was sweet of him. Then he blew it by saying, "Speaking of stinky," and gestured to the toilet with his eyebrows raised.

"I just have to pee," she said, affronted.

"Well, I don't, so hurry up."

"Turn around, then!"

"Oh. Right." He walked over to the entryway and stood there blocking it with his back to her until she was done.

She wasn't about to stay in the room while he did his business, so she ducked through to the next pipe, where the guard was waiting. He looked bored until she came in, then he openly leered at her.

She ignored him and rummaged around in her bag until she felt a round, flat object: her compact mirror. She wasn't concerned about looking attractive - especially not around lowlifes like the guard here, but she'd rubbed her eyes when she got up before she remembered all the eye makeup and wanted to check it. The mirror had a row of tiny LED lights that showed her she looked like a raccoon. All she could do with the guard looking on was wipe the edge of her finger around her eyelids. It didn't help much.

She sighed, closed the compact and glanced around the pipe. It was a storage area with shelves filled with necessities like toilet paper and cleaning supplies.

It occurred to her that Jason would need new dressings on his wounds. She turned to the guard. "Is there anywhere I can get some bandages?"

He snorted and his eyes shifted to her quills. "You poke yourself?"

"Um, yeah, all the time, but they're not for me."

He waved a hand. "If you can find 'em, help yourself."

She moved down the aisle between shelves, searching. There wasn't a discernible shelving system, but eventually she found a box of cotton balls, an industrial-sized bottle of antiseptic, and a can of pseudo-skin.

When Jason came out of the latrine, she held up her finds.

"Yeah, okay, that's a good idea," he said. He dropped his bags and stripped off his shirt.

The guard said, "The queen's waiting, you know."

"It'll only take a minute," Bryn assured him.

She peeled off all the bandages she'd applied yesterday. It was hard to tell in the low light, but the wounds looked inflamed. She quickly swabbed them with the antiseptic, wincing for him as he let out a few gasps of pain, then she stepped back and thoroughly sprayed each wound with pseudo-skin.

"That feel better? The can says it has a numbing agent in it."

He made a '*whew*' sound. "A little, yeah. Thanks."

The pseudo-skin took a few minutes to dry. Because the guard was looking on impatiently, she began to blow on Jason's back to hurry the process along. When she moved to the wound next to the Gila monster xenograft and gently blew on it, he stepped away and said, "It's dry enough."

He put his shirt back on. She offered to carry his bags for him, but he shook his head and tucked them under his arms.

The guard said, "Are we done now, or do you all want to clip each other's toenails, too?"

"That's incredibly amusing," Jason said, sounding anything but amused. "Do you know who I am?"

"Everyone knows who you are," he replied, but she noticed he was quick to back down.

In the dining room pipe, Maddy was sitting at the table eating. Today she wore a man's camouflage field jacket over a lacy black bustier. Her long blond hair was in one thick braid pulled forward. She looked up when the guard appeared and said, "Yes, yes. Send them in."

When she saw that Jason and Bryn were carrying their bags, she asked, "Planning on leaving?"

Jason glanced at the guard, who'd settled near the doorway. "Still not sure if we're welcome."

"Sit." Maddy stared down at her plate. Even in the low light, Bryn saw worry lines etched on her face.

Jason pulled out the chairs in front of two place settings and they sat and waited. After a few minutes, Maddy said in a subdued voice, "Thanks for the supplies. I wouldn't be eating now if it weren't for what you brought."

"Why's that?" he asked.

"Poison. At least, that's what we think. The effects are too rapid and too severe to be an illness. We lost two more last night. I have my holo techs working on identifying a common link between the victims, and my bioengineers are trying to isolate the toxin."

The same servant woman from last night entered with two plates and two glasses of a liquid that glowed fluorescently in the lighting. She set the plates and drinks in front of Scott and Bryn and left without a word. Jason immediately began to dig in, but Bryn looked down at the steaming pile of what looked like corned beef hash from a can and swallowed.

"Are you a vegetarian?" Maddy asked.

Bryn picked up her fork. "No."

"Well, that must have been a blessing for you after what your father did. It would have been funny, though. I mean, imagine if you had really strong beliefs about killing animals and he went and did that." She gestured to Bryn's quills.

"Yeah, funny," Bryn said. She put a bite of the hash in her mouth and hoped Maddy wouldn't continue.

"My father was willing to do anything for me and my brother; that is, until he found out I liked boys. That didn't go over so well."

Bryn was saved from having to come up with a suitably sensitive response by someone who appeared in the doorway and waited there uncertainly. Maddy said, "Come in, Vespa. Have you discovered anything?"

It was the female tech Bryn had seen yesterday at the holo table. She held a holopad in one hand. She took a few steps into the pipe and stopped, as if she was afraid to get too close to Maddy. "Yes-yes-yes, we think so," she stuttered, nodding rapidly.

"Well what is it? Tell me."

Vespa took another step into the room and held out the holopad, fully five feet from Maddy. "Everyone who got sick was seen with this man."

Jason jumped up, took the holopad from Vespa and gave it to Maddy.

"Thank you, Dragila," she said, shooting the terrified woman an annoyed look. She frowned down at the holopad and then handed it back to Jason. "I don't know him. Do you know him? Who is this?"

"Never saw him before," Jason said.

Bryn glanced over. "Oh, wait. That's Junk."

"Who?" Maddy and Jason said at the same time.

"Dillo had him bring in the boxes..." she trailed off and looked down at her breakfast.

Maddy's mouth fell open and she put her hands to her throat. A low sound escaped, like a moan that began to build until it became a full-fledged scream of fury. She shoved her chair back and swept her hand across the table. Her glass and nearly empty plate flew into the curved biopolycrete wall and shattered. Vespa cringed by the door as Maddy snatched the holopad from Jason. Then she stalked out of the pipe, bellowing in a man's voice, "Dil-*lo*!"

Chapter Nineteen

When Scott left Shasta's office, he passed Deputy Director Unger in the hall. Unger didn't acknowledge Scott - didn't even seem to notice him. His face was florid with anger as he headed straight for Shasta's door. Scott didn't envy her; he was just glad he'd escaped before the fireworks.

At his desk, he checked his messages. One was from Mia, confirming that Robert Cruise's neighbor had died from the super typhoid and asking Scott to meet her for lunch at the Holo House Cafe so they could discuss it. The other was from one of the detectives who'd shut down the massage parlor where Cruise's girlfriend had worked. Scott called him back and got the girlfriend's name and address. Lucky for him, Candace 'Candy' Barton hadn't been caught up in the raid.

She lived in the same neighborhood as Cruise, but a few buildings down. It took Scott twenty minutes of driving around to find a parking spot, and he was aggravated by the time he fed the meter. He had to walk six blocks to Candy's building, which was nearly identical to Cruise's in every way. Her apartment was on the second floor and she answered the door after his third knock. She was heavyset and had shoulder-length, pink-streaked brown hair. She wore no make-up to cover her acne-pocked skin, although her complete lack of eyebrows suggested she usually painted them on. Dressed only in a man's t-shirt that came to mid-thigh, she leaned against the doorjamb and said wearily, "Can I help you?"

"Candy Barton?" Scott asked, flashing his badge.

She let out a heavy sigh. "Dude."

"Is that a yes? Are you Candy Barton?"

"Um..." She straightened up but lost her balance and stumbled to one side. "Yeah...yeah. S'me."

"May I come in? I'd like to speak to you about Robert Cruise."

It was obvious Candy was high on something, and she confirmed it by smiling beatifically and slurring, "He's sooo good to me - brought me some shrooms! You want some?"

Scott couldn't help smiling back at her. She'd already forgotten he was law enforcement. "Sounds good. What kind?"

She turned and walked into the living area, which had a battered couch, stained coffee table and what looked to Scott to be a first-generation holovision. Clothes and garbage were strewn everywhere, and the stench of rotten, moldy food nearly made his eyes water. She picked up a plastic bag from the coffee table and waved it in the air. "Mad Eye. Nothing but the best from my Junkie."

He was a little surprised to hear that Cruise had given his girlfriend Mad Eye Mushrooms, which were specially bioengineered to be a potent hallucinogen, highly sought-after in the black market, and highly illegal. If Cruise was taking orders from Fournier, as the XIA assumed, that made him a member of the XBestia gang. He'd be taking a big chance purchasing drugs from a Mad Eye dealer - unless he'd gotten them second-hand. The quantity in the bag Candy was waving around would be worth thousands of dollars. No way Cruise could afford them unless he'd made a big score recently.

"Wow," Scott said in an exaggeratedly friendly voice. "Those look fresh, too. Where'd he get 'em?"

Her puffy eyelids closed until she was looking out at him through mere slits, and her head went slowly back, forming an impressive double chin. "Who are you again?"

"Cougar," he said, holding his hand out.

As expected, her eyes went wide at the sight of his xenograft. "Whoa, dude."

"So where's Robert now?" he asked.

She shook her head, sighed again and subsided onto the couch. Her t-shirt slipped off one shoulder and he saw a small rectangular xenograft in dark fur. He wondered if it was supposed to represent a candy bar. She seemed about to doze off sitting up, so he said again, "Where's Robert?"

Her eyes closed and she slumped over onto a pile of dirty clothes. "Out."

"When's he coming back?"

She giggled, eyes still closed. "Next time he's lonely."

"Candy?"

He waited a moment to see if she would respond, and when she didn't, he gently poked her shoulder.

She was out cold. He took the baggie out of her slack hand, went into the bathroom and emptied it into a toilet that looked like it hadn't seen a scrub brush in years. He used his foot to depress the handle and flushed the mushrooms down.

Chapter Twenty

For the next four hours, the underground home of the Mad Eye gang became a frantic hive of activity. Every available soldier was put to the task of finding Junk, who, it was eventually determined, must have slipped out sometime during the night. Those who were known to associate with him were then paraded before Maddy. She sat in a throne-like parlor chair set along the inside rim of the unfinished fountain. Dillo stood to the right of her, looking like the grim reaper in his long coat, and the fake Munnu stood on her left. Hundreds of people gathered around the fountain, which resembled a circus ring, an impression that was emphasized by a spotlight someone had set up on the second level and aimed at the center of the circle. Each acquaintance of the accused was made to stand within its bright light.

Maddy had settled down considerably since flying into the early morning rage that had awakened all of Edgemere, but Bryn wasn't fooled. The Mad Eye queen was deeply disturbed by recent events, and her calm demeanor was only a thin veneer.

She asked the same questions of each person who knew Junk. It was clear the vast majority of them did not know him well. Whenever she waved her hand to dismiss the latest one, her mask of patience slipped a little bit more.

Bryn stood next to Jason in the crowd, trying to ignore the gnawing hunger in her belly. After word of the poisonings got out, probably no one here had eaten much. She wanted more than ever to go home, and not just to raid Carla's refrigerator. The pullout bed wasn't any great shakes but compared to a cot in a room crowded with unwashed xenofreak soldiers, it seemed like nirvana.

She wondered when she would have the opportunity to talk to Jason without having to worry about being overheard. She wanted to ask him why he thought it wasn't safe to contact the XIA. He'd said they needed to disappear until he could find out who else was involved, but it didn't seem like he was in any hurry to do so. Unless he thought Maddy knew something? One thing Maddy *had* to know, at least, was that her brother was dead, since the imposter was wearing his face.

The spotlight brought color to this section of the formerly monochrome Edgemere. The man now called Munnu was, indeed, wearing a red jacket. Since it was unlikely he, too, was an albino, his hair must be bleached to be that almost-white shade. She thought maybe she saw the tiniest bit of darkness at the roots. He seemed to spend an awful lot of time staring at Jason with glittering, malevolent eyes. Jason didn't notice; he was focused on the queen's spectacle.

The people standing closest to them stirred as if a breeze had blown through. Heads turned and murmurs swelled. There was a disturbance somewhere. Bryn heard a faint shout and the crowd thinned as people moved towards the main entrance. Someone nudged her and she looked around. It was Esmie, the old woman who'd accosted her yesterday. Bryn expected the toothless woman to start in again about recognizing her, but instead, she slipped something surreptitiously into Bryn's hand and melted away into the crowd. Bryn looked down at the object: an earbug, a cheap one, like the kind children bought out of a gumball machine, where you could record a simple message for your friends to listen to. She wasn't eager to listen to anything the crazy old hag had to say, so she slipped it into her pocket and forgot about it.

There were more shouts from the crowd, and Bryn thought she made out the name 'Junk.' Someone standing next to her said, "They caught him! He was trying to sneak back in. What a moron!" She and Jason were jostled as people moved to make a path for a group of soldiers hauling a man roughly along. As they pushed him into the circle, the latest man under the spotlight scurried away.

One final shove sent Junk to his knees in front of the queen. The crowd hushed and all eyes focused on Maddy. Her head tilted to one side and she blinked several times.

"I don't think we've had the pleasure," she said.

Junk looked up but said nothing. His lip was bleeding, and one eye seemed to be swelling closed. He'd either fought capture or the guards took out their anger on him.

"Which," she continued, "rather surprises me, considering your actions."

"What am I accused of?" he asked.

She stood. "Three people are dead. Several more are dying. Young and old. All innocent."

Junk ducked his head, staring down at the bare concrete without replying.

"Shall I take your silence as an admission of guilt?"

When Junk still didn't answer her, Maddy crossed her arms over her chest, the muscles in her jaw working. As the seconds ticked by, the tendons stood out on her neck as she continued to tense up like a string drawn on a bow. Even from as far away as they were standing, Bryn cringed a little as she watched the pressure build. Everyone stood enthralled, waiting for Maddy to go ballistic.

When the eruption finally burst forth, it consisted of a name screamed at the top of her lungs.

"Dragila!"

Bryn looked at Jason, astounded.

Without hesitation, he dropped his bags and abandoned her, elbowing his way to the front of the crowd. Maddy raised an arm and pointed at him, crooking her finger to beckon him. To Bryn, it seemed as if Jason flicked some internal switch, turning the simple act of walking across the ring into a display of power, a subtle swagger that held every eye in fascinated suspense. When he stopped a few feet away from Maddy, she said something quietly to him, after which, to Bryn's further astonishment, he moved back, peeled off his shirt, and tossed it outside the ring.

He thrust his clenched fists in the air, his muscular arms contracting in a classic bodybuilder flex, and began to strut in a slow circle around Junk so all could see the fierce dragon on his back with its uplifted wings. The angry-looking scabs, glistening with their covering of pseudo-skin, only served to make the sight that much more intimidating.

Jason bared his teeth in a snarl, practically growling with aggression, before turning to the crowd and shouting out - inciting them with one word: "*Justice!*"

Pandemonium broke out as men and women pumped their fists into the air, stomped their feet and repeated the word over and over at the top of their lungs.

In Bryn's world, justice involved giving certain rights to the accused. Somehow, she doubted Junk was going to be afforded that courtesy. Jason moved towards him, his shadow looming over the now cowering xenofreak. Maddy raised her hands and the crowd quieted.

"This is how it's going to work," Jason said to Junk, speaking loudly so everyone could hear. "The queen will ask you a question. You will answer quickly and truthfully. If you do not, I will begin the slow process of reducing you to a sticky, red stain. Do you understand?"

84

Junk cowed away from him and nodded rapidly as the crowd chanted, "*Stain, stain, stain, stain!*"

Maddy raised her hands again and silence quickly fell. Bryn marveled at the control she had over her subjects. Now that their queen was about to question the man who was responsible for killing their own, they hung on her every word.

"What," Maddy asked in a pleasant tone, as if she were addressing someone over afternoon tea, "kind of poison did you use?"

Junk's dull expression changed drastically. He shook his head, pleading. "It wasn't poison, I swear!"

Jason jerked his arm back, but Maddy held up a hand to stop him. "Then what was it?" she asked.

Junk mumbled something no one but Maddy and Jason could hear. Maddy's eyes widened and she staggered back a step, her face incredulous. Jason gaped at him, his arms dropping to his sides.

"And *you knew*?" Maddy exclaimed. "You knew this, but you came here and infected everyone you came into contact with?" She spat the word 'infected' at him.

Junk seemed to perk up a little, and even managed a little bluster. "Xenos are immune! It only affects people without xenografts. I never meant to hurt anyone."

"You never meant..." Words seemed to fail her. She spun on her heel and in an inflectionless voice said, "Kill him."

"*Wait!*" Junk held out his arms towards her, begging. "There's more! I was sent here."

Her chin went up and after a moment her head turned, and she looked down her nose at him. "By whom?"

Junk's Adam's apple bobbed up and down as he swallowed nervously. "Make me a deal."

She laughed derisively. "I'd rather make you an example."

"You need to know this. You need to know what he's planning."

"Fine. I'll torture it out of you." She gestured to Dillo and Munno. "Take him to the dungeon."

Junk shouted after her, but his pleas were drowned out by the crowd as they began chanting, "*Stain, stain, stain,*" again. Jason stepped back as Dillo took one of Junk's arms and Munno took the other. They hauled him to his feet and propelled him after Maddy, who walked regally across the compound to her pipe lair.

Chapter Twenty-one

When Scott arrived at The Holo House Cafe, Mia was already sitting at a table on the patio, giving her order to the waitress. She'd pulled her long hair back in a casual ponytail today and was dressed in jeans and a plain pink t-shirt.

He sat in the chair next to her so he could keep an eye on the blood donation center and tried not to be offended when she tossed him an apologetic smile and switched chairs.

The waitress lifted her eyebrows at him. "Would you like a moment to decide?"

"No," he said. "I'm in the mood for mushrooms. What have you got?"

She listed the applicable menu items and he ordered a grilled steak and mushroom sandwich.

After she left, Mia asked, "Have you seen the news?"

"No, I've been working."

She slid her holo tablet across the table and activated a clip. A middle-aged male anchor had a picture of the courthouse displayed over his left shoulder and Scott instinctively knew this was going to be bad.

The anchor said, "What do four superior court jurors have in common with six county courthouse employees? Well, this reporter is sorry to say two are dead and the rest are clinging to life at Middleborough Hospital. If you're wondering if a terrorist bomb went off, then you'd be far from the truth. News 8 reporter Terriann Brunswick has the story."

The holo switched to a dark-haired female reporter standing in front of the hospital.

"Family members say they've been denied access to see their loved ones, who've been struck down with typhoid fever, a bacterial infection contracted through eating or drinking contaminated food or water. Hospital administrators are not calling this a quarantine situation, but my sources tell

86

me the patients are all contained to one ward, and personnel coming in contact with them are required to wear personal protective equipment. News 8 Medical Correspondent Keith Johnson told me it's unusual for someone in the United States to die of typhoid, and yet two of the ten victims have already succumbed. Family members have been given no explanation as to how the disease was contracted, but courthouse employees have since been advised to thoroughly wash their hands after visiting the restroom, and public drinking fountains in the courthouse were shut off. As an additional safeguard, government employees all over the city have been advised to wear facemasks - something my sources tell me couldn't possibly protect them from a simple outbreak of typhoid. Perhaps, as one official, speaking under the condition of anonymity, suggested to me, the masks are a misguided precaution. Or, as the same official said, 'Keep your eye on this one. It could be big.' Terriann Brunswick reporting for News 8 from the downtown courthouse."

The view switched back to the male anchor, who launched into another story. Scott stopped the clip. "Has Shasta seen this?"

"She's the one who sent me the link. Apparently, your deputy director - Unger?" When Scott nodded, she continued, "wasn't too happy about it."

He waited while the waitress deposited their meals on the table and answered as soon as she left.

"What'd he expect? People are dying. You can't just sweep that under the rug."

"I would hate to be in his position, though. No matter what he does, criticism will follow."

He shrugged. "The price you pay for power. If it was your family member who died, would you be content with a 'we didn't want to panic the public' explanation?"

"Of course not. Have you made any progress finding Robert Cruise?"

"I know where he isn't. How about you? Any headway on the typhoid?"

"Two of the eight people still in quarantine seem to be responding to a new class of antibiotics, but they were also in the group who were previously immunized. And we've identified a mutation in the flagellum."

"Uh, you're gonna need to dumb that down for me." He took a big bite of the sandwich and had to grab for his napkin as a dribble of juice headed down his chin.

"Flagellum." She held up a finger and wiggled it. "The tail bacteria swim with."

He took care to finish chewing and swallow before responding. "You know...I was exposed to it."

"What? The typhoid? How?"

"Cruise isn't the first person the XIA identified as being a possible carrier. A xenofreak named Dundee is suspected of infecting the first non-xenos who came down with it. I had contact with him."

"And I'm just now finding this out?" She looked dumbfounded.

"I wasn't exactly briefed on what you do and don't know, and it just now occurred to me to mention it."

"Has anyone ever tested you?"

"Of course they did."

"And?"

"And...I don't know the results."

She sighed, turned in her seat and lifted a hand, trying to catch the waitress' eye.

"What are you doing?" he asked.

"Getting this to go. Yours too."

"Please tell me you don't plan on making a pincushion out of me."

She snorted delicately and said, "Afraid of a little needle? Guess I'm not the only one with a phobia."

"Funny."

He started to say more but caught a movement out of the corner of his eye. Across the street, a slight figure was lurking in the alley between the blood donation center and the building next to it. Even without being able to see her clearly, he knew it was Padme.

He glanced regretfully at his sandwich, but said, "Sorry, Doc. Gotta go."

She sputtered a protest, but he ignored her and leaped the fence to cross the street.

Whatever had prompted Padme to come out in broad daylight had to be important. When he got close enough, she turned, walked down the alley and stopped by a dumpster. She was wearing a bulky parka with the fur-lined hood drawn forward to conceal her cow ears. For the first time since she'd reappeared in his life, he got a good look at her face. What he'd mistaken last night in the dim light as dark circles under her eyes now looked more like faded bruising, as if someone had been using her as a punching bag.

"Are you alright?" he asked.

"I found Bryn for you."

"What?" It was the last thing he expected her to say. "Why would you do that?"

"Technically, the information dropped into my lap. She's at Edgemere with a Mad Eye lieutenant. Is he the missing agent? Wait, no, don't tell me. It's best if you do not confirm that."

Padme had never been one to talk much, but she was practically babbling now. Her nervousness was palpable, but he didn't dwell on it.

"Is she okay?"

"She's sleeping with him." She said it with a casual twitch of one shoulder, but her gaze was unflinching, like a hawk's.

Scott blinked, trying not to react. After a moment, he asked, "How do you know?"

"Fournier has his spies. He's creating an army - did you know?"

"An army of typhoid carriers?"

"He calls them his assassins."

"How many does he have?"

"I don't know. Lupus hasn't confided the details to me."

"Is Dundee still alive?"

"Very much so."

"And his sight?"

"Restored. Bryn should take care to avoid him in future."

Scott was going to ask her what she meant by 'restored,' but she asked, "Did you mean what you said last night?"

He almost asked, "What part?" but instead went with, "Every word."

"Four months ago, when we were vacating Fournier's facility, I had a backup copy of the nanoneuron program in my bag, but I...lost it."

He remembered what Bryn told him - that Padme had thrown a gym bag at her to distract her, and then locked her in the control room. If Bryn hadn't broken through the ceiling and escaped, she would have burned to death.

Scott pushed his true feelings aside and said sympathetically, "Fournier must have been furious."

Her face went pale, as if just the memory of it pained her. "I recreated the program from scratch, but this time, I added a - well, let's call it a subroutine to make it easier for you to understand. You know the program can stimulate the nanoneurons to produce fear or pleasure."

"Uh, yeah, thanks. I do know that."

She looked down at her feet. "I had to."

"I know why you did it. But Bryn - she didn't deserve that."

89

"Didn't she?"

"We're *not* together." Technically, it was true. Since the fire, he'd done as Shasta advised and kept their relationship to a warm friendship. Not that it had been easy.

A mildly calculating look passed over Padme's face. "Next time I'll send her pleasure, I promise."

"No, don't do -"

She cut him off. "Let me finish what I was saying. I do not have a lot of time."

He nodded.

"In the previous version of the program, Fournier was the only one who had access to control the nanoneurons of his bioengineers, surgeons and lieutenants. Only he could activate their fear."

Fournier's most trusted lieutenant was Lupus, although 'trust,' as the rest of the world defined it, probably wasn't in the criminally deranged doctor's vocabulary. Lupus had been brainwashed - conditioned to obey him; punished with fear and rewarded with pleasure.

Padme continued. "Remember I told you the savant helped me write the program in the first place?"

"Yeah."

"Well, after the fire, he never met up with us at the alternate location. He disappeared, so Fournier found another programmer to work with me. Not with me, but to oversee what I was doing. As luck would have it, this man was not as astute as the savant and I was able to create a back door to get to Lupus. I can activate the fear, but only once."

"Why once?"

"Fournier hasn't had to use it on him since he went through the loyalty conditioning. Lupus would definitely mention it to him and then they would become suspicious."

"Can't you just turn it on until it gives him a heart attack like with Abel?"

"There's no guarantee that would happen. In many ways, the loyalty conditioning accustomed him to the sense of fear. He relishes seeing it in others because he has felt it so many times himself."

Lupus had once been an undercover XIA agent just like Scott. What Fournier had done to him was horrible, and the things that Lupus had done to others since he'd been conditioned were just as horrible.

"Why are you telling me this?" he asked.

"I know where Lupus will be tonight. If you intercept him, and I activate the fear, it will disable him enough for you to kill him."

Scott's sense of fair play immediately rejected the idea, but he didn't say so. He thought fast and decided to agree to the setup in the likely event Shasta would give the go-ahead to capture Lupus instead. It would be a huge betrayal to Padme, one that she would be unlikely to forgive him for, but the XIA would give a lot to get their hands-on Lupus and the information he had.

"I'll do it," he said.

Chapter Twenty-two

The crowd dispersed within two minutes. Jason put his shirt back on, picked up his bags and said to Bryn, "I'm starving. There was never any poison, so let's eat."

Instead of heading for the queen's lair, he led her to one of the store areas; the one that was lit up with lanterns. Inside, a bar made from old barrels with wooden planks laid across them took up one wall, and mismatched tables and chairs lined the other. Someone had painted a mural that stretched around to all three concrete walls; a southwestern scene complete with mesas and cacti and a sunset. There were no customers.

A portly grey-haired man stood behind the bar, and within the circle of his arms he held a woman with short, dark hair. Neither of them had obvious xenografts, but most of their skin was covered up with the winter clothing they wore against the frigid Edgemere air. The man appeared to be comforting the woman, but as soon as she saw Jason and Bryn, she cleared her throat and stepped away.

"Hola, Dragila," she said. "What can we get for you?"

"Is that tamales I smell?"

"Si. And for the lady?"

Bryn smiled and said in Spanish, "Tamales are my favorite."

The woman turned and disappeared through a doorless opening in the wall. Jason pulled a rickety stool out for Bryn, set his bags on the floor, and sat next to her. The man behind the bar held up two clear glass mugs and Jason nodded. When the full mugs were set before them, she realized to her consternation that they contained beer.

She swallowed her protest and instead took a sip as if she drank alcohol all the time. The truth was: she'd tasted it a few times but hadn't liked it.

"May I please have a glass of water?" she asked.

"I am sorry, señorita, but we have no clean water to spare."

"Porky is new to Edgemere's ways, Carlos," Jason said. He turned to her with the obscure explanation of, "Supply and demand."

The woman came back out with two smallish plates, but they were heaped high with tamales and refried beans. Jason dug in immediately, but after a few bites he looked at the woman, who lingered near the back door.

"Where's Antonio?" he asked.

Her lips turned down in a disconsolate frown and she spun around and left. Carlos answered for her, "He's in the back. Sick."

Jason stopped with his fork halfway to his mouth and then lowered it. "I'm sorry."

Carlos nodded sadly, eyes glistening with unshed tears. He waved a hand vaguely and said, "I'm going to check on him."

After he'd gone, Bryn asked, "Is Antonio their son?"

Jason nodded.

"Why don't they take him to the hospital?"

He gave her a sidelong look. "I don't know. But everyone here has something to hide. Do you think they'd live in these conditions otherwise?"

So Carlos and his family were hiding from the law or from immigration or both. It was unlikely they had health insurance if they were forced to live here.

"What did Junk say?" she asked. "He was infecting people - on purpose?"

He shoved a big bite in his mouth and nodded again.

She thought about the first time she'd visited her father in prison. It was the only time he'd been willing to talk about why he'd made a deal with Fournier, why he'd arranged to have her kidnapped and xenografted. He'd said Fournier had been looking for ways to capitalize on a mutated form of typhoid one of his xenos had contracted. He'd justified what he'd done to her by claiming it was for her protection. A curious web of truth and lies.

"Xenos are immune to whatever is making everyone sick," she said.

"That's what the man said." He took several swallows of beer.

"And he was sent here."

"Yep. Eat."

She cut one of her tamales with the side of her fork and began eating, thinking if Junk was sent here, it could only have been by Fournier. But if it was an intentional attack by the XBestia, what could Fournier gain by killing off non-xenos, most of whom were children?

The tamales were good, but every once in a while, she encountered a bit of jalapeño that was too spicy for her liking. Her nose began to run, but there were no napkins on the bar. She reached into her jacket pocket for one of the napkins she'd put there from yesterday's fast food meal. When her fingers closed on it, she felt the earbug Esmie had given her.

She pulled it and the napkin out of her pocket. A joke about crazy old ladies was on the tip of her tongue, but a cautionary internal voice stopped her. What if the earbug had been given to Esmie to pass along to Jason? What if the XIA knew they were here and were trying to contact him? Bryn decided to listen to the message before giving it to him, because she suspected if she didn't, she'd never know what it said.

She lifted the napkin to her nose and bent over to blow into it. While her head was down, she snuck the earbug into her right ear, getting poked by a few of her shorter quills for her effort. With her fingernail, she flipped the 'on' switch. Immediately, a voice began to speak. It was a female voice, not Esmie, but not anyone else Bryn recognized either.

The message was short: "Stay the course."

Bewildered, she took the earbug out again and went to put it back in her pocket, but it slipped from her fingers and clattered to the floor.

Jason glanced down and frowned. "What's that?"

Hastily, she got off the stool and bent to pick it up. Always conscious of the possibility that someone was watching and listening, she handed it to him rather than tell him what it was.

He bent down, turned his head and pretended to scratch his ear, but she knew he'd put it in. After several seconds, he 'scratched' again and took it out. Then he stood, and without looking down, let it roll out of his hand onto the floor. He casually stepped on it, crushing the fragile electronic device and kicking the pieces to scatter them.

Without a word, he sat back down and tucked into his meal.

Bryn put a bite in her mouth, pensive. If the message hadn't meant anything, Jason would have given her a strange look, as if to say, 'That was weird.' But he hadn't. He'd deliberately destroyed the earbug and was quite obviously avoiding the topic entirely.

Stay the course.

What did it mean? She decided it was a message sent by the XIA. They wanted Jason to keep doing what he was doing. But what was he doing?

The beer tasted awful, but she was thirsty, and the spicy food didn't help matters, so she drank most of it. The unaccustomed alcohol gave her a weird feeling in her chest and shoulders unlike anything she'd experienced before. It lingered after they finished their meal and Jason paid for it. As they were leaving Jason said to Carlos, "Let me know if you need anything."

Carlos raised hopeless eyes and replied, "A miracle?"

Bryn put a hand to her chest and felt tears of sympathy start. She was supposed to be acting like a 'tough xenofreak chick,' but how could she pretend to be heartless when confronted with a parent's worst nightmare?

To her surprise, Jason said, "You have my prayers."

"Thank you, my friend." Carlos turned away.

As they left the warm lighting in the makeshift restaurant for the weird fairy-like green of the main mall, Dillo arrived, flustered and breathless. "Dragila! There you are. Come."

He turned and headed for the queen's lair. Jason fell easily into step beside him, but Bryn, even with her long legs, was forced to trot to keep up.

"Interrogation over?" Jason asked him.

"Yes."

"XBestia send him?"

"Who else?" Dillo's massive shoulders rose and fell.

Jason stopped asking questions. Bryn still had a million of them.

The control room rang with the sound of boots clanging on the metal flooring as soldiers rushed to and fro.

Maddy was leaning over her three holo techs, Munnu by her side, as ever. She glanced over and said, "Dragila. Good."

As they got closer, Bryn saw that the large holo in the center of the table was now displaying a schematic of Coney Island - XBestia territory. Maddy waved her hand and the 3D map rotated. She spread her fingers to zoom in.

"The Bungholes are here. We know one of his lieutenants has a presence there, but there are hundreds of units."

Bryn recalled the day she and Scott had gone to Coney Island. The day they'd hauled that poor Panda to shore and gotten shot at by the ARA. The Bungholes were temporary housing units the government had set up after hurricane Poppy, which were then abandoned and taken over by the XBestia.

Her arm rose and she found herself pointing. "Number nine."

"What about it?" Maddy snapped.

"That's the unit where the lieutenant will be."

"And just how," Maddy said in her softest voice, "do you know this?"

Jason had tensed up by her side, but Bryn didn't falter. "I was there. After I found out my father was the one who arranged for my kidnapping, I ran away. I got...involved with one of my kidnappers. My shrink said it was

Stockholm syndrome. Anyway, he took me to Coney Island. The number nine bungalow was the one designated for the lieutenant."

Maddy regarded her for a moment, her eyes narrowed. "What makes you think number nine is still being used for that purpose?"

"They call them the Bungholes because they're disgusting. Number nine was the only one that was...clean."

Munnu, who never spoke, said, "How convenient that you happened to be here today to give us this information."

Bryn knew he wasn't Maddy's real twin, and yet strangely, he had her voice, accent and all. There were no visible scars to show where the real Munnu's face ended and the imposter's skin began; scars themselves were a thing of the past unless a person wanted them. Bryn noticed that the imposter had bags under his eyes and blotchy patches on his cheeks as if someone had slapped him.

"No, no, Munnu," Maddy said, with a raise of her hand. "I would like to hear more about our guest's visit to Coney Island. What else did you learn that could be of use to us?"

Bryn had no idea what the Mad Eyes were planning, but she didn't think it would be a good idea to tell them about the tunnel that led from Bluto's restaurant to the building behind it - the building that turned out to have been owned by Fournier himself.

"Nothing else, really. I was only there for a day. It's not - it's not like here. There weren't any children, not that I saw anyway. It was a filthy, lawless place."

"Hm. Yes, well, 'bestia' does mean beast, does it not?" Maddy clasped her hands and looked around her as if she'd come to a momentous decision.

"Prepare the fleet." Her voice was laced with undisguised relish, as if she'd been waiting all her life to utter her next words: "We attack at dawn."

Chapter Twenty-three

Scott had briefed Shasta by holophone on the way back to headquarters, but she quizzed him again when he got to her office.

Her focus wasn't on what Padme said about Bryn being at Edgemere, or about Fournier building an army of 'assassins.' It wasn't even about the trap Scott agreed to spring on Lupus. She was fixated on the details of Padme's comment about the missing programmer.

"She said he disappeared? Like, he'd been killed, or he just didn't show up?" Shasta was sitting in her desk chair with her legs crossed, the top foot bouncing in an agitated motion.

Scott tried to remember the specifics of the conversation. "She said, uh, he never met up with the rest of them after the fire."

"But she didn't tell you his name?"

"No. She always referred to him as 'the savant.'"

Shasta looked down, her gaze darting around randomly, as if her eye movements represented each change in the direction of her thoughts.

"Prodigious savants are not common," she said, almost to herself. Then she looked up. "Did you meet him?"

Scott thought about the tour he'd been given of Fournier's underground facility right before it had been destroyed. All of the bioengineers and doctors he'd met had seemed odd, but there'd been one man who wouldn't look him in the eye and refused to shake his hand, just like Mia. He tried to recall the man's face, but it had been so long ago, and he'd only seen him briefly.

"Maybe," he said doubtfully.

"Scott, this is important."

He lifted his hands. "There was one guy it could have been...wait a minute. I remember what she said now, before, at the Warehouse. She mentioned that one of the engineers I met invented grease, the cold fire, and another one - yeah, I met him. He had to be the guy who wouldn't look at me. Savants have trouble making eye contact, right?"

"Assuming he's on the autistic spectrum. Can you describe him to a sketch artist?"

He grimaced. "Shouldn't I be prepping for the Lupus op?"

"We have plenty of time for that." She reached for her holophone.

Twenty minutes later, he was sitting in a cubicle next to an agent named Marty, trying to remember details that hadn't impressed him much at the time. Marty was an older Asian gentleman trained in the use of a specialized facial feature compositing program. He patiently prompted Scott to remember whatever he could, but Scott must have been making pained faces, because Marty finally said, "Relax. Here."

He got up and crossed the cubicle to an electric teapot. He poured hot, amber liquid into a white china cup and handed it to Scott.

"I'm more of a coffee guy," Scott said, but sipped the tea out of politeness. It was fragrant and sweet but had a strange aftertaste.

After about fifteen more minutes of responding to Marty's soft, monotonous voice, he realized he felt strangely languid. "What was in that tea?"

"Nothing but natural theanine," Marty replied. "Have you ever been hypnotized before?"

"No, why?"

"No reason. Except that you're especially susceptible."

"What does that mean?"

"Look." He pointed to his holoscreen, where there was a completed face with a high forehead, broad cheekbones and heavy-lidded eyes that looked down and to one side.

"Oh, hey. That's him. Wow, you're good."

Marty rolled his eyes. "Okay, I think I've got enough to work with here."

"Great." Scott stood, feeling like he'd missed something.

He headed straight for the Op-Prep room, where he met up with Shasta, two com tech operators and two agents he had only a passing acquaintance with. The first, Ryan Boardman, was a few years older than Scott, but as a new agent, had significantly less on-the-job experience. He was blond and blue-eyed and had matching xenografts on each hand - the spiked protuberances from the spiny part of an alligator's hide, like two scaly sets of brass knuckles. His xeno name was, in fact, 'Knuckles,' and he was a hand-to-hand fighting expert.

The other agent was Tina Lo, a tall, lanky middle-aged woman who'd transferred in from Los Angeles a few months ago. She'd been a helicopter pilot in the Fourth Iraq War. Her xenograft was hidden under her clothing, but Scott had heard it was an unusual one. She'd undergone a double mastectomy to fight breast cancer, but instead of scars, she'd opted to have a porcine strip grafted to her chest. Shasta had chosen her because she was also an experienced amphibious armored vehicle pilot.

"I wish it were any location other than Coney Island," Shasta said. "If things go south, it'll be hard to get a clean-up crew in there."

"It'll be fine," Scott replied. "It's the Bungholes we need to avoid, and Bluto's is a half mile away."

Shasta shook her head. "That's not what I'm worried about. You know I contacted my informant at Edgemere this morning. She said tension was stretched very thin between the Mad Eyes and the XBestia."

Scott exchanged a look with her. She'd told him earlier that the informant had managed to pass a memo earbug to Bryn, but that Bryn may not have realized what it was. Even if she had, and had passed it on to Alton, it would be highly dangerous for him to attempt to contact the XIA while he and Bryn were still at Edgemere. Like Fournier, Maddy Singh was hypervigilant about security.

Scott was taking lead on the op, and once the details were ironed out, he and the other agents inserted their earbugs and conducted com tests with their tech team. A slow-moving hover drone was dispatched to the location in advance to provide a secure connection between the com team and the earbugs.

Then the agents were outfitted from head to toe with lightweight, level three bulletproof, knifeproof clothing designed to look like normal clothes. They wore ballistic vests underneath that could be inflated at the pull of a cord to become aqua vests. Each of them had inspected and tucked their weapons of choice and extra ammunition into the multiple hidden pockets of their disguises. Scott hoped they didn't have to use any firepower, but it was best to be prepared in case, as Shasta put it, things went south.

They left headquarters at eleven o'clock, long after darkness had fallen. It took over an hour for Lo to drive them to the controlled access self-storage facility located southeast of Crescent Beach where their transportation was located. All was quiet in the well-lit, fenced yard when Lo parked on a strip of gravel out front. A security guard escorted them to the unit and waited until Lo held her palm under the holoscanner and the green light lit up, before leaving them to it. The orange corrugated metal door rolled smoothly upward and a light in the ceiling came on. Inside squatted what was, to all appearances, an ice cream truck.

Boardman laughed. "Is this the wrong storage unit?"

"No, no, don't let it fool you." Lo patted the hood of the vehicle affectionately. "This is a ninth generation Urban Amphibious Armored Vehicle, made to look completely innocuous in order to easily get to and from conflict within the city. See these panels?" She pointed and Scott saw that the entire exterior of the UAAV was tiled like a space plane. Lo said, "Right now it's in display mode, so you see the ice cream truck graphics, but with a flick of a switch they become adaptive camouflage panels, which change color, pattern, and light to mimic whatever the omnidirectional cameras see in the background, from all directions wherever we happen to be."

"Like a cloaking device?" Boardman asked.

"More like a cuttlefish," Scott said.

Lo's wide mouth curved in a smile. "Yep. Just like a cuttlefish hides in plain sight on the sea floor or a chameleon blends in with the leaves. It's not perfect technology, but in low light conditions, the human eye can be effectively fooled with this baby." She stroked the hood now, like a proud mama. "It's quiet, too. Almost silent engine operation."

She slid open the side door and ushered them in. Scott sat shotgun. The seating was typical of the average maxivan, but the gauges and gadgets on the ceiling and dash looked like something out of a space plane, too. Lo drove into the alley before getting out and closing the storage unit door. It was a short drive to the street that paralleled the beach. She took them past several blocks of houses on the landward side until they came to a park-like, forested area. When there were no other cars on the road, she drove up and over the sidewalk onto the sand and went straight into the water.

"Are we camouflaged?" Boardman asked, as Lo changed gears to convert the UAAV to amphibious mode. "Because if a pedestrian sees an ice cream truck driving into the ocean, that's going to get us some attention."

"No worries," Lo replied. "If someone sees us, they'll call the police. Tech team'll intercept it and advise the locals to stand down."

In Scott's earbug, he heard one of the techs say, "So far no call."

The UAAV rocked in the surf before settling low on the surface of the water.

Lo pressed a button and said, "Watch this." Exterior screens slowly slid down over the windshield, back, and side windows, but the view outside remained mostly unchanged. She looked at Boardman. "Does that answer your next question?"

He laughed. "I take it we're invisible *now*?"

"Like ninjas." She said with a brief widening of her eyes. "Better settle in, it'll take a while to get there."

Scott leaned back in the comfortable bucket seat and closed his eyes. Before he knew it, he'd drifted into a much-needed catnap.

Chapter Twenty-four

Nearly every able-bodied xeno at Edgemere had been put to the task of readying 'the fleet,' which turned out to be a ragtag collection of watercraft housed in one of the store areas. Most of the boats were one or two-man kayaks, but there were a few canoes and inflatables in the mix. Bryn wondered how they planned to get the boats out of the underground mall. The only way in or out that she knew of was the main drainage pipe lined with mushrooms.

All the efficient bustling around, with the men and women of Edgemere wearing grim expressions and bristling with weaponry, reminded her of the ARA soldiers' preparation when Kareem Williams had kidnapped her. She'd been terrified then. Now she was scared for a different reason: Maddy quite nonchalantly assumed that Jason - *and* Bryn - would participate in this endeavor.

The plan was to launch the boats in the predawn hours and row around the Rockaway Peninsula. Coney Island was northwest of the tip of the peninsula across about three nautical miles of water, and the Bungholes were just north of the beach. Maddy wanted the attack to happen before it got light out and before the Xbestia had a chance to fully wake.

Bryn hadn't been looking forward to attempting the trip in one of the small boats. She'd been on the open ocean only once before, when she and Scott had gone out on the Wavecruisers to fetch the panda. Even in broad daylight, the ocean swells had made her feel small and insignificant, as if her belly were exposed to some vague but looming threat.

As it turned out, Maddy had a small yacht berthed in a nearby marina, and since Jason had been assimilated into the personal guard protecting her, he and Bryn had a less up-close-and-personal appointment with the ocean. She hoped the yacht was in better shape than the 'fleet.'

As the newest member of the royal guard, Jason was given a private 'chamber' within Maddy's drainpipe lair. He and Bryn retired there soon after preparations for the assault were complete.

The chamber was a small room built at the back of one of the top-level pipes, with a curtain for a door.

"God, I need a shower," she said as she dropped her bag and settled down on the one small cot. "Or at least some clean water to brush my teeth and wash my face."

"I can take you to the showers," he replied. "But the water quality is questionable, and I can't guarantee privacy."

She thought about the leering guard from this morning and responded, "No thanks. It's probably better if I smell like a goat anyway."

She hunted through her bag for a clean pair of underwear and ordered Jason to turn around as she peeled off her jeans. After she finished changing, he said, "Be right back," and disappeared. She sat on the cot and tried not to think about tomorrow. Was Jason really planning on going through with it? Protecting Maddy as she fought her way to the lieutenant's Bunghole unit? The plan was to capture whoever was inside and torture information out of them, much like Junk had been tortured to admit who'd sent him. Maddy's goal, a lofty one in Bryn's estimation, was to find out where Fournier was holed up.

To Bryn, the whole scenario had seemed more and more unreal as the day went on, but she'd already experienced the lawlessness of xenofreak society and knew that unless something or someone intervened on her behalf, she would soon be thrust into the middle of this conflict.

Jason should be the one ensuring she wasn't put in danger, but he hadn't given her any indication that he had a plan to get them out of this. She'd begun to suspect he was using their inability to communicate with each other here as a shield to keep her from questioning his motives. Surely the danger from whoever else had been involved with sending that FBI agent after them couldn't be any worse than dragging her into a firefight.

She pulled her bag into her lap and reached inside. She wanted to take Scott's stuffed panda bear out and hold it, but she settled for stroking its fake fur and staring sadly into its black button eyes.

Jason came back inside, and she zipped up the bag self-consciously. He said, "Best I could do," and tossed her a plastic canister. The label read, 'Saniwipes.'

She muttered a grudging thanks and pulled a few of the disposable cloths from the canister. They were lemon-scented and intended for a kitchen countertop, but she scrubbed her face and under her arms anyway.

After she'd finished, she pulled several more, handed them to Jason and said, "You're getting pretty ripe, too."

He grinned and responded, "I'm just trying to blend in," but he obliged her, pulled off his shirt, and ran the wipes under his arms. When he was done, she offered to check his wounds. He got the flashlight out of his bag and let her inspect them closely. The scent of lemons mixed with the faint smell of sweat rose from his body. She should have found it unpleasant, but for some reason, it reminded her of Scott.

"This one still looks bad," she said, referring to the deep gouge in his trapezius muscle. "But the pseudo-skin is holding."

As he reached for his shirt, she impulsively put her fingertips against his Gila monster xenograft. She knew the pebbled orange and black skin was sensitive, knew he didn't want her to touch it, but something made her do it anyway - perhaps simply the need to get a reaction of some kind out of him.

She got more than she bargained for. The air left his lungs in a shuddering exhale as his torso curled slightly in on itself. She heard him swallow convulsively before he said huskily, "Unless you want me to throw you down on the cot right now, I suggest you stop doing that."

She pulled her hand away quickly and scooted over so she wasn't touching any part of him. He pulled his shirt on and turned to her, gaze impassive in the green light.

"I'm sorry," she said. "I didn't mean to-"

"Yes, you did."

Her mouth dropped open, but no words came out. She'd be lying if she denied it, and she was a bad liar. She wanted to give him a plausible excuse but didn't really have one other than plain curiosity. She'd been intrigued by the way he'd responded in the past; had wondered why touching the graft had such a powerful effect on him. She couldn't imagine the physiological reason for it, but then again, there was no way for any human being to know how another animal felt. Perhaps a Gila monster's skin had a part to play in the animal's mating ritual and that function somehow translated itself to Jason's nervous system. Just like her quills responded to her arousal by going flat to her head - but her quills were tied to her nanoneurons, something Jason had never had implanted in his brain.

Regardless of the reason it affected him so strongly, she honestly didn't know why she'd done it. She wasn't attracted to him. He was twice her age, and besides, she wanted Scott. *Didn't she?*

Jason sighed. "Maybe tonight we should sleep at opposite ends of the cot. I don't like to take my shoes off in case we need to leave suddenly, but it's probably for the best."

She nodded and watched as he unlaced his shoes, peeled off his socks and got a fresh pair out of his bag. She followed suit, feeling like a complete idiot. They settled side-by-side on the narrow cot, turned away from each other's feet.

Within a short period of time, his breathing became even, and he began to snore lightly.

Unfortunately, sleep eluded her. The shame of having inadvertently made a pass at him faded quickly enough, but she couldn't stop thinking about why she'd done it, and why she'd questioned her feelings about Scott. He and Jason were superficially alike in that tall, dark, dangerous kind of way. Both were essentially 'off-limits' to her because of their jobs, but she didn't think that was influencing her. As she finally felt herself cross the threshold of sleep, she acknowledged that what was really bothering her was the similarity between her situation now and when she'd first been thrust into the heart of xenofreak nation. Scott and Jason were both in a position to keep her alive - a powerful attractant that she was afraid was beginning to blur the two men together in her mind.

She finally dozed off, and sometime later, began to dream. Like all dreams, this one had no cohesive substance; it was just a mishmash of images and actions that made little sense. And since dreams occur during REM sleep when the sleeper is close to wakefulness, exterior forces such as sound are easily incorporated into them. When the pleasure hit, just like the fear she'd experienced two nights ago, it had the brief effect of changing the course of her dream. She'd been browsing an open-air market in India for glycerin soap with live, fluttering butterflies embedded inside when she found herself face-to-face with her mother, alive and well and smiling at her with shining eyes. Bryn had never been so happy, so excited, so full of yearning.

The transition from sleep to wakefulness came directly afterwards, as the sensations shooting through her body intensified and brought her to awareness. She gasped and arched her back and must have vocalized her response because Jason was suddenly a dark shadow in her field of vision.

"Bryn! What's wrong?"

She couldn't speak, couldn't move other than to squirm in response to the wonderful feelings pulsing through every pathway in her nervous system.

"Oh, no," he muttered, sliding his hands beneath her shoulders and knees and lifting her into his arms.

She closed her eyes tightly and cried out. He couldn't possibly know that wherever he touched her, however impersonally, frissons of delight radiated outward like ripples in a pond. She wanted to tell him, wanted to say it wasn't fear that had taken control, but didn't have the strength of will to form the words.

Vaguely, she felt movement as he began walking, carrying her. She heard him say, "We need to get you away from the signal," but the words had no meaning.

It felt good. It felt *so* good, but something deep in her consciousness knew it was wrong, knew it was not real. It was her nanoneurons creating a false sense of exultation, just like Scott had said happened to him.

The brief flash of insight was dashed away when Jason said, "I can't take you down the fire pole. Can you do it? Bryn!"

He released her legs and her feet hit the floor, but her knees immediately buckled. His arms tightened around her to keep her from falling, crushing her to his chest. As if of their own volition, her hands lifted and she turned his support into an embrace, sliding her fingers up his back, savoring the taut feel of his muscles. It seemed impossible for the pleasure to intensify, but when she encountered his xenograft through his shirt and he took a quick indrawn breath, an added dimension of passion joined the equation. She felt each tiny muscle at the base of the quills on her scalp respond by pulling them flat to her head.

"What the *hell* are you doing?" His voice was thick and growly, and just the sound of it - the unvoiced response in it - sent an unexpected jolt of desire coursing through her midsection.

It was too much. In one sane portion of her mind she knew what would happen if she couldn't stop herself, distract herself somehow, but as if the nanoneurons in her brain wouldn't let her dwell on the negative, the thought evaporated under the onslaught.

Her legs were no longer useless. She leaned into him as her left hand dropped to his lower back. Her thumb hooked one of the belt loops on his jeans and pulled him closer. The mere contact of hipbone to hipbone kindled a fierce heat that rushed straight through her. Her head fell back, her lips parted, and she looked into his eyes just as the pleasure abruptly stopped.

With a groan of capitulation, he kissed her, and even though full control of her body had been returned, she found herself caught up in the residual excitement, hungering for the tempest to return. That need manifested itself in a fervent response to his kiss, but she felt the loss of the

106

pleasure keenly. Being in his arms was nice, but the unenhanced sensations she experienced now left her unsatisfied, empty even, like she'd lost a limb and was tormented by its phantom. Still pressed up against him, still desperately returning kiss for kiss, tears began to course down her face.

He must have felt them, because he tore his mouth away from hers. Breathing heavily, he said, "Bryn."

She sniffed and disentangled her hand from his belt loop to wipe at her tears. "It's gone. I'm okay now."

For the first time since she'd met him, he looked uncertain. "That wasn't...I thought you were supposed to be scared."

She took a deep, trembling breath, aware that his arms still encircled her. "Apparently, Padme has a choice between sending fear or pleasure." Her voice broke on the word 'pleasure.'

Jason's face slowly crumpled in confused repugnance. His hands loosened their hold and dropped to his sides. "That's-"

"Horrible?" She thought of her dream and the sheer joy she'd felt at knowing her mother was alive. She thought about what she'd almost given him, a man she'd met less than two days ago. It was another sharp reminder of his similarity to Scott.

He stepped back and she realized they were standing by the fireman's pole in their stockinged feet. On shaky legs, she brushed past him and went back into their little room. A moment later, she heard him come up behind her as she stood staring at the cot, fighting off a return of the tears.

His breathing hadn't quite slowed to normal. "I can sleep on the floor if you want."

"No." She shook her head. "Just promise me if it happens again, you won't - touch me."

He didn't touch her now, just leaned around her so she could see his face. "I didn't know what was going on. Earlier when you..."

He trailed off, but she knew what he was trying to say.

"Your xenograft," she said. "I don't know why I - I shouldn't have done that. I can see why you might have come to the conclusion that I..." now she trailed off.

A humorless laugh escaped him. "Whatever Padme did to you is kind of like what happens to me, isn't it?"

She shrugged helplessly, but asked, "Can you control it?"

"Usually. But just now you were so..."

"Intense?" The tears threatened again.

"Don't cry, okay? I hate that." But he said it gently.

"I just want to go home," she whispered.

His head jerked a little to one side and his expression instantly changed to one of warning. As if she could read his mind, she knew he was going over their actions and words since Padme had attacked, trying to determine if any of it would give them away in the event Maddy's holo techs were listening. Their conversation had been the first open one they'd had since arriving here - and could have put them in more danger than they'd been *since* arriving.

By mutually unspoken decision, they climbed onto the cot and settled back down for the night. Bryn thought she was going to be kept awake by reproachful thoughts but found herself so utterly wrung out that she slipped quickly back into slumber.

Chapter Twenty-five

Lo woke him up with a nudge to his shoulder. "Hey, Van Winkle. Wakey-wakey."

Scott sat up, stretched and yawned. "Sorry about that. Haven't gotten much shut-eye the last few nights."

"Here you go, Boss." Boardman passed him a thermos.

Scott removed the cup, unscrewed the lid and inhaled the welcome scent of coffee. He poured some of the dark brew into the cup. Normally, he didn't drink it black, but he needed an infusion of caffeine to chase away the residual grogginess. He took a sip and said, "Strong."

Boardman shrugged. "The stronger it is, the less you have to drink. Don't want a full bladder when things get dicey."

"*If* things get dicey," Lo said. "But you also don't want a shaky trigger finger. Moderation in all things."

The coffee was so strong it was almost thick. Scott took one more sip and set it aside. "What time is it?"

Lo gestured to a holoclock on the dash at the same time one of the techs said in his ear, "Go time in two hours."

Scott looked out the windshield. They were maybe a hundred yards offshore, and tonight there was no fog to obstruct the view. Lo handed him a pair of round-lensed spectagoggle tactical optics and he fit them over his eyes. There was no switch to activate them - to all outward appearances, they were nothing special.

Scott said, "Check," and his lens display lit up.

"We see what you see," one of the techs said. "Remember that if you have to make a pit stop."

"Oh, you guys are high-larious."

"You're the one drinking coffee."

Scott turned his head to look back out the windshield and squinted his eyes to zoom in on the beach. The remnants of the boardwalk and the buildings that had survived Hurricane Poppy were slowly deteriorating from neglect, but the building housing Bluto's Bar and Grill was intact. The establishment would be closed now, or nearly so, but a party of Xenos, four men and two women, had started a fire in one of the battered metal garbage cans out front and were laughing and horsing around, clearly inebriated.

He shifted view to the alley between Bluto's and what remained of the shack next to it. He could just see the wall of the building at the end of the alley, the same building in which he, Bryn, and Carla had encountered Nosferatu and his gang. The tunnel Fournier had built between that building and Bluto's was, according to Padme, how Lupus would be entering Bluto's tonight in order to conduct business with Phaco, the manager.

Lupus had traveled in the dark of night ever since Scott had known him. With the face of a wolf, he couldn't exactly move around incognito, so he used the cover of darkness to skulk around doing business for Fournier. He would not be easy to bring in. He'd been Army Special Forces before becoming an XIA agent. He was the first to pose as a member of the XBestia, and the first to go missing. Padme told Scott that Lupus himself had killed and disposed of the next agent who had attempted to infiltrate the gang. Fournier had complete control over him, turning a once-admirable man into his own personal executioner.

All because of the nanoneuron program Padme had helped create.

She'd talked of sending Bryn pleasure as if it would make up for the fear, but Scott knew it was just as bad. Fear and pleasure may be on opposite ends of the sensation spectrum, but if a person was forced to experience either one against their will, it was a violation plain and simple.

He remembered how he'd felt when Padme first demonstrated it; when she'd pulled off her shirt and straddled him in her control center. Just the touch of her body pressed up against his sent his desire spinning almost out of control. If he hadn't hit the escape button on her holo keyboard...

Scott's train of thought stopped dead and he swallowed a sudden lump in his throat. If Padme could be believed, Bryn was right now sleeping in the same bunk as Jason Alton. Objectively, Scott knew she would be in less danger among the Mad Eyes if she posed as Alton's girlfriend; knew instinctively that was why they were, as Padme put it, sleeping together.

He fought a flood of angry adrenaline as he remembered the calculating look on Padme's face when she'd 'offered' to send Bryn pleasure. She hadn't said it to placate him - it had simply occurred to her that she had the power to push Bryn completely away from him. All she had to do was time it right.

Chapter Twenty-six

A noise like the clearing of a throat woke her. She opened her eyes, startled and disturbed to find Maddy standing over them. The Mad Eye queen was outfitted in an all-white pantsuit, with gold buttons and fringed epaulets on the shoulders. Her hair was loose and wavy from the braid she'd worn the previous day. She held a holopad in one hand.

Jason sat up and asked, "Is it time?"

"Not quite yet," Maddy replied. "I had a few things I needed to discuss with you and your...friend."

Jason swung his legs over the side of the cot and reached for his shoes. Maddy said, "No, don't. First, explain this."

She activated the holopad and held it out. Just as Bryn had feared, Edgemere's hidden cameras had caught last night's entire scenario. It was beyond weird to see herself writhing in Jason's arms as he carried her to the fire pole; beyond embarrassing to watch a replay of the clinch that followed. It would have been an easy thing to explain if it were only a holo, but their words, too, had been captured.

After the holo stopped, Maddy drew her finger backwards along the progress bar until Jason's voice was heard saying, "We need to get you away from the signal."

"What did you mean by that?" she asked.

Jason inhaled deeply through his nose and let it out slowly. "The nanoneurons in her brain were being stimulated via cell signal."

Maddy's eyes widened and she blinked a few times. "Really."

He nodded once. "We'd hoped being here, underground, would block it."

"Ah, yes, well, that would normally be the case, but you see, I had a signal booster installed. Wouldn't want to miss all those loving calls from my father."

111

With her finger back on the holopad, Maddy went forward to when Jason said, "That wasn't...I thought you were supposed to be scared," and Bryn's response, "Apparently, Padme has a choice between sending fear or pleasure."

"This interests me greatly," Maddy said. "I don't suppose you have information on how this was accomplished?"

Bryn said, "When I was in the hospital, the doctors told me their scanners couldn't read my nanoneuron program; that Fournier had his own program created and they couldn't disable it."

"Most excellent." Maddy's voice dripped with envious admiration. "And Padme is...?"

"Fournier's programmer."

"I *love* it. Since there's no way to remove nanoneurons, once you flip the switch on fear or pleasure, all the victim can do is run and hide. Yet another reason to get my hands on one of Fournier's lieutenants."

She shut off the holopad.

"Now for the other matter I wanted to discuss with you. My other contact in the FBI has informed me that they found the body of my brother. It's only a matter of time before that information gets back to my father. Dragila, when you told me Munnu was an imposter, I never did get your answer as to how you knew. Would you care to enlighten me now?"

"I saw the body."

"And then you, a recently escaped criminal, called the FBI to inform them?" Maddy's face was the picture of pleasantness.

Jason hesitated just a bit too long, giving Bryn the impression he still hadn't come up with a plausible cover story and was frantically thinking one up on the fly. Luckily, she'd mentally concocted an account she thought would cover all their bases, one that blended enough truth in with the fiction that she hoped she could tell it convincingly.

"We didn't call anyone," she said, ignoring Jason's sharp look. "When I helped Jas-Dragila escape custody, I took him out to this place I knew of - an old missile silo where my friends and I used to hang out. The top level was converted to a house, but no one's lived there for a while. The main entrance has got some heavy-duty security, but I knew a secret way in. We got comfortable and the next thing we know, this big guy with a gun busts in. You know, shoot first, ask later? He thought he'd killed Dragila and wanted me to help him move Munnu's body. But Dragila shot him and found out he was FBI. We ran."

"And came here to warn me," Maddy said, looking at Jason thoughtfully.

He shrugged. "Plus, we went to the silo in the first place to get her underground, away from cell signals. She pissed off the XBestia, and if they stimulate her nanoneurons long enough, it can kill her."

"Better and better," Maddy murmured.

"I figured it'd be safe here," he continued, "since the feds have never messed with Edgemere."

Maddy's laugh held no mirth. "Yes, well, that may change soon, since the agent you killed was my man."

Jason's head went back in surprise. "You knew Munnu's body was at the silo?"

"No." Her jaw clenched. "Antonovich was supposed to have thoroughly disposed of it, but since he didn't it's obvious he was planning to double-cross me. And I see from your face you have come to the wrong conclusion. I did not kill Munnu. He got into a fight and was mortally injured. The man who is posing as him is one of my seven younger brothers, an outcast like me, as well as a near-perfect tissue match, so he doesn't have to take too many anti-rejection drugs. We had very good reasons for the charade, I assure you. However, it will all be moot now that he's come down with the sickness Junk brought us."

"Oh, no," Bryn murmured as Jason asked, "He's not a xeno?"

"He is *now*," Maddy said. "I brought a xenosurgeon in last night as soon as we realized he'd contracted Fournier's deadly little germ. Let's hope whatever imparts immunity kicks in in time."

Jason rubbed his chin, which had grown dark with stubble. "Are you going to postpone the attack?"

Maddy straightened resolutely. "Of course not. Now I have even more reason to rain fury down upon the XBestia. Plus I've gone to great lengths to prevent word of the attack from getting out. No one has been allowed to leave and all transmissions have been monitored. It will be a complete surprise. But without Munnu - without my brother - I'm forced to trust in you more than I have in the past, Dragila. I hope it will not turn out to be misplaced."

Jason reached for his shoes and looked up at her with a small smile. "Stay the course."

Maddy's return smile had a quizzical bent to it, but she said, "Indeed."

Chapter Twenty-seven

"Is the drone in place?" Scott asked the com team, shifting in his seat. Almost two hours of fidgeting in the UAAV was not taking the edge off his anticipation for action.

In his ear, he heard, "Overhead now. Uh, hold on, possible target acquired. Sending holo."

Lo switched on the holo projector in the UAAV's dash. Because the live feed from the surveillance drone was shot from above, she squashed it almost to 2D so the image hovering between them wouldn't be so disorienting. Infrared showed a lone figure entering the building behind Bluto's. Even from above with only a heat image to work from, Scott recognized the large, slightly hunched figure as Lupus from the xenofreak's distinctively intimidating body language.

"That's him." Scott turned to Boardman. "This is it. Ready?"

Boardman settled his own pair of tactical optics onto the bridge of his nose. "Let's roll this rock."

Lo piloted the UAAV silently right up onto the beach about a hundred yards east of Bluto's. The partying xenos remained oblivious to the vehicle's presence. Scott put his arms through the straps of what looked on the outside to be a normal backpack but was in reality a portable stretcher made out of the same tough, slick material used by hunters to drag big game. He then slid open the door on the side facing away from the action, and he and Boardman jumped out onto the sand.

"Break a leg," Lo said. "I'll be waitin' in the getaway car."

There was a mild breeze off the ocean and the cold night air chased away the last of the residual sluggishness. He walked casually alongside Boardman in case anyone saw them, but they didn't head towards Bluto's. Instead, they took a straight course across the beach and over the partially buried boardwalk to an alley between the nearest structures, or rather, the crumbling walls of what used to be structures.

In his ear, Scott heard Lo say, "You're platinum," which he took to mean the xenos out in front of Bluto's still hadn't noticed them.

Even with night vision, it was slow going picking their way through the alley, which was cluttered with rubble and garbage, but they needed to circle around to the same building, same entrance, Lupus had used.

In his ear, a tech said, "Hold on. Picking up some heat. Looks like three - no, four - incoming - what are those?"

"Canines," said the other tech.

"Okay, looks like a pack of dogs at your six o'clock."

Encountering even one dog on Coney Island would likely result in a confrontation, but four meant a wild pack was on their trail.

"I got this," Boardman said. He pulled a plum-sized object from one of his pockets.

"No noise," Scott said quickly.

Boardman held the object up.

"Is that a dodo egg?" Scott asked.

"Yep."

'Dodo egg' was the nickname for the hard-to-come-by dodecahedron smart grenade; smaller than a standard-issue pepper spray canister, and each of its twelve sides had motion sensor equipped nozzles that not only detected when the target came within the spray zone, but released the caustic liquid in the target's - or multiple targets' - direction.

Scott admired it for a second. "I didn't get one of those."

Boardman pulled the pin and lobbed the egg into a clear space about ten yards behind them. "Pays to flirt with the munitions clerk."

They didn't stick around to watch. When they reached the exterior door to the building Lupus had entered, they heard several yelps echoing through the alleyway.

"Canines are in retreat," one of the tech guys reported. "Oh, and we got a faint heat signature of your target after he went into the building. Sending you the schematics to show where he disappeared."

A map of the building appeared in the upper right quadrant of Scott's optics. A circle with the words 'You Are Here' was placed by an exterior door and a big X by a doorway in a corridor.

Scott said, "Yeah, that's the closet that leads to the tunnel."

"Let's hope we don't lose com once you boys go underground."

"If so, see you on the other side," Scott said.

"Roger that."

The door was reinforced and locked. Boardman pulled a slim leather case from one of his pockets and unzipped it. He chose a couple of metal tools, and in a cool two minutes picked the lock.

"You gotta teach me how to do that when this is over," Scott said.

Boardman turned the handle and opened his mouth to reply, but as soon as he cracked the door, an ear-splitting alarm began blaring.

"Damn it, I thought the building had no power!" Scott shouted so the techs would hear him over the noise.

"It must be battery operated," one of them responded, his voice perfectly clear in Scott's ear despite the din.

Scott reached around the edge of the door and pushed it open. It was pitch black inside the building, but his optics made it seem bright as day. A car battery sat on the ground just inside the door. He located the trip wire that had set off the alarm and yanked hard on it. The earsplitting sound abruptly stopped. Padme hadn't said anything about the building being booby-trapped, which meant one of two things: she didn't know, or this was a set-up. He could only hope for the former and trust his instincts that it wasn't the latter.

In his ear, a tech asked, "Are we aborting?"

Scott's eyes shifted to the corner of his optics, where the building schematic was still displayed.

"Negative on the abort."

He tapped Boardman on the arm and gestured that he should follow. He went left down the corridor with the idea in mind that they circle around and catch Lupus from behind - assuming he was the one who came to investigate the alarm. As soon as they rounded the first corner, however, Scott spotted another car battery and threw his arm out to stop Boardman. With his optics, he zoomed in on the battery posts. Another wire was hooked up to them, but Scott doubted this one had an alarm at the other end. He visually traced the wire along the baseboard, up the wall, and onto the ceiling, where a camera dome was mounted. If it was the same type of camera Fournier had used in his facility, it would be transmitting a sharp night image to whoever was on the receiving end, presumably Lupus.

"We're made," he said. If the alarm hadn't changed this from a stealth operation to an all-out offensive, the camera sure did.

"What now, boss?" Boardman asked.

Scott held up a hand and made a pinching motion with his fingers to indicate they should split up and come at Lupus from front and back. Boardman nodded and went back the way they'd come. Scott continued on, keeping his head down so the camera didn't pick up his face.

According to Padme, she'd kept his secret - Lupus and Fournier still had no idea Scott was an XIA agent. She said she'd been *persona non grata* these last four months, but she *was* privy to the fact that, like the savant, Scott was considered to be missing in action. Which was a good thing as far as Scott was concerned, since the last time he'd seen Lupus, the wolf-faced man had caught Padme caressing Scott's cheek and had gone all savagely possessive on him.

In his ear, he heard Boardman say, "Another camera down this way." Then one of the techs said, "Heat sig coming from the tunnel!"

Scott reached the reception area where he, Bryn and Carla had been confronted by Nosferatu's men. He pulled his gun and double-checked that the ammo clip he'd loaded was the one with plastic bullets. Shasta had requested, very politely, that they please bring Lupus in alive, something that wouldn't be easy if the op continued to deviate from the plan.

He rested his shoulder against the wall before poking his head around to look down the final corridor, catching a glimpse of Lupus standing in front of the closet that led to the tunnel, an assault rifle gripped in his meaty hands. He wasn't wearing optics, so he'd be blind inside the unlit building, unaware that Boardman and Scott could see him just fine.

Quietly, Scott said, "I've got visual. Target is heavily armed."

He'd barely finished speaking when, without bothering to lift the gun sight to his eye, Lupus rotated his torso in Boardman's direction and let loose with a burst of gunfire that ripped right through the wall.

In his ear, he heard Boardman gasp and say, "I'm hit! He's got AP shells!"

As the nose of the rifle began to swing Scott's way, he turned and dove for the ground, covering his head with his arms. Bullets tore through the wall all around him. In his ear, Boardman said grimly, "Flash bang, baby," so Scott knew to close his eyes and brace himself. A second later, Boardman's stun grenade detonated with a booming concussion and a light so bright it penetrated Scott's closed eyelids.

When he opened his eyes, he could see through his optics, but his ears were ringing. Lupus, who'd been closer to the blast and wouldn't have known to close his eyes, would be temporarily blind, and the bang would have disrupted the inner workings of his ears. At the very least they'd be ringing like Scott's; probably though, he was temporarily deaf and unbalanced with vertigo.

Scott scrambled on all fours back towards the corridor, noting the bullet holes in the wall. Lupus had aimed low, possibly anticipating that his target would take cover. It was a miracle Scott hadn't been hit, but he didn't stop to contemplate his luck. He knew he might only have seconds to take advantage of Lupus' disorientation.

Lupus, however, may have been blind, deaf and dizzy, but there was nothing wrong with his trigger finger. He'd had military training same as Scott - he'd know that standard procedure following a flash bang grenade was to rush the target. Before Scott could even look around the corner at him, he started shooting again. The assault rifle was equipped with a thirty-round magazine, and Lupus emptied it into the walls, ceiling and floor all around him. All Scott could do was duck and cover again and hope that if he got hit his body armor held up better than Boardman's. As soon as the shooting stopped, he gritted his teeth and got to his feet to take another quick look, gun ready.

To his shock, Lupus was only about three feet away from him, holding the spent rifle up to his left shoulder to take advantage of the night scope and freeing his right arm for an attack. Scott didn't even have time to recoil before his former XBestia superior came at him with a knife, probably his favorite hunting knife, a wickedly serrated 14-inch blade that had the blood of dozens of people on it. The knife ripped through Scott's leather jacket but was stopped by his shirt and vest. Lupus yanked it free for another stab attempt, but he'd had to lower the rifle to get close enough for the first hit and was now effectively blind again.

Scott was too close to fire his weapon - even plastic bullets could be lethal at close range. His first instinct was to disable Lupus with a throat strike, but that could also kill him, so he struck the underside of his chin with the heel of his hand. Instead of attempting to fight the much larger man hand-to-hand, Scott skated backward to put some space between them before shooting at his legs with the plastic bullets.

Lupus flailed around in the dark, swishing the knife through the air before his knees buckled and he fell like a colossal tree toppling in the forest. It was impossible for Scott to make out any expression on Lupus' wolf face, but he did see his black lips move as if he was saying something.

Scott's ears might still be ringing, but they worked, because one of the techs said, "Multiple heat sigs approaching the building, but your entrance point is still uncompromised. Shasta says abort and get out *now*."

"Understood," Scott replied quietly.

Scott wouldn't dream of going against a direct order, but he had to actively stifle his resentment. He looked down at Lupus, who had grabbed his shins and was rolling around in pain. At least at this point, Scott could get away clean, with Lupus none the wiser as to who had broken into the building.

In the lower left corner of his optics, the time was displayed. It was still sixteen minutes until Padme was scheduled to activate Lupus' nanoneurons and flood him with fear. But since the mission hadn't exactly gone according to plan, her sacrifice would be in vain and Lupus would know what she'd done.

He didn't have time to contemplate the price she would pay for her duplicity. Part of him really wanted to end Lupus here and now, but even if he was the sort of person to do such a thing, it wasn't something he could get away with - not with the com team privy to his every move.

He jogged past Lupus, keeping his head down again after spotting another camera on the ceiling. He was focused on getting to Boardman and getting out, but Lupus' hand suddenly shot out and grasped his ankle. Scott hadn't built up enough momentum to lose his balance entirely, but he staggered and hopped on his remaining foot. Lupus brought the rifle around and smashed it into the back of his knee, though, which did bring him down. Faster than he would have given the big man credit for, he was on him, wrapping his arms around him from behind in a full nelson.

Scott still had his gun and no longer had compunctions about possibly killing Lupus. He bent his wrist down and fired in the direction of Lupus' lower body. His hearing must have been nearly restored, because not only was the gunshot report loud, he had no trouble making out Lupus' profane response. Still, it took a second shot to get the big man to release him.

He tried to get to his feet, but to his astonishment, Lupus lunged for him again, this time catching him around the chest from behind in a bear hug that pinned his arms down. The constriction across his chest was so powerful he felt as if his ribs were about to crack. This encounter was the first time Scott had been on the receiving end of Lupus' fighting skills; he now had first-hand knowledge that Lupus' reputation as a formidable opponent was deserved.

Instead of attempting to wrestle him, which would clearly be tantamount to wrestling a bear, Scott fumbled under his shirt for the pull on his bulletproof aqua vest. When he yanked the cord, the vest inflated instantly, adding several inches to his girth and effectively loosening Lupus' grip. Scott threw his head back and connected with something solid. Lupus grunted and released him.

He rolled away but had a feeling Lupus would only keep coming. He had one chance and that was to bluff his way out of this. The plastic bullets were useful as a temporary distraction, but Lupus had been conditioned to endure pain and fear. It was a serious flaw in the plan; one that Scott hoped didn't get him killed. Swiftly, before he lost his advantage, he lifted the gun and placed the barrel against the fur on Lupus' forehead.

"Even a plastic bullet will scramble your brains from this distance," he said.

"Cougar?" Lupus asked in his deep, rusty voice. Scott cursed inwardly, wishing he'd thought to disguise his own voice.

Lupus bared his teeth, but not in his customary snarl. It was something Scott had rarely seen before on the wolf-faced man: the approximation of a smile. In a voice that held actual welcome, Lupus asked, "Where you been all this time, boy?"

Chapter Twenty-eight

Hours before first light, Dillo had picked Maddy, Jason and Bryn up near the main entrance of Edgemere's underground mall in an all-black Hummer E8 with tinted windows. Maddy didn't get in right away, preferring instead to stand watch until the last of the small boats was launched and her vengeful and well-armed people were on their way to Coney Island.

While Bryn had stood shivering next to her in the frigid early-morning air, Jason excused himself to make a quick trip to his truck. He'd come back with the narrow bag that contained the rifle he'd used to kill the FBI agent; the man Maddy had said was named Antonovich.

The drive to the marina on the bay side of Rockaway Peninsula had been short, and they were met at the dock by four of Maddy's soldiers. The captain of the yacht had the 58-foot vessel ready to go. After seeing the barely seaworthy 'fleet,' Bryn had wondered whether the yacht would even be safe, but once on board, she'd quickly realized she needn't have worried. The vessel may have been considered small as yachts go, but it was sleek, powerful, and state-of-the-art.

In the stern cockpit, Bryn had sat next to Jason and Dillo on comfortable and spacious leather seating out under the stars, while Maddy took the chair next to the captain at the helm under the roof. The soldiers stood halfway between, two on each side of the yacht, holding their semi-automatic weapons out over the water like dogs hanging their heads out of a car.

The captain had run without navigation lights, but they passed no one else on the water. If anyone on shore had seen them, it would have been as a ghostly silhouette. The pace Maddy set had been excruciatingly slow; they'd barely moved fast enough create a wake, or even a breeze strong enough to stir the coarse hair at the base of Bryn's quills. Still, Coney Island had come into sight well before any of the smaller craft arrived. The captain had made anchor some distance from shore as Maddy anxiously studied the radar holo. Communication between the yacht and the fleet had been nonexistent. Maddy had declared 'radio silence' in order to avoid attracting the harbor police - or alerting the XBestia to their arrival.

The yacht was anchored east of the fleet's expected landing point, and Bryn had been relieved to discover Maddy had no intention of joining the fight. She'd given her people the location of bungalow number nine and a very good incentive to be the one who brought the occupant to her alive: a large quantity of cash.

Now Bryn looked out over the water to shore, trying to get her bearings. She'd navigated these waters just once before, but the experience was indelibly imprinted on her memory. That 'adventure' had occurred in broad daylight, though. This late at night, the shoreline had a very different profile. Some areas of Coney Island were still legitimately occupied and had basic city services like water and electricity, but lights were few and far between. If it weren't for the faint orange haze in the sky from the city lights of Brooklyn, it would be hard to distinguish between the water and the shore and the sky.

Bluto's was the most obvious establishment along the boardwalk, and she thought she could pinpoint it by what appeared to be the remains of a garbage fire out front. She knew from Carla, who used to date the owner and work there as a waitress, that the bar closed late, often staying open until three or four a.m. It was likely closed by now, as dawn began to lighten the eastern sky.

From her vantage point standing over the radar holo in the cockpit, Maddy rubbed her hands together gleefully and said, "Here they come! Should be making shore soon."

Chapter Twenty-nine

When Lupus asked him where he'd been all this time, it threw Scott off so badly he answered without thinking, "Avoiding you."

Lupus laughed and swatted Scott's gun away. "Yeah, that was probably a good move. I wasn't very happy when I saw you with Padme."

"There was nothing going on," Scott said, feeling like he was always denying being involved with someone.

"Maybe not, but she told me she wished there was."

Scott got to his feet and deflated his aqua vest. "Well, I don't care what *she* wanted, I didn't encourage her - I'm not suicidal."

Lupus stood too, and reached into his jacket pocket. Scott tensed up until light appeared from a holophone. Lupus muttered, "Knew I should have brought a flashlight."

There was a noise from the front of the building and a light swept across the entrance to the corridor from the front lobby. Lupus called, "Over here!"

Scott wasn't sure what to expect when six of Lupus' armed goons crowded into the lobby and stood waiting for their orders. He didn't for a minute think he was 'forgiven' for the sin of having attracted Lupus' woman, but he also knew he'd be dead already if that was Lupus' intention.

Lupus pointed to two of the xenos and said, "You and you - go get the other one." He jerked his thumb over his shoulder towards the end of the corridor where Scott assumed Boardman was laid out, hopefully still alive.

Lupus snatched the flashlight out of another xeno's hand and shined it in Scott's face. The optics instantly adjusted to the brightness as Lupus asked, "Night vision specs?"

"Yeah."

Lupus grunted and put his holophone back in his pocket. "What's with the plastic bullets? And what the hell are you doing here anyway?"

In his ear, Shasta's voice said, "Tell him you came to warn him that the Mad Eye gang is going to attack the Bungalows - tonight."

Scott's blood went cold, but he didn't have time to wonder how Shasta had gotten that intel, or to worry about Bryn.

To Lupus, he said, "I heard the Mad Eyes were planning on opening a can of whoop-ass on the Bungholes tonight. Thought that info might get me back in your good graces."

"You don't say. And how are they fixing on doing that?"

Shasta said, "By boat. ETA ten minutes. Get out of there."

"Same way I got here," Scott said. "By boat. They should be making landfall any time now."

Lupus stared at him for a moment, then waved a hand at his remaining men and told them, "Don't just stand there, go greet our guests when they arrive."

The xenos filed out and Lupus turned back to Scott. "I got eyes and ears out at Edgemere and didn't hear nothin' about any invasion."

Scott was spared having to come up with a good story when the two xeno's Lupus had sent to get Boardman returned, hauling the limping agent between them. Scott hadn't heard Boardman's voice in his ear since he'd tossed the flash bang grenade, so it was a relief to see him alive, even though his pinched face looked anything but well.

Even though he was injured, Boardman made an effort. He nodded politely at Lupus and said, "Hey."

Without a word, Lupus stripped the optics from Boardman's face, made a fist around the flashlight he was still holding and punched him in the face. The two supporting xenos let go of Boardman's arms and he fell to the ground.

"That's for the grenade," Lupus snarled. "My damned ears are still ringing."

Flat on his back, Boardman raised his head and said weakly, "What was I supposed to do? You shot me."

Lupus made a move like he was going to go after him again, but Scott said quickly, "Knuckles has a big mouth, but he's got mad skills in the ring."

Lupus was a betting man and a big fan of grease fights. Scott hoped to appeal to his sense of greed at the thought of obtaining a new fighter.

It worked; Lupus ran the flashlight over Boardman, lingering on the injured agent's wicked-looking xenografts. He finally turned his attention to the optics in his hand. As soon as he'd snatched them from Boardman's face, the com team shut down transmission - Scott knew because his own display had gone blank. When Lupus fit Boardman's spectagoggles to his face, he would see no time, no map, nothing to indicate the optics were anything other than standard night vision goggles.

Lupus was also unaware that the round spectagoggles gave him the appearance of the Big Bad Wolf dressed up as a steampunk Granny. Scott bit back a highly inappropriate laugh.

Thankfully, Lupus didn't notice. He glared at the two hovering xenos and said, "What you waitin' for? Go get you some Mad Eye action."

They grinned and ran off.

Lupus turned his attention back to Boardman. "Where you hit?"

"Leg." Boardman gestured to his right thigh.

"Well, you better get up and walk on it, boy. I don't particularly feel like taking on a Mad Eye mob tonight."

Boardman sat up and laboriously got to his feet. "Yes, sir."

Lupus started down the corridor but paused when his pocket buzzed. He pulled out his holophone and glanced at it, but instead of putting it on display he held it to his ear and snapped, "What?" After several seconds of listening, he said shortly, "I'm well aware of that."

Something about Lupus' manner told Scott the caller was Padme. It was confirmed when one of the techs said in his ear, "Call intercepted," and then he heard her voice: "-says it looks like there are dozens of boats. And the alarm went off in the building next to Bluto's. Where are you?"

"Standing here with an old friend. But you already know that, don't you?"

For a tense moment, Scott thought Lupus was revealing his hand; telling her he knew of her plan to have Scott kill him.

But she didn't miss a beat. "Yes, I'm watching the camera footage."

"Then why didn't you just say that? Always playing your damned games." He hung up on her and shook his head at Scott. "If she wasn't pregnant, I swear to Dog I'd kill her myself."

"Who, Padme?" Scott asked, trying to hide his shock.

"Who else? Come on, show me this boat of yours."

Scott put his arm around Boardman's waist and helped him as they made their way out of the building. Lupus headed on a straight path to the beach, down the same alley Scott and Boardman had come through on the way in. It seemed too good to be true that Lupus was walking to the UAAV under his own steam, unaware of what awaited him. Which, as far as Scott was concerned, was a heck of a lot better than having to subdue him during the flood of fear Padme was supposed to have dosed him with. The plan had been to drag his large, bound and unwilling body through the cluttered alley

125

and across the beach, which would have been left for Scott to do alone since Boardman was in no shape to help.

Scott's optics display was still dark, but he knew the time had to have passed by now: Padme hadn't activated his nanoneurons on schedule. She'd been witness to the fight; witness to everything that was said and done. Did she realize Scott's intention was to capture Lupus all along, or did she simply think he'd failed to kill him? Either way, he should have known she wouldn't leave it to chance. She'd planned on watching from afar all along.

Chapter Thirty

Bryn's teeth had begun to chatter uncontrollably. Jason offered her his jacket but didn't attempt to move closer or, heaven forbid, put his arm around her. Even though the warmth of his body still lingered in the heavy leather jacket draped over her shoulders, she was freezing. She clenched her jaw to stop the rat-a-tat, but every time she relaxed, it started up again. Maddy finally exclaimed, "For bugger's sake, they're going to hear you on shore. Come here!"

It was much warmer under the roof at the helm, and the captain made it warmer by adjusting the fan nearest Bryn to blow heat on the back of her legs. Maddy continued to examine the holo radar and ignored Bryn as she, too, bent over the display.

The swarm of red dots representing the fleet was coalescing near shore. There were several other dots here and there, but they didn't seem to concern Maddy. Bryn noticed one blip that was quite close to the yacht and almost touching the shoreline. She turned and looked for it but saw nothing.

"What?" Maddy asked.

Bryn shook her head, but Maddy persisted. "You have a very expressive face and just now you looked positively constipated. What did you see?"

Bryn pointed to the blip and waved a hand to indicate the shore. "According the radar, there should be a boat between us and Bluto's."

"What's a Bluto's?" Maddy asked.

"It's a bar and grill." She pointed again. "See that light? Bluto's should be right about there."

Maddy frowned down at the radar and then held her hand out towards one of her soldiers and snapped her fingers. He immediately moved forward to hand her a pair of binoculars. She stepped close to the window and lifted them to her eyes. After about a minute she muttered, "Curious."

Bryn waited.

Maddy bent her torso one way and then the other. "*Quite* curious."

Dillo appeared at her side. "What is it?"

Maddy handed him the binoculars. "Look at waves directly beneath that light there. Do you see how they're breaking?"

Bryn didn't see a thing; it was still too dark, but assumed the binoculars had night capability or something.

"Uh-huh," Dillo said. "I see it. Like there's a glass boat right there."

"An invisible boat. But not invisible to radar."

Jason joined them, and Dillo passed the binoculars to him.

"It's not very big," Dillo said, looking down at the radar holo. "Who do you s'pose it is?"

Maddy crossed her arms and then brought the knuckles of her left hand to rest against her upper lip. "Well, if it's Harbor Patrol they've certainly upped their game."

Bryn was the only one who saw Jason's face after he slowly lowered the binoculars. She'd spent the last two days in close company with him, and even though he had very few 'tells,' she picked up on the flicker of concern in his eyes.

He knows what it is, she thought. Which probably meant the invisible boat was XIA.

Chapter Thirty-one

Just about nothing had gone according to plan, but all they had to do was play it cool until they got to the UAAV, where Lo was waiting with enough firepower to convince even Lupus that it'd be best not to resist. As Scott helped Boardman over and around the junk cluttering the alley, he suddenly remembered the dodo egg, which may or may not have depleted itself of pepper spray when the wild dogs encountered it.

Lupus had forged ahead and would be almost upon it. He was still wearing Boardman's optics, which would protect his eyes, and his face was furred, which would protect his skin somewhat, but his mouth and canine nose would be vulnerable.

Scott started to shout a warning, but it was too late. He heard a faint 'pssst' sound as the dodo egg went off, followed by Lupus crying out in a surprisingly high-pitched voice. Boardman said, "Ah, jeez. Go on ahead. I'll catch up."

Scott glanced up at the sky, which was beginning to lighten, but not enough for Boardman to see his way through the alley, a virtual minefield of rusty metal and splintered boards.

He reached up to his goggles and said, "Take my optics," but Boardman replied, "I got my holophone. Go!"

Scott jumped over a heap of garbage that looked suspiciously like it was squirming, pushed past an overflowing and foul-smelling dumpster, and wove his way through haphazardly stacked piles of beams and boards to where Lupus was bent double, coughing and swearing.

Scott stayed back, out of Lupus' reach in case the big man lashed out. "You okay?"

The reply was garbled, but Scott thought he said, "Can't...breathe."

Scott fought off a surge of irritation. This *would* be the perfect opportunity to fully take control of the situation by using his stun gun, but the electric shock would incapacitate Lupus' muscles, and since he was already having trouble breathing, he might suffocate.

As if to illustrate the need to hurry, a faint burst of gunfire erupted somewhere down the beach.

"Can you walk?" he asked.

An angry growl was the only response, but Lupus began staggering toward the end of the alley. Scott looked around for the dodo egg, but it was gone - Lupus must have kicked it away. Boardman caught up with them, but when Scott made a move like he was going to help him, the other agent waved him off and said, "I'll be right behind you."

Scott went after Lupus, who had stopped on the boardwalk. Wheezing heavily, he gestured out at the water. The UAAV was still in camouflage mode, but Scott knew its general location. There was something else out there, though. In his ear, Lo said, "Welcome back. And, yeah, we got company."

Out on the water, several hundred yards from shore, a dark shape was silhouetted against the lighter sky. Lupus struggled to speak between laboriously indrawn breaths. "Your...boat?"

Whoever was manning the other watercraft seemed to be in stealth mode, too, since there were no running lights. Scott had a bad feeling about it, but the other vessel's presence did give him an idea. He hadn't thought how to lure Lupus out to the UAAV when it was essentially invisible.

"Yeah, that's it," he said. "Come on."

Chapter Thirty-two

When the sound of gunfire echoed out over the water, Maddy snatched the binoculars from Jason and turned to look at the Mad Eye boats.

It was light enough now for Bryn to see them just converging on shore. The plan had been for the invading Mad Eyes to land quickly before stealthily moving into XBestia territory, but something must have gone wrong because there were men on shore shooting at the boats. The cracking and popping sounds increased and now Bryn heard faint shouts and screams. From this distance, the men on shore looked like ants. They began to fall under an onslaught of bullets from the incoming boats.

Maddy lowered the binoculars. Her angry face, highlighted by the bluish light shining up from the holo display, looked positively sinister. She turned to Dillo and said, "They knew."

Dillo held his hand out for the binoculars. For a moment, Bryn thought Maddy might throw them at him, but she handed them over.

He looked. "There were only five or six men on shore. If someone warned them, there'd be a whole lot more...hold on...ahh, here they come."

Bryn saw them pouring across the boardwalk, collectively shouting and waving their weapons like a barbarian horde. They rushed to meet the occupants of the boats that had made it to shore.

"How did they *know*?" Maddy said through gritted teeth.

"They must have posted a look-out," Jason said.

Maddy treated him to a dour look that shot his suggestion down. "They're too stupid and disorganized for that. Someone tipped them off."

"Wait," said Dillo. He'd turned and was looking toward Bluto's. "I see something."

"Well, what is it?" Maddy snapped.

"Two men on the beach, headed for that invisible boat." He passed her the binoculars with a huge grin. "And you're not going to believe who it is."

Maddy lifted the binoculars and looked. After several tense seconds, she lowered them again. On her face was a look of utter glee.

"Captain?" she asked cheerfully. "How close can you bring us in?"

Chapter Thirty-three

Lupus made it halfway across the beach before collapsing. He rolled onto his back gasping for breath. Scott was no veterinarian, but the wolf-faced man's canine nose and thin black lips looked swollen. He knew from basic training that some people reacted more adversely to pepper spray than others. From the sound of Lupus' labored breathing, he must have inhaled some of the caustic liquid. If his lung passages closed up, Scott would be left hauling a dead man.

He quickly assessed the situation. The boat shadowing them had begun moving closer. It was very likely they'd spotted the UAAV on radar. It was *un*likely they were friendlies. Boardman had just stepped onto the beach and was shuffling his way through the sand towards him.

"Lo, I need you," he said, before pulling the backpack from his back and unzipping it. A flick of his wrists and the stretcher pack unrolled, the stabilizing bars snapping automatically into place.

"They spotted us," Lo replied.

"Affirmative. Lupus is down, Boardman is shot, and we need your muscle." Scott set the stretcher in the sand, knelt by Lupus' side and heaved him onto it.

The UAAV motor revved and in seconds Lo had driven it onto the sand and stopped nearby. Scott glanced up. It looked like an ice cream truck again. Lo slid open the side door, jumped out, and took the back end of the stretcher.

The com team must have repositioned the drone, because one of them said, "The unknown vessel has launched an outboard. You've got two incoming. Get out of there!"

Scott and Lo heaved Lupus into the UAAV, then ran together to assist Boardman. One on each side, with his arms over their shoulders, they lifted him and pounded across the sand. To the right, half a mile up the beach, the Mad Eye and XBestia gangs were killing each other. Isolated patches of orange light flickered from several locations along the boardwalk. Clouds of billowing smoke indicated the light came from buildings that had been torched. Far off sirens began to wail. Ahead of them, to the left of the UAAV, the two men from the unknown vessel landed. The taller of the two had hulking huge shoulders. Both were armed with rifles.

Scott and the others were twenty yards from safety when Boardman said, "We're not going to make it. Leave me!"

"The hell with that," Lo said. She ducked out from under Boardman's arm and pulled her gun. Scott swore, but he knew why she'd done it. Of the two of them, he was stronger and could get Boardman to safety faster than she could.

"Federal agent!" she shouted. "Drop your weapons!"

Scott didn't hesitate; Lo was wearing body armor and could handle herself, and he wasn't about to squander her gambit by standing around waiting to see what the two armed men would do. He bent down, hefted Boardman in a fireman's carry, and ran.

Chapter Thirty-four

After Maddy sent Dillo and Jason ashore in the little outboard, she broke her own radio silence rule to call someone. Bryn tried to stay out of her way as she paced back and forth, staring at her holophone and muttering, "Pick up...pick up."

Bryn had begun chewing on one of her fingernails, eyes glued to the outboard as it zoomed closer to shore. The sky had gotten lighter, but darkness was still hours away from being completely dispelled.

"No one's answering!" Maddy let out a frustrated cry and threw her holophone at the windshield. It slid across the dash and clattered to the floor.

The captain turned to her with eyebrows raised. "Maybe they're busy."

"I need *them*..." she jabbed a finger at the beach where the gang fight was still raging, "to go *there*!" she turned and pointed to where Jason and Dillo were just landing. "Lupus is i*n that truck*!"

Bryn shrank away from Maddy's fury, pressing her nose against the cold glass. The shore was some distance away, but she clearly saw two people helping a third walk to the invisible boat that had quite bizarrely turned into an ice cream truck and driven onto the beach. She couldn't make out their faces in the low light, but one of the helpers was a woman and the other a man with goggles over his eyes. When the woman broke away and yelled that she was a federal agent, Bryn hoped Jason and Dillo would back off, but they didn't.

Dillo yelled back, "We just want the wolf man!"

The woman responded by diving to the side and simultaneously firing at them. Jason and Dillo dropped flat. After that, everything happened so fast it was like a blur. The woman continued to fire while rolling towards the ice cream truck. Dillo and Jason also took cover on the ground and fired back.

In the meantime, a group of xenos, Bryn wasn't sure if they were XBestia or Mad Eye, seemed to be making their way up the beach. Several fires had broken out and the windless morning did nothing to dispel the smoke, which expanded in the air and drifted across the sand.

The man with the goggles appeared from behind the truck with a gun in each hand. He laid down a hail of bullets that allowed the woman to run for the shelter of the truck. Just when Bryn thought the 'federal agents' were going to get away, Dillo took aim and picked the goggled man off - and from the way the man's head jerked back before he fell, it looked like he'd been hit in the face.

The xenos coming up the beach were flat-out running now, chased by another, larger group. The ones being chased must have been Mad Eye, because they headed straight for Dillo and Jason, who began shooting at their pursuers. Most of the newcomers were carrying firearms, but none were shooting, and Bryn suspected it was because they were all out of ammunition.

She glanced back at the truck just in time to see the woman use the distraction to attempt to pull the fallen man to safety, but Dillo saw her, too, and quite casually turned and shot her.

Bryn's fingernail had been bitten to the quick. She moved on to the next finger, watching the carnage on the beach, horrified, but unable to look away. Six Mad Eyes made it to safety behind Dillo and Jason. Ammunition was shared, and the newcomers gained a quick advantage over their pursuers, who retreated out of range.

The far end of the beach was almost completely obscured by smoke now, but the sirens had gotten louder, and she made out flashing red and blue lights that indicated the police had arrived. The pursuing XBestia must have seen the lights, too, because they scattered, running for the safety of the buildings along the boardwalk that had yet to catch fire. Dillo waved the surviving Mad Eyes over to the outboard. It wasn't big enough to hold them all, but three climbed aboard and the other three held onto the side as they strained the little motor and headed for the yacht.

The arrival of the police was apparently Dillo and Jason's signal to attack the ice cream truck full force. They fired on it, but the bullets ricocheted off - the strange vehicle was obviously reinforced, and since the occupants didn't drive away, it was clear they felt safe inside.

But Dillo wasn't going to give up that easily. He approached the fallen man, who was still alive and moving. Bryn saw him step on the man's arm and take his gun, tucking it into his waistband. Then he grabbed him by the hair, lifted his head and placed the barrel of his own gun against his skull.

"Fair trade!" he shouted. "The wolf for this one, or I blow his brains out!"

Chapter Thirty-five

The bullet that hit Scott's optic lens had glanced off the shatter-resistant plastic, but still slammed the goggle frame into his eye socket hard enough to knock him briefly unconscious. He'd woken to a massive headache, unable to see out of his left eye. Lo had been shaking him, urging him to get up. His vision in the uninjured eye was blurry - he wasn't sure if the lens was clouded or what - but he'd seen her take a shot to the chest that sent her flying.

He was glad when she dragged herself inside the truck and shut the door. He certainly didn't blame her for leaving him. She'd taken a huge risk coming back for him in the first place. Her body armor would have absorbed the brunt of that shot, but she'd be bruised at best and incapacitated at worst depending on where the bullet hit her. He'd been flat-out lucky that his optics had deflected the kill shot, but Lo had nothing protecting her head from a similar shot.

Not that he felt lucky when the man with the huge shoulders took his weapon and lifted his aching head by his hair. The barrel of the gun resting against his temple was warm. He tried to think of a way out of the situation, but gun-to-the-head scenarios didn't offer many options.

After the man made his demands, another voice came from behind - one that he instantly recognized. *Alton.*

"No time to negotiate," Alton said. "Cops are coming. Don't kill that one, he's not a fed - look at his hands."

The man tilted Scott's head back and pushed the broken optics up onto his forehead. "What's your name?"

Scott still couldn't see out of the injured eye but was relieved to find his other eye worked just fine. The dark-skinned man looking down at him had a deceptively kind face.

"Cougar," he said.

"I've heard of him," Alton said quickly. "He works for Lupus."

If Alton was attempting to save him, Scott thought pointing out he was an XBestia was probably not the best way to go about it - although the alternative was to admit that Scott was a fed. Either way, he was expendable. But the man grunted and said, "Well, then I guess he'll have to do."

He let go of Scott's hair while Alton patted him down, took his extra ammo clips and then bound his hands behind his back with his own zip tie. The gun against his temple never wavered, and when he was forced to his feet, he saw why. Lo had cracked the side window of the UAAV and she and Boardman were pointing their weapons at them. Neither of the agents would have recognized Alton since they hadn't been with the XIA for long and he'd been on assignment for the last six months. Scott tried to give her a reassuring look, but the man grabbed his arm and pushed him toward the ocean.

He fully expected his usefulness to expire as soon as they got out of range of Lo's gun, but for some reason, they seemed to want him as a hostage. One of the Mad Eye soldiers had arrived back at the beach in the outboard, and they forced Scott aboard.

The trip to the yacht in the little boat was unpleasant. His head injury had brought on dizziness and nausea that the motion of the waves only exacerbated. He kept the coffee he'd drunk down for as long as he could but ended up vomiting over the side. After dry heaving until he thought he was going to turn inside out, he heard Shasta in his ear, saying softly, "Clear your throat if you can hear me."

Scott was relieved to hear her voice. His throat was raw from vomiting, but he cleared it.

"The drone will not be able to keep up with the yacht," she said, "We will lose com with you very soon. Alton's assignment is crucial. You will follow *his* lead. Clear your throat if you understand."

Scott didn't understand, not really. Last he heard, Alton's assignment had been to protect Bryn, but Shasta's words confirmed what he'd begun to suspect anyway - that Alton's orders had reverted back to his original assignment the moment he'd gone back to Edgemere.

"Agent Harding?" Shasta prompted.

For the first time in his career with the XIA, he felt the urge to argue with his superior. But even if he could, he didn't have any idea what Alton's assignment was. He had no choice but to trust that it *was* crucial.

He cleared his throat.

"Maddy Singh has cameras everywhere," Shasta continued. "Watch what you say. If there's any way for you to dump this earbug, do it before she has you searched."

Scott's hands were bound and the earbug's design prevented it from being knocked loose even if his aching head could withstand the good shaking that would require. He tried to get a nonverbal message across to Alton, but the other agent was avoiding making eye contact. For the time being, there was nothing Scott could do about the earbug.

He was grateful when the outboard arrived at the yacht, if only because the larger boat was more stable in the water. Alton kept hold of his arm, as if he was claiming him. Once on board, Scott looked past the Mad Eye soldiers crowding the bridge and saw Bryn, staring at him with her mouth slightly open. Moments later, he braced his legs as the powerful vessel turned and retreated from the area, which would sever contact with the com team.

They were on their own.

On the bridge of the yacht, a masculine-looking blond in a white suit seemed to be in charge. In an accented and effeminate-sounding male voice, she said, "Who have we here? Anyone useful?"

"He's Lupus' right-hand man," Alton said. It was a blatant exaggeration, but Scott wasn't about to dispute it. He realized now why the Mad Eyes attacked the UAAV - to get to Lupus. Alton must be trying to convince them that Scott was second best.

The blond let out a loud, dissatisfied sigh, followed by, "Take him below."

Alton pushed him forward and down some steps. Bryn appeared by his side, saying quietly, "Let me help."

"It'd be better if you didn't," Alton replied. God, Scott was beginning to hate that guy.

"Just try and stop me."

There was no one else below deck in the salon. It was a compact, opulent space, like a mini apartment with cherry wood cabinets, marble countertops and a thick carpet. Alton pushed him toward a settee and said, "Sit. Don't talk."

Scott sat, but immediately began testing his bonds to see if he could free his wrists. Alton hadn't tightened the zip tie excessively, but he hadn't left enough room for Scott to break loose.

Bryn went over to a mini refrigerator and came back with a frozen pack of peas. She gently placed it against his eye. He'd never seen her with such heavy black eyeliner on, but it didn't hide the worried look in her eyes.

Her expression told him all he needed to know about his injury: it didn't look good.

He couldn't resist saying, "You're a sight for sore eye."

She laughed a little, even though she looked like she was going to cry.

"I said shut up," Alton snapped.

"I heard you." He turned his head away and tilted it at an angle, hoping Alton would see the earbug. He didn't.

The sound of footsteps on the stairs alerted them that someone was coming. It was the blond. She sauntered slowly over, turning her head this way and that as she appraised him. Behind her hulked the man with the huge shoulders. He held Scott's gun casually in one hand.

"Cougar, is it?" the blond asked.

Scott knew Maddy Singh was a transgender woman; there was no question in his mind that this was she. "Yes, ma'am," he said.

Her chin came up. "Polite. I like that. What I don't like is mysteries. How did you know we were coming?"

By 'you' Scott knew she meant the XBestia. He couldn't very well tell her the truth, that Lupus hadn't known until Shasta had given Scott the intel. He had no idea how Shasta had known - unless her informant had told her, and she'd withheld the information from him so he'd be focused on the op instead of worrying about Bryn. But Maddy was waiting for a response and he'd better give her a plausible one.

He decided to go with the simplest, hardest to disprove answer. "Someone on shore saw the boats coming and raised the alarm."

"Okay. I'll accept that - for the time being. What were the feds doing there?"

"I don't know."

Maddy pursed her lips and made a *tsk* sound. "Lie. I don't like lies and I don't like liars. Do you know what I do to liars?"

It was a rhetorical question, but Scott felt she wanted an answer anyway. "No."

"Sadly, you're going to find out unless you stop. But I will give you a chance to redeem yourself. Where's Fournier?"

Scott had known he was in pretty deep as soon as he'd been taken prisoner, but he'd hoped with Alton in the picture he'd somehow get out of it. Maddy might as well have asked him to instruct her how to flap her arms and fly to the moon. He gave her the only answer he could: "I don't know."

To his surprise, she said, "Well, that I actually believe. We'll talk more about it later." She said it pleasantly enough, but Scott knew it was a threat.

"I do have one more question, though." She turned to Bryn. "Is this your ex-boyfriend?"

Chapter Thirty-six

Bryn didn't even get a chance to deny it before Maddy exclaimed, "My God, your face isn't just an open book, it's an instruction manual. I have really enjoyed having you around these last few days. Seriously, Bryn, you and Dragila have been terribly entertaining all by yourselves, but with the ex-boyfriend added to the mix, I can't *wait* to see what will happen. And you know what's the most interesting thing of all? The incredible series of coincidences that brought us all together, just like Munnu said."

She stopped talking to look from Bryn's face to Jason and then to Scott. "I don't know what you people are playing at, but I *will* find out."

Dillo stepped forward, and with a casually limp wrist, waved the gun in his hand at Jason. "You fired a lot of bullets out there today, Dragila. Didn't hit a damned thing, though. Someone as familiar with guns as you."

Almost as if by accident, he squeezed the trigger and shot Jason in the chest. Bryn screamed as he slammed up against the wall, grabbed the front of his jacket and slid to the floor.

Maddy winced and put her hands to her ears. "Oh, stop with the screaming already! It's your boyfriend's gun and it's loaded with plastic bullets. He'll be fine. For now."

Jason was breathing heavily and in obvious pain, but the hand he took away wasn't covered in blood. Dillo made sure they all saw him switch to a different gun.

Bryn stood frozen to the spot, watching and waiting for Maddy's next move.

"So," the Mad Eye queen said to Scott. "Why would an XBestia bring plastic bullets to a gun fight?"

Scott didn't respond.

Maddy's lips curled in a feral smile. "Brilliant. You've learned to stop lying. That's step one." She moved into the tiny kitchenette and opened a drawer, sliding a long knife out of its block. "Step two is a whole lot more fun. For me, of course."

When Maddy turned, brandishing the blade, Bryn wasn't surprised to see her gaze turn towards her. It was logical that she would threaten Bryn to get Scott or Jason to tell her what she wanted to know. Bryn felt her quills respond to the danger by puffing up around her head. Maddy must have noticed, because her eyes narrowed in interest.

"Fournier is a sick, sick man, but I have to admire his inventiveness," she said. "He had to have known he was giving you a way to protect yourself when he grafted those quills onto your head. Don't you think?"

Bryn lifted her shoulders in a tentative shrug, never taking her eyes from the knife that Maddy was now twirling around in her fingers, the metal flashing as it reflected the salon's track lighting. She was relieved when the motion of the yacht slowed and she heard the captain's voice over the intercom, "We've arrived at the dock."

Maddy rolled her eyes and adopted a resigned expression. "Probably for the best. The salon isn't really equipped for this, and I would hate to get blood on the carpet. Dillo, would you do the honors?"

She put the knife back in the drawer and left, leaving Dillo to herd the three of them on deck. He recruited two of Maddy's soldiers to strip Jason's jacket off, frisk him thoroughly, and tie his hands behind him. Bryn, who was clearly not considered a threat, was left unbound.

In their new status as prisoners, they were no longer welcome in Maddy's car. They traveled in the open back of a pickup truck with the soldiers. Dillo sat across from them with Jason's bag on his lap, nonchalantly going through it.

By the time they got back to Edgemere, the sun had risen on another cold, clear day. They were taken directly to the 'dungeon,' the same place Junk had been taken the day before. It turned out to be just another sealed off and converted biopolycrete pipe, except it was some distance away from the stacked pipes that made up Maddy's lair. Several cinder blocks had been laid along both edges of the pipe to keep it from rolling. A low, rickety platform with stairs was pushed up against the only entrance. Inside, to Bryn's surprise, Junk was still there and still alive - barely.

He was handcuffed to a metal railing that was bolted to the curved wall and extended horizontally the entire length of the pipe. Shirtless, bloody, and from the smell of it, left in the dungeon so long he'd been forced to soil himself, he barely lifted his head when Dillo gestured them in.

Bryn expected Dillo to handcuff them to the railing, too, but he just shook his head at Jason in disappointment and slammed the door.

Unlike the rest of the pipes in Maddy's hive-like lair, this one didn't have a light source. Once the door closed, darkness surrounded them except for a sliver of barely detectable green light all around the door. Bryn reached out to Scott, touching his jacket, feeling around to his hands, to the soft fur of his xenograft. Her fingers encountered the plastic tie that bound his wrists together and she tugged on it. She wished she had a knife or a pair of scissors, or even the tweezers Carla had packed for her. Dillo hadn't bothered to check her, but even if he had, she had nothing more useful in her pocket than her tube of lip gloss and maybe some lint.

She took a shuddering breath and slipped her arms around Scott from behind, resting her chin on his shoulder blade. She felt him grasp the hem of her jacket and lean slightly back against her.

"Don't talk," Jason said.

She clenched her teeth against a rush of resentment. "About what? The weather? Because it looked like a really freaking nice day out there."

Jason didn't reply, which made her even angrier. They wouldn't be in this mess if it weren't for him. If he hadn't brought her here despite the danger. "Is this what they had in mind when they told you to 'stay the course?'"

"You have no idea what you're talking about," he snapped. "And if you don't shut up, I'll have to shut you up."

Scott pulled away, but she kept her hands on him and felt him turn around to face towards Jason's voice. "Don't make me say the obvious, Alton." Bryn hoped by that he meant that Jason would have to go through him to get to her.

"This is what she wants," Jason said, enunciating each word. "For us to fight amongst ourselves."

Bryn laughed. "Well, we might as well get it all out in the open now, since she's only going to torture it out of us later. And frankly, I'm not up for that."

"No one's going to torture anyone." Scott sounded more confident than the situation warranted, but then again, he always knew more than he let on - maybe rescue was imminent and all they had to do was stay calm and wait. She tried to take comfort from that, but from the darkness, a third voice chimed in. It was Junk, who slurred, "Yesh she will...she will..."

Scott said quietly, "Don't listen. It'll be all right."

"Water," Junk whispered.

Chapter Thirty-seven

When Alton had patted Scott down back on the beach, it had been a deliberately cursory search that was just for show. For Dillo's benefit, Alton had made a point of removing Scott's extra bullet clips from his pockets, but Scott knew he'd felt and overlooked the diver's knife in its ankle sheath and a narrow object in a concealed pocket on Scott's right thigh. That object happened to be Shasta's birthday present to him - the auto injector filled with a powerful tranquillizer.

On the deck of the yacht, Dillo had taken pains to strip Alton of his weapons, but fortunately hadn't done a second search of Scott, who was already bound and had been doing his best to seem cooperative.

Shasta had warned him that Maddy Singh had cameras everywhere, and he doubted the 'dungeon' was any exception. Alton had ordered them not to talk because someone was always watching, picking up on every nuance of their conversation to report back to Maddy. An escape attempt would be foolhardy, but Scott had another plan, one that he had to instigate and carry out quickly, before the watchers figured out what he was up to and responded.

Bryn was still standing in front of him, clinging to his jacket. He bent at the waist and put his forehead against the front of her shoulder, pushing his spectagoggles back down over his eyes. It hurt when the frame settled down over his injury, but once he'd gotten the optics in place, he could see in the dark out of his good eye again.

"What are you doing?" she asked.

"Nothing. I just need to sit down."

He walked over to the wall next to the door, on the opposite side of the pipe from the handcuffed man. The flooring was metal and seemed level, but he felt an almost imperceptible shift as his weight rolled the pipe against the cinderblocks wedged along the outer edge. The interior walls were curved, which might make his next move more difficult. He turned around and lifted his left foot behind him, simultaneously falling back against the wall and trapping his foot against his thigh. Even though his hamstrings cramped up from the unnatural position, it was an easy matter of reaching back for his ankle with his bound hands. He managed to hook the handle of his dive knife with a claw and flip it around. It took only seconds to slice through the zip tie. He immediately retrieved the box with the auto injector from its hidden pocket, opened it and grasped the cylinder in his right hand like Shasta had shown him.

The watchers responded more quickly than he'd anticipated. The door to the dungeon was just beginning to swing open when he grabbed Bryn's wrist and jabbed her in the thigh with the auto injector.

"Ow!" she exclaimed. "What was...oh, I feel funny..."

Scott let the knife clang to the floor in order to catch her as she fell. When Dillo appeared in the doorway, framed by the strange green light of Edgemere, Bryn was already on the verge of unconsciousness.

Scott held up the spent auto injector. "Now you can't torture her."

"We can still torture *you*." Dillo shrugged. He gestured to the injector. "And what is that? Knock out drug? She'll come to eventually."

Scott had known he was just buying Bryn time. He'd also realized rescue was not forthcoming. Shasta would be unaware that Alton's cover had been blown, since the yacht had taken them out of range of the hover drone before Maddy had informed them they were under suspicion. Maddy might not know who Alton was working for - yet - but it was unlikely his mission could be accomplished now.

Scott had one card left to play, but first he had to convince Maddy Singh to let him play it.

Chapter Thirty-eight

Bryn woke on a hard surface. Her mouth was open and her tongue so dry it took her a while to work up the spit to wet it again. She was intensely thirsty, and her stomach ached from hunger. She was lying on her back, and when she turned her head, the first thing she saw was a bright light pointed at a bloody, shirtless man slumped against the wall of the pipe, one arm handcuffed to a rail.

Memory flooded back. The man was Junk, but where were Scott and Jason? She sat up stiffly, glad it wasn't pitch dark anymore, until she realized the light was not directed at Junk.

"Jason!" she gasped. She attempted to get up, but dizziness overtook her, and she stumbled and fell forward onto her hands. Her elbows shook and she felt feeble as a newborn as she crawled over to him. As she got closer it was clear she was far better off than he was. His face had been battered, and by the dark streaks beneath his nose, the majority of the blood on his chin, neck and chest appeared to have come from there.

The door was closed; they were alone in the dungeon. She put one hand on his shoulder and checked the pulse in his throat with the other. This was the second time since she'd met him that she was grateful to feel the fluttery rhythm of his heartbeat under her fingertips.

"Jason, can you hear me?"

Both of his eyes were bruised and swollen, but he opened them somewhat and said weakly, "Yeah."

She almost asked, "Are you okay?" but didn't, because it was obvious he wasn't.

"Where's Scott?"

"Gone."

Her heart skipped a beat. "What do you mean?"

"Made a deal with the devil."

Chapter Thirty-nine

The truck Maddy had given him couldn't possibly be emissions compliant. It was parked outside of Edgemere's underground mall in the middle of a thick copse of holly bushes that had grown to the size of trees. It took Scott several tries to start the piece of junk, and when the engine finally turned over, a cloud of blue smoke shot out the exhaust pipe. When he got out onto the road, he hoped he wouldn't get pulled over for a pollution violation.

It had been easier than he expected to convince Maddy to let him go. He'd explained that he had a contact in Fournier's organization and that he could convince that contact, with force if necessary, to tell him where Fournier was.

"And what is this contact's name?" Maddy had asked.

"Padme."

Maddy had shifted her gaze to Alton. "The same Padme who sent Bryn that lovely dose of pleasure last night?"

Scott scowled. So he'd been right. Padme *had* waited until Bryn and Alton were bunked down together before activating her nanoneurons.

Alton had the grace to look uncomfortable, but Maddy saw Scott's reaction and seemed to be enjoying herself. He wondered how she knew about Padme but realized it didn't matter. There were other, more important things for him to focus on.

Now driving the beat-up old truck, he headed straight for the blood donation center, determined that every aspect of his plan would fall into place. Bryn's life was hanging in the balance.

"If I even *think* you're contemplating double-crossing me," Maddy had said, "I will kill her. If the feds so much as sniff downwind of us, she'll be the first to go."

To further ensure his compliance, she'd had her holo techs wire him. They'd confiscated his earbug and bulletproof aqua vest and taped a long-range listening device to his chest. It not only transmitted his voice and the voices of those nearby, but it recorded his heartbeat, so if he removed it, they'd know instantly.

"I go where you go," Maddy had said, in an eerie echo of what the com techs said to him yesterday before the Lupus op.

He got lucky and found a parking space in front of the blood bank building, but right away he realized something was wrong. A sign was taped to the glass of the main door. It said, 'Closed indefinitely for FDA violations.'

He looked up at the corner of the building, but the camera he'd contacted Padme with was gone. He took a deep breath and let it out slowly, mentally backpedaling. So far, no good on the first leg of his plan to save Bryn. Time to institute the much less desirable back-up plan.

He was reaching for the ignition when someone rapped on the passenger's side window. He turned, expecting for some reason to see Padme, but it was Mia. Her hair was pulled back in her customary loose bun and her cheeks were pink from the cold. Her breath left condensation on the dirty glass as she lifted a hand and mimed rolling down the window.

The truck didn't have automatic windows, so he leaned over to roll down it down manually.

"I had a feeling you'd come back here today..." she trailed off after getting a good look at his face. "What happened to your *eye*?"

"Nothing. It's fine."

He wanted to ask her if the CDC or XIA shut the blood donation center down but was conscious that Maddy was listening. The Mad Eye queen still didn't know for sure who Scott worked for, and he'd prefer to keep it that way.

"Fine? It looks horrible. Have you seen a doctor?"

"Yeah, I was just headed there now." He reached for the ignition again.

"Oh, no you don't!" Before he could stop her, she opened the door and jumped in. "No more disappearing acts. The world's gone nuts and you're never around when I need you."

Scott wanted to get her out of the truck, but found himself asking, "What's happening?"

"What's happening?" She looked at him like he'd lost his mind. "Coney Island? The riots? The fires? It's a war zone. Where've you been?"

In the middle of it, he thought. But he said, "Busy."

"Well, last I heard, they called out the National Guard. And things are only going to get worse."

"How's that?"

"That news reporter who did the piece on the typhoid? She got fired and isn't too happy about it. She's been screaming conspiracy theory to anyone who'll listen. Saying the typhoid is killing off non-xenos."

He started to respond, but the harsh sound of screeching brakes interrupted him. He turned to look out the driver's side window and saw that a black Hummer had stopped in the street so close to the truck he wouldn't have been able to open the door more than a few inches. He couldn't see through the Hummer's tinted windows, but he heard a car door slam as someone got out on the far side. In his rear-view mirror, he saw two dark-clothed figures appear at the back of the truck.

They'd followed him.

He reached for his weapon before he remembered he didn't have one. Mia's door opened abruptly, and a semi-automatic rifle was thrust past her into Scott's face. The second man reached in and grabbed her arm, pulling her roughly from her seat.

She took a breath to scream, but the man clasped a hand to her mouth and dragged her away. Scott expected a bullet to his head, but the gun-wielding man didn't fire. He backed away and ran around to the Hummer. Seconds later, the Hummer - and Mia - was gone. No way Scott could catch them in this ancient truck.

He bent his head towards the microphone hidden under his jacket and shirt. "Maddy," he said, trying to keep his voice even; trying not to let his fury show. "That was *not* Padme."

It hadn't been part of Scott's plan for Maddy's soldiers to kidnap Padme, but obviously it had been Maddy's intention all along. She clearly didn't trust him to get Padme to talk and thought her methods would be more effective.

"The woman your moronic soldiers just snatched is named Mia Padilla and she's completely innocent. She's a doctor, not an XBestia, not even a xeno. Please let her go."

He stopped talking, knowing that Maddy had heard him but had no way to respond back. He sighed. "I'm going now to talk to Padme, the *real* Padme, to lure her out. If your soldiers show up again, I guarantee I'll fail. Let me keep my end of the bargain."

He only hoped it wasn't already too late.

Chapter Forty

Not long after Bryn came to, the door to the dungeon opened, a woman was thrust inside, and the door slammed shut again.

The woman was a petite Asian with long black, tied-back hair, very pretty and very upset. She'd fallen to her hands and knees but sprang back up and flung herself at the door, screaming in another language. She threw a full-blown fit, banging on the door with her fists and kicking at it with her boots. When it became obvious that her anger had no effect on her captors, she turned to Bryn and Jason, breathing hard and still ready to fight.

"Where am I?" she demanded.

"Edgemere," Bryn replied.

The woman looked wildly around the interior of the dungeon before reaching up with both hands to push her disarrayed hair out of her eyes. She focused on Jason then, on the handcuffs and the blood.

"Who are you?" she asked.

"I'm Bryn and this is-"

"Jason," he said.

Bryn glanced down at him, startled that he'd given his real name. She wondered if it meant Maddy knew who he really was - if she'd tortured it out of him when Bryn was unconscious. He hadn't wanted to talk since she'd awakened, but she'd taken that to mean they still needed to watch what they said. It was possible they'd already beaten it out of him, though; that all the secrets were now out in the open.

Jason was staring at the woman. "Why are you here?" he asked.

"Good question." She turned back to the door, kicked it again, and shouted, *"Why am I here?"*

To everyone's surprise, the door opened. Dillo stood on the threshold. In his right hand, he held an expandable black baton with two metal electrodes protruding from the end. He slapped the narrow end of the baton into his left palm and asked, "Do you know what this is?"

152

The woman lifted her chin in defiance but took a step back.

"That's right," Dillo said. "It's a couple thousand volts of *shut the hell up*."

"Dillo!" Maddy's voice was like a chastising mother's. "I'm sure our guest realizes she'd be better off cooperating with us. No need to threaten."

Dillo's upper lip twitched, but he stepped aside. Maddy had changed her outfit and was now decked out all in black: tights, high-heeled boots, and a long, sequined sweater with a cowl neckline. She took a few steps inside and stopped, biting her lip and looking the woman up and down.

"Mia, isn't it? You are *so* cute." She wiggled her fingers near her head. "Even with your hair all disheveled like that."

"What do you want with me?"

Maddy made an exaggeratedly contrite face. "You are here...by mistake. Well, sort of. Actually, we thought you were someone else when we...oh, I'm trying and failing to think of a euphemism for kidnapped...but anyway, after Scott so helpfully pointed out you were a doctor, I thought, we've already got her, why not keep her? As it happens, we could use a doctor."

Bryn had never heard Scott mention anyone named Mia before, doctor or otherwise. The entire scenario was confusing, and from the look on Mia's face, she didn't understand it either.

Mia looked down at Jason. "It seems to me you wouldn't need a doctor if you didn't treat people like animals."

Maddy laughed. "Oh, not for *him*! He can rot in his own filth. No, we have rather a lot of sick people that need attending to, but you see, it's not your run-of-the-mill illness. I had my techs check you out - Dr. Mia Padilla of the Centers for Disease Control - and I thought, who better? Since you're from the main office in Georgia, I'm guessing the CDC sent you here in the first place to investigate whatever is killing my people. Am I right?"

Mia wrapped her arms around herself as if she were trying to contain her wits. She looked at Bryn's quills, Maddy's eye and Dillo's shoulders. Jason's back, with its Gila monster xenograft, was facing away from her, but her eyes lingered on the tattoos covering his arms. After a moment, she said, "Edgemere...is this a community of xenofreaks?"

"We prefer the politically correct term 'xeno,'" Maddy said. "But, yes, we are an alternate living facility - a sort of commune, if you will. The xenos among us aren't sick, though. It's their children, and the elderly who've never been grafted. We've already lost several people."

"They died? At what hospital?"

Maddy shook her head. "No hospital."

153

"What morgue?"

"No morgue."

Mia's eyes widened. "I see. We believe this disease is spread by a carrier; one person who had contact with each of those who contracted it. Would it be possible to identify that person?"

"He's been identified and dealt with."

Bryn watched Mia's face, sympathetic to what she must be feeling. It wasn't easy for a normal person to assimilate all that was Edgemere. Bryn had gone through the same gamut of emotions when she'd been kidnapped by the XBestia, and the lawlessness and brutality of xenofreak society still had the power to shock her.

"I'll look at your sick," Mia said, "but not because you're threatening me. I'm a doctor; I can't walk away from someone who needs help. But that also means I can't walk away from this man." She gestured to Jason. "Let me help him first."

Maddy shot Jason a withering look but said, "Done. What do you need?"

Chapter Forty-one

When Mia told Scott that Coney Island was a war zone, she wasn't exaggerating. The chaos had spilled over into every neighborhood on the peninsula and authorities had responded by blocking off access to the general public. Police and military presence was everywhere. The streets leading into Coney Island and Brighton beach were blockaded by soldiers. The subway to Coney Island had collapsed after Hurricane Poppy, but the one to Brighton Beach, which normally ran on a limited schedule, had been shut down. People were being allowed out, but not in.

Scott parked the old truck on a side street two blocks from the nearest barricade. He found an all-purpose wrench in the glove compartment and popped the hood. After disconnecting the grimy battery, he wrestled it out and tucked the heavy block under one arm. Then he started walking. Using the thick smoke in the area as a screen, he traversed alleyways, climbed fences into backyards, and somehow managed to avoid the soldiers.

Dodging the roving gangs of xenofreaks was another story. The first group he encountered was a threesome, teenage thugs hopped up on testosterone and reveling in the mob mentality. They didn't see him coming down the alley because they were too busy harassing a family of four; a man, woman and two children, who, from the packs on their backs, appeared to be fleeing from the violence.

The father had a shotgun pointed at the trio. His wife and kids were backed up against the brick building behind him.

One of the xenos laughed and said, "I think Daddy woulda shot us by now if he had the guts."

"I think Daddy woulda shot us by now if he had enough *bullets*!" another said.

The third xeno, a beefy, acne-pocked brute with a shaved, tattooed head and what looked to be bat wings sticking out above his ears, lunged forward in a feint designed to intimidate. The entire family flinched away, but the father said in a thick Russian accent, "I vill shoot!"

Scott didn't particularly want to get involved, but even if he didn't have to pass by on his way through the alley, his sense of fair play wouldn't let him abandon the family to whatever the xenos had in mind.

He deliberately set the battery down and scuffed his shoe against the tarmac. When the xenos turned to look, he waved casually. "Hey."

Bat Boy, who appeared to be their leader, asked belligerently, "What do you want? Can't you see we're busy?"

Scott spread his legs in a challenging stance and held his arms out slightly from his body, elbows straight and claws extended.

"I'm in a bit of a hurry," he said, lifting one hand and gesturing them over with a coolly assertive twist of the wrist.

Bat Boy laughed. "You wanna take *us* on?"

The other two xenos exchanged uneasy looks but abandoned their quarry to follow Bat Boy as he advanced on Scott. As they got closer, Scott assessed their potential skills. Of the three, Bat Boy was clearly the biggest threat, but his bulk was mostly fat. He stomped as he walked, shifting his weight from foot to foot in a near waddle. Scott doubted he was fast, and his arms were on the short side, so his reach would be limited. He struck Scott as the kind of bully whose fearsome appearance got him what he wanted without having to put much effort into it.

The other two flanked him; his toadying wingmen. Both were the kind of skinny that could mean they were typical teens with abysmal eating habits, but in this neighborhood probably meant they were tweakers. They'd be more likely to fight dirty, if at all, while their leader would come at him like a tank.

Sure enough, as soon as Bat Boy got close enough, he took a swing that Scott easily sidestepped. Scott didn't wait for a second swing; just danced in close and jerked his knee up, connecting solidly with Bat Boy's groin. The xeno doubled over with a groan and Scott shoved him to the ground. Before the other two could react, he stepped on Bat Boy's throat and held his hand out to them, claws prominently displayed. "Next throat gets ripped out."

Bat Boy's friends decided to run.

Scott lifted his foot and stepped over the prone xeno, ignoring his choking gasps. To his surprise, the family hadn't moved from where the xenos had cornered them. He pointed back down the alley to the fence that opened onto a field. "Head that way and you'll run into some soldiers who can get you out."

156

The father shook his head. "Ve can't."

Scott didn't ask why, he just assumed they were illegals. "Well, head that way anyway. You'll be safer from looters closer to the soldiers."

The woman said something sternly in Russian to her husband, gesturing emphatically to the two frightened children and then pointing in the direction Scott had advised them to go. After she finished bawling him out, she turned to Scott and said, "Thank you for helping us."

"My pleasure." He picked up his battery and walked to the street end of the alley, glancing back in time to see the parents kick out at the fallen xeno in passing.

The second group of xenofreaks he encountered were loosely gathered on the boardwalk not far from Bluto's. They seemed disinterested in him until he tried to walk past them towards his goal - the building he and Boardman had broken into the previous night. Then a dark-skinned man with a big belly called out, "Ain't nobody gonna loot dis here property, Mistah."

Scott changed course until he got close enough to see the man's face. It was Phaco, the manager of Bluto's, with his huge, protruding lower canine teeth, courtesy of his warthog donor. Last time Scott had seen him, they hadn't exactly met on good terms, but Phaco was standing there like a walking, talking barrier that he would have to breach.

"I'm not going to Bluto's," Scott said.

"Is dat Cougar? Your face don' look so pretty. Where you been?" Phaco eyed the battery under Scott's arm.

"Laying low." Scott was conscious of the microphone under his clothes, conscious that Bryn's time was short. He wished he'd been able to contact Shasta to verify that the UAAV had made it out of the area, but couldn't while Maddy was listening. He didn't see the vehicle anywhere, and fervently hoped it wasn't because it was stranded and camouflaged again. Lo had been hit, but she'd had her vest on. The most likely scenario was that she'd recovered and driven the UAAV to safety.

Padme had to know by now that Lupus had been taken by the XIA. She'd seen and heard enough this morning to figure out that Scott had double-crossed her, which would have been confirmed when Lupus didn't return to their hideout. But there was an excellent chance that Phaco didn't know anything. Padme would play dumb with Fournier, erasing any evidence of what had happened to Lupus so her part in it wouldn't be discovered. And the XIA wouldn't put Lupus in the system where just anyone could find out he'd been arrested - no, he'd be underground somewhere by now, guarded very carefully. Fournier would eventually come to the obvious conclusion that Lupus had been killed in the fighting.

"Look," Scott said to Phaco, holding his free hand out in a placating gesture. "Lupus sent me to get something out of the building behind Bluto's. He had to ditch it when the Mad Eyes showed up last night."

Phaco's tiny, pig-like eyes squinted in distrust until all Scott could see was flesh. "What is it?"

According to Padme, Lupus had met with Phaco last night to 'conduct business.' Phaco, more than anyone, would know whatever Lupus had on him - especially if he'd given it to him. Scott's only option in the face of Phaco's suspicion was to bluff. "If he wanted you to know, he would have asked you to get it for him, wouldn't he?"

Phaco laughed. "No. I ain't his gofer. 'Sides, I already know what it is. Come on, we'll see what we can find. Dere was looters in dere earlier. Lucky dey din't burn da place down."

Scott didn't want an escort, but there was nothing he could do. On the bright side, when they got there, he didn't have to attempt to break in, because Phaco pulled a set of keys out of his pocket and opened the same lock Boardman had picked. Scott tried not to dwell on how long ago that had been, and how long it had been since he'd slept.

It wasn't pitch black anymore. Sunlight came from the front of the building, brightening the gloom so that even the back hallways were navigable. Probably, the looters had broken through the boarded up front windows. The car battery that had been wired to the alarm was no longer on the floor. For that matter, the alarm was no longer mounted on the wall. Even the wire was gone. The looters had definitely been here. He hefted the battery under his arm, glad he'd decided to bring it. He started to go to the right, where they'd encountered the first camera, but Phaco said, "Nah. Dis way."

"Yeah, hold on." Scott jogged to the right anyway, rounding the corner and looking up. He'd expected the looters to take the battery, but they'd gone to the trouble of climbing up on something to get to the camera, too. Nausea struck, twisting his guts. He had only one chance left.

He rejoined Phaco and they walked down the hall. When they reached that corner, Phaco frowned at the bullet holes in the wall and ceiling. "What happened here? Dis waddn't no looters."

Scott pretended to be just as puzzled. "No bodies."

Phaco pointed at a dark stain on the carpet. "Dat look like blood to you?"

It *was* blood. Boardman's blood. Scott shrugged. "Maybe." He leaned his head around the corner and looked. No battery. No camera. No way to contact Padme.

For some reason, Carla's words came back to haunt him. "How you gonna to fix *this*, hero?"

Chapter Forty-two

As a show of good faith, Maddy not only provided Mia with medical supplies, but she gave Bryn and Jason the opportunity to use the toilet and afterward, sent food and beer. This time, Bryn wasn't at all hesitant about drinking the awful stuff - it quenched her thirst, and that's all she cared about. The resulting buzz did nothing to alleviate her anxiety, however.

She knew from what little Jason had told her that Scott was out trying to negotiate her release. The fact that his plan hinged on the cooperation of Padme did not reassure her. Padme herself had attempted to kill Bryn - why would she agree to save her now? Of course, Scott may not be planning to *tell* her that Bryn's life was on the line. Either way, she couldn't imagine what he could do or say that would get Padme to give up Fournier's location.

After they'd been escorted back from the bathroom, Mia requested that if Dillo insisted on handcuffing Jason again that he put the cuffs on his other wrist, which wasn't bruised and scored from the metal.

When the medical supplies arrived, she latched onto a box of surgical gloves like she'd discovered a long-lost friend. Bryn noticed she painstakingly pulled two pairs onto each hand. Did she think she would catch something from Jason? Maybe she'd put two and two together and come to the wrong conclusion that Jason was the carrier Maddy had told her had been 'dealt with.'

Bryn was sitting cross-legged on the floor across from Jason when Mia began her examination. She cleaned the blood from his face and chest and put butterfly bandages on a cut on his cheek and another on his bottom lip. She gently palpated his nose, speaking quietly to herself as if she was taking notes, "There's no deformity, but edema and epistaxis indicate possible nasal fracture."

"Oh, it's broken," Jason said. "I heard it go."

160

She shined a pen light into his eyes and said, "Periorbital hematoma on both eyes with no hyphema. Pupils are fine. Any loss of consciousness?"

"I don't remember. I was unconscious at the time."

"Any double vision?"

"Which one of you would like to know?"

"Headache?"

"Yes, it does."

"Confusion?"

"I'm sorry, who are you again?"

Mia let out a heavy sigh and said, "Possible concussion, definite smartassery."

She took his chin in her hand and said, "Open."

He obliged and she looked inside his mouth. "Do any of your teeth feel loose?"

He laughed a little. "I think there are one or two that *aren't* loose."

Bryn saw Mia's lips thin a little as if Jason's flippant remarks were getting on her nerves. Bryn was frankly astonished at how different he seemed, almost as if he was...flirting.

Mia knelt down and concentrated next on his torso, impersonally touching around his ribs. "Multiple contusions," she muttered. "Does this hurt?"

He flinched away and she said, "Rib may be fractured. You need an x-ray. Relax your abdominal muscles, please."

Jason's defined eight-pack pooched out slightly. Mia poked and prodded for a minute and asked, "Can you relax more than that?"

"No."

She said, "Hm," and then, "Will you get up and unbutton your jeans for me, please?"

He straightened up onto his knees but rattled his cuffs to remind her he only had one hand.

She said, "Right," and unbuttoned them herself. "I'm just going to pull them down past your hips to get a better look at this bruise, okay?"

He glanced over at Bryn, brows knitted in chagrin. Maybe it was the effects of the beer that made her smile back and deliberately not look away. She hadn't enjoyed much in the last few days, but Jason's discomfort was coming close.

Mia pulled down the zipper and let his pants sag to the floor.

"I'm not taking off my drawers," he said.

Mia seemed to be concentrating on a bruise that extended down under the waistband of his 'drawers,' a pair of navy-blue boxer briefs.

"Okay," she said. "If you won't let me examine you, can you at least tell me if the beating extended," she shrugged slightly, "below the belt?"

Jason's face went stony. "Would you be able to do anything for me if it had?"

Mia appeared taken aback for a moment, but admitted, "Not here."

"You know they're just going to start in on me again once you're done, right?" he asked.

"Why are they doing this?"

"I pissed 'em off."

"Are you the carrier?"

"If I were, you'd be infected by now, wouldn't you?"

"It's typhoid. It's *not* air-borne." Something in her tone made it sound to Bryn like she was trying to convince herself.

Jason pulled his pants up and yanked on the zipper with his one free hand. "Well, either way, it's your lucky day. It wasn't me."

She blinked and looked away. Bryn knew relief when she saw it. Possibly to cover her reaction, Mia said, "Turn around, please."

With his left arm handcuffed to the rail he could only turn so far, so Mia got up and walked around him. She was short; even on his knees his head came up almost to her chest. Bryn knew the moment she caught sight of his xenograft because even in profile, her face froze in what Bryn could only describe as horror.

"Is that a - a-?"

"Gila monster?" Jason asked. "Yeah."

"Aren't they poisonous?"

"Their bite is, not their skin - but don't touch it."

From the look on her face, Bryn figured the last thing Mia wanted to do was touch it, rubber gloves or not.

"These wounds on your back - when did you get them?" she asked.

"Couple days ago."

She sighed. "This one needed stitches, but it's too late now. Looks infected. Who treated you?"

Bryn raised her hand. Mia gave her a sidelong look and said, "I assume you have no medical training?"

"I'm eighteen."

"So? I graduated college at eighteen."

Bryn couldn't help it, she burst out with, "Brag much?"

Mia's cheeks colored. "It's just a fact."

The door to the dungeon opened with an ominous squeal and Maddy and Dillo entered. Maddy addressed Mia, "All done then?"

Mia glowered at her. "Are you going to continue to torture this man?"

"Not if he tells me what I want to know."

Bryn let out a silent sigh of relief. Maddy didn't know Jason was XIA.

Not yet, anyway.

Chapter Forty-three

Scott was so overwhelmed and exhausted he felt like he was going to vomit. He hadn't slept, hadn't eaten, hadn't even had anything to drink for - *how long*? He put a hand to his head, trying to think clearly. All he knew was that Bryn was still in Maddy's dungeon - and Mia, too, probably. It was unlikely Maddy had just let her go. The only thing that had kept him going was his determination to save them.

He had no Plan C.

"You don' look so good." Phaco said. "What happen to your eye?"

"Lupus." In a round-about way it was true.

"No s'prise. So where he say dis item was s'posed ta be?"

Scott couldn't very well walk away now. He could try, but doubted he'd get far in his condition. Woodenly, he set the useless battery down, went to the closet and opened it. It was empty - the looters had taken the janitorial supplies that had been in there last time Scott had come through the tunnel. He tried to recall which corner of the back wall would open the secret door. Carla had banged on the top left corner from the other side, so he made a fist and hit the top right. The back of the closet swung silently open. He turned to Phaco, who nodded and said, "*Now* I believe you. Ain't nobody know 'bout da tunnel."

Scott went first, descending the ladder. Halfway down, Phaco closed the back of the closet, enveloping them in darkness. His voice was irritated, "You brought a big-ass car bat-ry but no flashlight?"

"Sorry. I didn't want anyone to steal my truck."

Scott heard the little 'boop' sound a holophone makes when it's activated, and a circle of blue light appeared above him. Phaco made grunting sounds with each step down the ladder and was winded by the time he got to the bottom. He swept the area with the light from the phone. "Where is it?"

Scott sighed. The jig was up. The fictional item he was supposed to retrieve wasn't about to manifest itself. There was nothing left to do but summon the energy to knock Phaco unconscious-

"Oh, dere it is," Phaco said.

To Scott's astonishment, a green pleather, zippered bank bag sat in the middle of the low-ceilinged tunnel ahead of them. Lupus really had left something behind. He ducked down and went forward to pick it up, but when he stood, he forgot about the low roof and cracked his already aching head. He leaned his shoulder against the wall and felt himself sliding down until his knee hit the ground.

"I tink Lupus did a number on you." Phaco held his hand out. "Come on. Let's git you sometin' to eat and drink. Mebbe dat fix you up."

Scott mumbled, "Thanks," and took his hand.

Fifteen minutes later, he sat on the couch in Phaco's back office. When he wasn't gulping down hot coffee, he was shoveling heaping forkfuls of scrambled eggs and hash into his mouth. When he'd finished, he belched and said, "Damn, you're a good cook."

Phaco ran a finger up and down one of his tusks. "Dat what dey tell me."

A crash sounded somewhere out in the restaurant. Phaco must have assumed some looters had gotten past the xenos outside, because he said, "Oh, no dey don't," and went out the door.

Scott wanted nothing more than to lie down on the couch and take a much-deserved nap, but that wouldn't help Bryn. He looked around the room, remembering when he'd been here before, after he and Padme had 'escaped' federal custody, and then again with Bryn, the day she'd decided to become a xenofreak.

That day, she'd shown him for the first time how strong she really was. She'd lost everything, but still had the capacity to trust. But, as recent events showed, she'd made the wrong choice in who to trust. Scott had never really earned it; had never been fully honest with her. If he had turned her away that day in this office, would she be lying unconscious in Maddy Singh's dungeon right now? Of course, by now she would have come to, would know that Scott had abandoned her to her fate - again. Were they even now torturing her to get Alton to talk?

He stood and paced to the desk. The computer was on, but was password protected. He sat in the chair and tried to log on anyway. Padme had used this computer. Maybe if he could get into it there might be a file somewhere, some clue as to how to find her. Even as he typed, he knew it was a desperate gambit that had no chance of working. He should be thinking about how to coax information out of Phaco - even if he had to use force.

He'd typed two random words without success and then entered 'Padme.' The red-lettered phrase 'incorrect password' mocked him, and then the login screen blanked out completely, probably because he'd exceeded the amount of login attempts. He stared at the black screen glumly before noticing the little blue light next to the holocam mounted above the old-fashioned 2D monitor had flickered on.

He focused on the holocam lens, instinctively asking, "Padme?"

Nothing happened. This wasn't her office. Most likely, Phaco had the holocam set up so it recorded anyone who attempted unauthorized use of his computer. Still, Scott's desperation made him say softly, "I'm sorry."

The black screen changed to a live shot of Padme sitting in front of a blank white wall. Scott's relief was profound, but he knew he had to focus on convincing her to help him - before Phaco returned.

"Hi," he said.

"You look awful."

"Thanks."

"And you lied to me." Her voice was cold.

"What do you think is worse, giving Lupus an easy death, or locking him up for the rest of his life?"

"He'll escape."

"No. He won't."

"Fournier is suspicious." Even on camera, Scott could see her left eyelid contracting in a minute nervous tic.

"He'll think Lupus was killed in the riots," he said. "But he *will* find someone to replace him."

"What is that supposed to mean?"

"You're not safe. You haven't been safe for so long you don't remember how it feels, do you?"

Her mouth worked with no words coming out.

"I can make you feel safe again," he said.

"As the wife of an XIA agent? Worrying about you constantly?"

Scott hoped his reaction didn't show on his face. He knew she was delusional about their relationship, but the depth of her self-deception shocked him. She'd so easily jumped to the conclusion that they would marry - something that had never been mentioned - never even occurred to him to lie about. The word 'love' had never even escaped his lips. It would be the most heinous of lies. Even so, for Bryn he would do anything, say anything.

"I don't have to work for the XIA. We can move across the country. I have friends in Seattle." He'd told her that once.

"That's right. You do, don't you? It's rainy there, though."

"You'll be my sunshine." It was sappy poetic garbage, but it made her eyes light up. Then, just when he was beginning to think he might have won her over, the light faded. Somehow, he knew what had crossed her mind.

"Lupus told me about the baby," he said.

Her face paled and then flushed. "Did he?"

"Do you want to keep it? Because if you do," he swallowed and prepared to tell her he would raise it as his own, but she interrupted.

"Do you think it is Lupus' child?"

Scott stared at her. He hadn't thought that, actually. At the back of his mind ever since Lupus had dropped the pregnancy bomb had been the question: whose baby was it?

She looked away at something off camera and said slowly, "The baby is a clone."

It made sense. The Lupus he knew wouldn't let pregnancy stop him from killing anyone, even if the baby was his. He was a monster, and Scott couldn't imagine him actually wanting a baby, especially not Padme's. She was his thing, his toy; he *owned* her. When Lupus found out about her feelings for Scott, he would've begun thinking of her in terms of her expiration date. The only thing Scott could think of that might hold him back from killing her was Fournier himself. Padme was important to Fournier. She'd created his nanoneuron program.

As for Padme, who feared and hated Lupus so much she'd contracted with Scott to have him killed, it seemed impossible that she would allow herself to conceive. There was always the possibility that during the four months she'd claimed Fournier had kept her prisoner, she'd had no access to birth control, but Scott didn't think that was the case. Lupus would have taken care of that.

Scott's adopted sister May had been Fournier's first attempt at cloning a human. She'd died because The Bestia Butcher had made mistakes in the cloning process, but Scott knew he'd tried again, using the same DNA - that of Bryn's mother. Nicola, the result of that second attempt, was alive and living in hiding with her 'father,' Fournier. It was logical to assume Fournier hadn't given up on his cloning experiments, but he'd need female bodies to use as incubators.

Bodies like Padme's.

167

And now she was confirming it. Still staring off into the distance, Padme said, "Fournier decided it would be the perfect punishment for losing the nanoneuron program, to make me carry it."

"Whose clone is it?"

She shook her head and finally looked into the camera. "I don't know. Someone important enough that Lupus didn't kill me when he found out I loved you."

Scott let that admission slide. He'd heard voices out in the restaurant. Trying to disguise his urgency, he said, "Come to me."

"There?"

"No." With a blinding suddenness, he remembered the wire. Everything he and Padme had just said to each other had also been heard by Maddy Singh. How could he tell Padme where to meet him without Maddy's soldiers making another kidnap attempt? As desperate as he was, he wouldn't condemn Padme to Maddy's dungeon. "Meet me where we saw each other last."

"The-"

"Shh! Someone's coming. I have to go. Phaco doesn't know I'm on his computer. Meet me!"

"Okay. I love you."

Scott looked into her brown eyes, thinking of Bryn's green ones, and said, "I love you, too."

Chapter Forty-four

Not even half an hour after Maddy took Mia away to examine the sick, she brought her back. This time, her conciliatory manner was absent. Bryn had noticed Maddy didn't like to get her hands dirty, ordering Dillo to do all the manhandling of her prisoners, but now he lurked in the doorway while Maddy stormed into the dungeon, a death grip on Mia's upper arm.

"Useless quack!" she exclaimed, propelling Mia forward until the smaller woman stumbled and fell.

Mia was a feisty one; Bryn had to give her that. She jumped to her feet and responded back with just as much heat, "They have a much better chance in a decent medical facility!"

Maddy pointed a stiffened, manicured finger in Mia's face. "I *told* you I can get anything you need."

"I *need* my freedom!"

Maddy lifted her arm like she was going to backhand her but stopped herself. Lowering her arm slowly, she took a deep breath, as if she was summoning her dignity. She tugged her spangly sweater down around her hips.

"So you refuse to help us."

"You have to help me help you. Give me the body of the carrier and let me go. An autopsy will go a long way towards confirming how this disease is spread, and then we can take measures to protect the public, including your people."

The body of the carrier? So Junk was dead. Bryn thought of Carlos and his wife, and their son Antonio. Had the boy died, too?

"Oh, I think it's a bit too late to protect my people. Now they just need saving, which according to you, can't be done."

"Your brother is doing remarkably well, as I said earlier. Of them all, he seems to be the one with the best chance."

Maddy closed her eyes. "And yet you still think giving him the xenograft had nothing to do with it?"

Mia opened her mouth and shook her head, finally saying in a near-whisper, "I don't see how."

"Just because you don't understand something, doesn't mean it isn't real."

Maddy put her hands to her face and rubbed her forehead between her eyebrows. "This has been one bloody awful day." She lowered her hands and her strange eyes drifted to Jason and hardened. "As for you, we have unfinished business, do we not?"

"No." He said it without the slightest trace of fear, as if he was calling an end to Maddy's games.

"No? So you're ready to talk? Because I'm a woman of my word, and since I promised 'Cougar' I wouldn't hurt his pet porcupine, I thought I'd see how you felt about our pretty little doctor having her fingernails pulled out...one...by...one."

Jason lifted a shoulder and looked Mia up and down. "She's not my type anyway."

"Okay," Maddy said. "That's fine. You've proven your manhood, Dragila, and your loyalty to whomever you work for. I get that. But how long do you think it will take for Bryn to break after the doctor starts screaming? I'm sure she knows who you are and will gladly tell me once the fun begins."

Bryn sat looking down at her hands, clenched tightly in her lap. Dillo stepped inside and closed the dungeon door with a finality that sent a shiver of terror down her spine. He took one step towards Mia, but Jason's voice stopped him.

"I'm surprised you haven't figured out for yourself who sent me."

Maddy let out an exasperated exhale. "It's just that there are so many organizations that want a piece of this." She ran her hands down her body. "Now stop stalling and tell me."

"Do you know what your father does with his money?" Jason asked.

"My father sent you?" A laugh escaped, sounding slightly unbalanced. "Surely you jest. He couldn't care less what I do."

"I didn't say he sent me. I asked if you knew what he does."

"He's a bloody multibillionaire. He does whatever he damn well pleases. Get to the point, if you have one."

"Are you aware of your father's influence over several key policymakers in the US?"

Maddy snorted. "I know his greatest dream is to see India surpass the United States as a global superpower, but no, I wasn't aware he'd been buying politicians, if that's what you mean. Really, that's just so tacky. They're a dime a dozen."

"He isn't just buying them. He's making them. And eliminating the competition."

"Eliminating as in killing? So? We all have our hobbies."

Jason's smile didn't reach his eyes. "Ever wonder why xeno legislation is never enacted?"

"Because the politicians you seem so fond of always tack on riders that makes the bills unacceptable?"

She said it sarcastically, but Jason was dead serious when he replied, "Exactly. And for the record, I'm not fond of *those* politicians. They're the problem."

"Uh-huh. I see where you're going with this. You'd like me to believe that my father is some kind of behind-the-scenes manipulator, wreaking havoc on America's political system - as if it needed any help imploding on itself."

"You know your father. Is it so hard for you to believe?"

"Oh, no, not at all. It actually makes perfect sense. If there really was a New World Order out there, my father would be in on it. I'm simply trying to figure out why you're here. I have *zero* influence over him. Munnu is the only one he cared about. As I mentioned previously, he doesn't exactly approve of my lifestyle. And trust me, as soon as he's notified that Munnu's body has been discovered I'll have less than zero influence. I will, in fact, be disinherited when he realizes I fooled him into thinking Munnu was still alive. But if you're trying to convince me to use that nonexistent influence based on the fact that xeno augmentation isn't regulated, I'm afraid you're barking up the wrong skirt. Why would I want it to be regulated?"

"The question should be: why doesn't your father? But that wasn't my bargaining chip. I was hoping to strike a deal."

Maddy eyed him skeptically. "You don't look like you've got much to bring to the table at the moment."

"What if I can stop the FBI from telling him about the real Munnu's death?"

"I'm sure they've already done so." But she didn't sound sure to Bryn at all.

Jason shook his head slowly. "I contacted my handler before the attack this morning and asked her to put a stop on it. Your father does not know. After you told me you had a good reason for substituting your

171

younger brother for the real Munnu, it occurred to me that your twin was the only thing keeping you in your father's good graces, wasn't he? I can ensure that you don't get disinherited and that your monthly allowance from your father doesn't stop."

For the first time since Bryn met her, Maddy had nothing to say. She stared at Jason until he said, "Have we got a deal?"

"What do you want in return?"

"Information."

Maddy's head went back. "About my father? I'm not exactly welcome in his little circle of cronies."

Jason smiled and repeated, "Have we got a deal?"

"Sure." Maddy crossed her arms and turned to Mia. "But the deal's off if *she* can't keep my brother alive."

Chapter Forty-five

Reenergized, Scott jumped up from the desk chair and rushed over to lock the office door, which might slow Phaco down a bit if he decided to follow him. He grabbed the green bank bag from the couch, tucked it into one of the big side-pockets of his pants, and ducked into the closet. He made his way back through the tunnel and retrieved his battery. On the way to the truck, he didn't let anything or anyone distract him.

Just before he started the ancient vehicle, he said, "Don't hurt them, Maddy. I've almost got what you want."

He had to stop at a gas station to fill the tank of the gas guzzler Maddy had so generously allowed him to use. Luckily, the green bank bag was filled with cash, about a hundred thousand dollars in one hundred-dollar bills. The cashier said, "What happened to you, man?" and he responded, "Got clocked with a line drive at a baseball game."

The cashier didn't seem convinced, especially after seeing Scott's xenoalterations, and made a point of carefully checking the two bills Scott handed him. Some years ago, it had been predicted that cash and checks would become a thing of the past with the advent of internet banking, but that hadn't happened. Too many people distrusted electronic methods of payment, but this guy seemed to distrust large bills, even though with inflation, they'd become more common than ever. He finally accepted the cash and gave Scott his change, eight bucks, which Scott used to buy a candy bar and an energy drink.

With traffic, it took well over two hours to get to the blood bank, but this time there was no parking to be had. He drove around for ten minutes before pulling a ticket at a paid parking structure four blocks away. After reaching the street, he jogged the whole way, even though the resulting raise in heart rate made his head feel like it was going to explode.

It was still light out, but the diner across from the blood bank building was hopping with the dinner crowd. Scott turned into the alley where he'd last spoken to Padme, and to his immense relief, she was there. He didn't have to fake the look of happiness he knew was all over his face. His plan had gone awry in so many ways, but here she was. Bryn was as good as free if he could convince Padme to tell him where Fournier was.

It was a big if, but he was confident he could do it. He *had* to.

"Hi," he said. "How long have you been waiting?"

"Half an hour. I was afraid you weren't coming." She tilted her head to the side and reached up to place cold fingertips against his forehead near the injured eye.

"Did you walk?" he asked, to forestall her questions.

She nodded and took her hand away. She was wearing the same oversized parka as the last time, her face dwarfed by the fur-lined hood. "I don't have a car. Was that you in that horrible truck that went by I think four times?"

He laughed. "Yeah. It's just a temporary ride."

"What is it you say in America? Nuts and bolts?"

"Bucket of bolts."

"Yes. Not inconspicuous."

"It'll get us out of the city."

She looked behind her as if she expected to find Lupus on her heels. "I can't believe I'm doing this."

"We'll be fine." He started to tell her about the money, reached down into his pocket with the intention of showing her the bank bag, when he heard her gasp. One look at her face and he spun around. The same two xenos who'd snatched Mia from the truck were coming down the alley. Double-parked in the street behind them was the black Hummer.

Padme let out a cry of despair and ran to the far end of the alley, where she was brought up short by a chain link fence that had barbed wire strung across the top.

Scott just stood there. How had Maddy known he would come back here? Unless...he looked down at his chest, where the wire was taped under his clothing. He closed his good eye briefly as the realization hit him. It wasn't just a microphone - it was also a tracking device. They hadn't followed him the first time, they'd simply tracked him. He was so exhausted he was making bad decisions, but he couldn't very well take the time to rest now.

He reached under his shirt and ripped off the tape holding the wire to his chest. Pinching the tiny microphone between his fingers, he said, "If you hurt one quill on Bryn's head, I *will* hunt you down." Then he tossed the wire into the nearby Dumpster and watched them come.

174

Neither of the advancing men was carrying a weapon this time. Maybe they were trying to keep a low profile since the diner across the street was so crowded, or perhaps they just figured he was a pushover since he hadn't resisted when they took Mia. He stepped out of their way and they both grinned in his direction as if he was in collusion with them.

"That's right," he said under his breath, arms by his sides where they couldn't see him flexing his claws. "I'm no threat..."

As soon as the first man passed by and was focused on cornering Padme, Scott took a sudden step forward and threw a swift, left-handed punch to the second guy's temple. It was the first time he'd ever deliberately aimed for the one location on the head most likely to kill, but he knew with a certainty that his decision to fight made this a kill-or-be-killed situation. Just because these jokers weren't waving their guns around now didn't mean they weren't armed.

His punch didn't knock the guy out as intended, but it did knock him down and stun him, giving Scott the perfect opportunity to bend down, yank up the guy's shirt and grab the weapon tucked in his waistband. The first guy turned to see what had happened and immediately fumbled for his own gun. Scott beat him to the draw.

He straightened up and held the gun, not as steadily as he would have liked, a few inches from the first guy's face, but had to back off to keep the fallen man in his limited field of vision. At the back of the alley, he could see Padme suspended halfway up the fence.

"Padme!" he called. "Let's go!"

As she dropped to the ground, Scott took the first guy's gun off him and then politely advised the two men to get into the Dumpster. Padme began to run over, but she stopped short and screamed, "*Scott, look out!*"

The shots rang out one after the other, four in all, each striking him in the back. He just had time to think, *The driver of the Hummer*, before he lost the ability to think at all.

Chapter Forty-six

The minutes ticked by slowly, not that Bryn had any idea what time it was. Maddy had ordered Dillo to remove Jason's handcuffs, and three sleeping mats had been brought in, complete with scratchy but warm wool blankets. Mia had gone back out with Maddy to hold vigil over Munnu, or whatever his real name was. Jason had wrapped himself up in two of the blankets like a burrito, lying down in a corner of the dungeon away from the bright light so he could sleep. Bryn, probably because she'd been unconscious for the greater part of the morning, was unable to do the same.

She paced for a while, feeling the floor shift slightly as the biopolycrete pipe rocked back and forth with her movements, but finally sat, trapped with her own thoughts.

More than once in the last few days she'd wondered why the XIA didn't just clean out the anthill that was Edgemere. Only when Jason had admitted to contacting his handler, whom she knew to be Shasta, did she figure out what 'stay the course' must have meant, and why Edgemere was tolerated. When he'd first appeared in Shasta's office, Jason was disgruntled about being pulled from his op to babysit her. Then Antonovich had attacked and Jason recognized Munnu's body. Had he ever really believed that someone else in the FBI was involved? Or had he exploited the situation to get into Maddy's good graces?

Whatever his motivation for bringing her to Edgemere, it was clear he'd since been working towards his, and the XIA's, goal, which was to get information on Maddy's father. And now it all hinged on Scott's doctor friend being able to pull Munnu through. She was concerned about her own safety if Munnu died, but not overly so. Jason had put Maddy on notice that he'd contacted Shasta. If Maddy killed them, there would be repercussions.

Probably.

Bryn wondered how much of Jason's motivation Scott had been aware of. Not much, at first anyway, if his reaction in Shasta's office had been genuine. He'd asked, "Why not me?" when Shasta had assigned Jason to the job. Plus, he'd pegged Jason as a Mad Eye, but hadn't seemed to know much else about him, or the op he'd been pulled from.

Things would have gone differently if Scott had been assigned to protect her. She thought about the cozy apartment in the silo and liked to think it would have gone *much* differently, at least until Antonovich showed up. Still, she knew that was just a fantasy. Maybe the reason she'd been so confused about her feelings lately was because she'd been slowly coming around to the realization that Scott didn't want *them* to be together. And as much as she'd come to care for him, she had too much self-esteem to keep making herself available to a brick wall. If only she could flip a switch and turn those feelings off.

It might help if she could stop thinking about him, but she was just wondering where he was when the door to the dungeon opened yet again. She expected it to be Maddy with news about Munnu, but was shocked to the core when Padme was escorted in by Dillo. He said, "You girls play nice, hear?" and left.

The moment her surprise faded, Bryn got to her feet and advanced on the smaller woman. Padme took one look at her livid face and began backing away, which only gave Bryn more confidence. She'd never been one to advocate violence, but there were some situations that more than warranted it.

"What are you afraid of, Padme? That I'm going to squeeze a little payback from your skinny little neck?"

Padme folded her hands over her abdomen and said quickly, "I'm pregnant."

As Padme intended, her words stopped Bryn cold - and also sent a cold wave of dread running through her.

Pregnant? With whose child?

As if anticipating Bryn's reaction, Padme added slyly, "And it's not Lupus' either."

I'm being played, Bryn thought, and shrugged off the moment of indecisiveness. "Well, I'm sure he's glad he dodged *that* bullet. And don't try to tell me it's Scott's. You're not going to manipulate me."

"It isn't Scott's, but he didn't care. He was trying to save me. We were going to leave together until-" her breath hitched in her throat and she looked around the dungeon like an animal caught in a trap.

Padme's large brown eyes shone with tears, *actual* tears, not the crocodile kind Bryn would have expected from her. Inwardly, Bryn cursed herself for being a softie. She wanted nothing more than to disabuse Padme of the notion that Scott was really her knight in shining armor, but the words wouldn't form. She knew what it felt like to be used. She glanced over at Jason, who'd awakened and was sitting there impassively watching.

She sniffed and crossed her arms, asking Padme, "Where is he?"

The tears in Padme's eyes spilled over as she shook her head, lips parted and quivering. "Gone."

It occurred to Bryn that she'd said, 'didn't care' and 'was trying,' as if talking about him in the past tense. Somewhere deep inside her, Bryn already knew, but she said, "What do you mean, gone?"

In her peripheral vision, she saw Jason stand and move towards her.

"Padme?" she urged in an exaggeratedly patient tone. "What did you mean?"

"They shot him."

Bryn sucked her lower lip into her mouth, biting down to keep from screaming at her, calling her a filthy liar. She felt Jason's hands on her upper arms, but she couldn't move, couldn't breathe.

Jason asked, "Who shot him?"

"The men in the Hummer. Then they brought me here."

"He's not dead," Bryn said.

Padme's tearstained face looked haunted. "They shot him four times. In the back."

"He had a vest on," Jason said, running his hands up and down Bryn's arms. "I felt it on the beach."

Dillo's voice came from the door. "We took it off him." He looked at Bryn. "For what it's worth, I'm sorry." Then he pointed at Padme. "The Mad Eye queen would like a word with you about a certain nanoneuron program."

After he took Padme away, Bryn broke down, gasping for air as her heart compressed in her chest. Jason tried to pull her into his arms, but even if her quills would allow it, she didn't want his comfort. She shoved him away, shouting, "No! You...*no*! Scott wouldn't be - he wouldn't be...if it weren't for *you*!"

Jason put his fist to his mouth and turned away. Bryn didn't have anywhere to go. There was no place to hide from her grief. She stood there in the middle of that insane place and sobbed.

Chapter Forty-seven

A woman's voice woke him.

"His vest was gone, but he was still wearing the bullet-resistant shirt and jacket from his earlier op. Whoever did it used a small caliber weapon, fired from some distance away. All four bullets were slowed significantly, only penetrating enough to cause flesh wounds. It's the head injury - and his eyesight, actually - that has the doctor worried."

Scott's vision was blurry, but he recognized Shasta's general shape and her voice. He didn't see anyone else in the room and couldn't figure out who she was talking to. Then she turned and he saw the light from the holophone in her hand.

"Hold on," she said, leaning over and peering into his face. "Agent Harding? Are you awake?"

He wondered why she couldn't seem to tell if his eyes were open, and then realized it was because only one of his eyes was *capable* of opening. He lifted a hand and found half of his head swaddled in bandages. A tube was taped to his arm and connected to a bag on a pole.

"He's conscious. I'll call you back." Shasta closed her holophone and got right to business, snapping, "Report, agent."

"Um..." he knew he needed to tell her something but couldn't seem to recall what.

Another person came up alongside his bed on the other side. A man's voice said, "He's in no shape for you to be grilling him." A light appeared, lancing into his eye, and then the man asked, "How many fingers am I holding up?"

Scott blinked, trying to focus. "Those are fingers?"

"Alright...ma'am, I'm going to have to ask you to leave."

Ma'am? I'm no ma'am, Scott thought before it got quiet again and he drifted off. Sometime later, he woke again, and this time his first thought was for Bryn. *Was she safe?*

His vision was still blurry, and it was dark, but he knew he was in a hospital room. He'd been shot - again. And Padme had been taken. He tried to sit up but realized that was a mistake as shooting pain radiated from his back. His next move was to turn his head in search of a call button, but that, too, sparked pain.

"Hey," he called, realizing as he did it that his voice sounded weak. "Someone!"

No one responded. He lay there feeling frustrated, but it didn't last long. He sighed and let his exhaustion and whatever drugs they'd given him pull him back under.

Chapter Forty-eight

After the storm came the numbness. Bryn sat on one of the sleeping mats staring at nothing. Every once in a while, she'd think of something Scott had said or done and the tears would trail down her face. They sent in some food and actual water, but she was too wrung out to eat. Jason came over to coax her into at least drinking, so she took a few sips to get him to leave her alone.

At some point, she lay down. The mat didn't do much to alleviate the hardness of the metal flooring, and the blanket smelled like dog. She slept fitfully, longing to be home.

In what she thought of as 'morning,' but could in actuality be any time of day, the door opened and Dillo ushered Mia inside. He seemed solicitous of her, which gave Bryn hope that their ordeal was about to end, but he just left without saying a word. Mia's head drooped and she seemed to be having difficulty keeping her eyes open. She headed straight for the remaining mat and sat on it.

Jason got up and brought her a blanket, draping it over her shoulders. "How is he?"

She looked up at him, eyes eloquent. "Dead. They all are."

Bryn felt like someone had punched her. She'd convinced herself that everything would be alright, and now their last hope had been snatched away.

"How did Maddy take it?" he asked.

"Hard."

He didn't probe further, and Bryn thought, *Why bother asking anything else?* Scott was dead and they were next.

"She went to bed," Mia said. "But I heard her tell Dillo to give the order for everyone to evacuate Edgemere."

A muscle in Jason's jaw jerked.

"Does that mean what I think it means?" Bryn asked.

181

He exhaled slowly, the air passing over his clenched teeth with a slight hiss. "She's going to disappear."

Bryn closed her eyes. "And so will we."

Chapter Forty-nine

"You were very, very lucky, young man."

Scott's doctor had round cheeks, a deep cleft in his chin, and his breath smelled like bacon. Those were the things Scott noticed most, as the doc got up close and personal in order to examine his eye.

"And not just because those bullets did as little damage as they did. You should have gotten immediate medical attention for this eye, but it appears you won't lose your sight. You're not going to be pretty while it's healing, but you get to wear a cool eye patch."

What, is this guy a pediatrician?

The doc spouted more *blah blah blah*, but Scott tuned most of it out. His injuries weren't life threatening and he wouldn't be blind, end of story. There were only two things he wanted to know, and the doc could only answer one of them.

"How long 'til I'm out of here?"

"I'd like to keep you another night for observation."

"But that's not necessary? I mean, if I wanted to leave, you couldn't hold me?"

From behind the privacy curtain, he heard Shasta's voice, "You're no good to me all banged up like that, Agent Harding. Just listen to the man in the white coat."

The doc leaned in and said quietly with his bacon breath, "I'd do what that one says if I were you. She scares me."

Scott impatiently suffered through the rest of the exam. When he and Shasta were finally alone, he asked, "Where's Bryn?"

With a negative twitch of her head, she said, "Edgemere, last I heard. I had intel from Alton that his op might come together after all."

"Alton's been compromised. Maddy Singh knows he's not who he seems. He and Bryn are under house arrest. I made a deal with Maddy to get them released, but she double-crossed me. Have you heard from Mia? Uh, Dr. Padilla?"

Shasta took in his rush of words with one eyebrow raised high. "I've been leaving messages for Dr. Padilla, but she hasn't contacted me. Why? No, wait. I have urgent business to attend to regarding a certain riot that has gotten out of hand, not to mention I'm late joining Deputy Director Unger in explaining the typhoid situation to the mayor. So please update me, from the beginning and as quickly and succinctly as possible, as to how you ended up in that alley looking like a sieve."

Scott gave her the short version of events, answering her questions as she fired them at him. When he'd finished, she stared at him like he was an alien who'd offended her deeply.

"Well, congratulations, agent. I'm not often at a loss for words, but I don't think the proper words exist to describe how messed up that op was." She sighed.

Scott felt like a complete failure. "I know what you're thinking. I should have found a way to contact you."

"That would have been nice," she said with only a trace of sarcasm, "but it sounds as if Maddy Singh made sure you wouldn't risk it. I'm not certain things are as bleak as you painted them, though. I had to sell my soul to the FBI, but it's given Alton an ace in the hole; he has something Maddy desperately needs. But Dr. Padilla's involvement complicates things and the timing couldn't be worse. Half my agents are here in the hospital and most of the department is out dealing with the riots. Alton's going to have to pull it out. We don't have the manpower at the moment for a rescue attempt at Edgemere."

"They lost a lot of people at Coney Island. It wouldn't be that hard."

"Maddy's men didn't harm you when they took Mia, and I suspect they wouldn't have shot you when they took Padme if you hadn't resisted. I don't think Maddy plans to kill anyone. Assuming she knows by now Alton is a federal agent, it would be a very bad move on her part."

"She was willing to start a war just to get her hands on Lupus."

"And now she's got someone even better. Padme would certainly be more useful to us than agent Quinones."

It had never occurred to him that Shasta might have known Quinones before he became Lupus. "Have you learned anything from him?"

"No. He's not cooperating." She stood and looked at her holophone. "I have to go. Do me a favor, agent Harding. I've got too many fires to put out. Stay put and don't start any more."

Chapter Fifty

"I am not going to kill you." Maddy stood framed in the doorway of the dungeon. "But I'm afraid I can't let you go just yet."

She wore a sober black suit, and a delicate pillbox hat, draped with dramatic black netting, was perched on her white-blond hair. Dillo, always the steadfast sidekick, occupied the space to one side of her, while Padme stood somewhat further back, head held high. To Bryn, Padme looked like she belonged there, which didn't surprise her one bit. If anyone could work the situation to her benefit, it was Padme.

"Cut the crap, Maddy," Jason said. "If you're not going to kill us, then let us walk out right now."

Dillo pulled his long jacket aside and revealed a pistol resting in the holster on his hip. "Recognize this?" he asked. "I'm loving your gun. Don't make me shoot you with it."

"Boys, boys," Maddy said, before taking a breath and addressing Jason. "I wish I could let you go, Dragila, dear, but I'm going to need a head start on you since Munnu's death rather negates our deal. It's patently obvious you and - the XIA I presume? We never clarified that - were merely tolerating my existence as a means to an end, but even the XIA won't be able to overlook the little matter of my driver having to shoot that other agent. In the end, it seems prudent to move my operations somewhere less, I don't know, blatant. I just wanted to stop by and thank you for all your...contributions."

She glanced proudly back at Padme. "I think things are going to work out just fine."

Jason held his hands out. "I'm sorry about Munnu, Maddy, really I am, but come on. You hate your father. Make the deal, get payback, and you don't have to leave. Win-win, right?"

"Oh, I do have to leave, and although the XIA is certainly a factor, it's not the only reason. Fournier is going to attempt to retrieve his former

185

asset," she held a hand out behind her and Padme clasped it, "plus, my father will be furious. I have been an embarrassment to him for far too long for him to suffer my existence once he finds out what I've done."

"We can protect you from him."

Maddy laughed. "Don't be ridiculous, it doesn't suit you."

"How can you just walk away from Edgemere? You count on your people and they count on you."

Even to Bryn, Jason was beginning to sound desperate.

"You're right, they do. And I will miss them. Who do you think built this place? I did. Not just this community, but the mall itself. And then that hurricane came along and all I had left was a ruined husk. The insurance company went bankrupt rather than pay out my claim and the monthly allowance my father deigned to send me wouldn't even cover the taxes on the land, so I was forced to find other ways to supplement my income. But I did it. My mushrooms have been quite fruitful, and that's not a pun since mushrooms are a fungi. Anyway, I'll be fine on my own and my p*eople* are just as self-sufficient. They'll find somewhere else to live."

"What's left of them," Jason muttered.

"What?" she asked, indignant. "Are you insinuating that I'm at fault for the massacre at Coney Island? Because I seem to recall that somehow the XBestia knew we were coming. And a certain federal agent had just snuck away to make a phone call to his handler." She thrust her chin forward pugnaciously. "You know what? I lied. I *am* going to kill you. As soon as we leave, I plan on turning off the pilot lights to the heating system and letting the methane from the bioluminescent bacteria flood the place. You would have gone peacefully to sleep, but you had to upset me and now you know."

"Actually, methane poisoning makes you sick," Jason said.

It was clear to Bryn that he was just stalling now - saying anything he could think of to prevent Maddy from leaving, or maybe even to provoke her into doing something that would give him an advantage. Dillo must have come to the same conclusion, because he pulled Jason's gun from its holster and fired point-blank at Jason's chest.

Jason collapsed to the floor as Mia screamed.

To Bryn, it felt like déjà vu, especially when Dillo laughed heartily and said, "I love these plastic bullets."

Maddy shook her head at him. "You're incorrigible."

The door swung shut with a resounding finality.

Chapter Fifty-one

Scott ate every bite of the bland hospital breakfast, wishing there was more. The pain medication he'd been given was strong, but he was too antsy to relax and enjoy it. Despite Shasta's assurances that Maddy wouldn't hurt Bryn, and her confidence that Alton's 'ace in the hole' would give him leverage, he wasn't convinced. He was just thinking about pushing the call button and asking for more food when two figures appeared in the doorway.

"Ahoy, Matey," said Lo. She was dressed in street clothes, but Boardman, standing next to her on crutches, wore a hospital gown.

Scott put a hand up to his eye patch and grinned. "Oh, you like that? Arrr."

"Hey, Boss." Boardman lifted his fingers from the grip of his crutch. "I hear you took four bullets to my one."

"Five if you count this." Scott gestured to the eye patch.

"I could have told you he was an overachiever," Lo said.

Scott waved them in. "Come on in, have a seat. I'd offer you a beer, but..."

Boardman sat in the one side chair and Lo stood by the bed. The levity faded as she patted his knee and said, "I'm glad you're okay."

"So what happened?" Boardman asked.

Scott gave them a similar version of what he'd told Shasta. Lo and Boardman took turns dissecting the op from their points of view. Then they told him that despite the blockades, the rioting had spread upward from Coney Island to some of the worst neighborhoods in Brooklyn. Once rumor of the deadly sickness originating with xenos had spread, the tide of violence turned. There were reports of non-xeno vigilante groups attacking anyone known to have a xenograft. Entire apartment complexes in the troubled neighborhood of Brownsville had been burned to the ground.

"The mayor declared a state of emergency," Boardman said. "I can't believe you went back to Coney Island and survived."

"I can't believe I shot at another agent," Lo said, grimacing.

Boardman lifted a crutch and poked her in the thigh with it. "You had no way of knowing."

"Yeah, well, I don't feel right just leaving him at Edgemere. I sure hope Shasta's right."

A voice came from the hallway. "Is she here?"

Lo turned, and Scott leaned to one side to see past her, wincing at the pain. An elderly woman, white hair hanging forward in two braids, said, "Shasta. They told me. *This* hospital."

"You just missed her," Boardman said.

The woman came into the room uninvited. As she got closer, Scott noticed her clothes were dirty and her braids mussed as if she'd slept on them. When she pointed at him and said, "You was there. Esmie saw. Now we all got kicked out," his first instinct was to hit the call button and tell the nurse someone had escaped from the psych ward.

But Esmie, if that was this woman's name, had said someone told her Shasta was here. That kind of information wasn't given out lightly. Of course, the old woman could have simply been listening at the door and overheard Shasta's name, but he didn't think so.

"Kicked out of where?" he asked.

"Edgemere. The queen abdicated her throne."

In an obvious effort to humor her, Lo said, "Okay. We'll tell Shasta you stopped by."

Esmie shook her head. "Esmie is Shasta's eyes and ears."

Lo put her hand on Esmie's shoulder and tried to steer her towards the door, but Scott said, "Wait. Are you Shasta's informant?"

Esmie smiled toothlessly. "Yes."

He thought about what she'd said. "The queen is leaving Edgemere?"

She nodded. "No more Mad Eye."

"And everyone's gone?"

"Maybe by now."

Scott looked at Boardman and Lo, alarmed. "Why would Maddy bail if she made a deal with Alton?"

"She took Padme, right? She's probably gonna hunker down somewhere Fournier can't find her," Boardman said.

"Then where's Alton?"

"Probably hasn't checked in yet. You did have his truck," Lo said.

"Bryn would have called me the minute she was freed," Scott said, but he wasn't so sure.

"The Bryn is still in the dungeon, and Dragila, and the China doll."

"Are they alive?" Scott asked, bracing himself for the answer.

"That's what Esmie needs to tell Shasta," she said, shaking her head. "Not for long."

Chapter Fifty-two

Instead of getting up and shaking it off like he had on the yacht, Jason lay flat on his back breathing shallowly, his features twisted in agony. Whether coincidental or deliberate, Dillo had hit him almost directly over the black circular bruise left when the plastic bullet had hit him last time. Mia knelt over him and, after only slight hesitation, placed her ear against his chest.

"Can you take a deep breath?" she asked.

"Ah...don't want to."

"Try."

Bryn bit down on a thumbnail as she watched his chest rise and fall.

"Again," Mia said.

"You're not...nice," Jason said, but he took another breath.

"There's adequate breath sounds, but I'm worried your rib may have splintered and perforated the lung." She looked up at Bryn. "We need to get him to the emergency room. If his lung collapses, he could die very quickly."

Bryn said, "Were you not listening? We're not going anywhere."

She looked around the dungeon. If Edgemere had really been abandoned, then Maddy's techs were no longer watching them. To test that theory, she went over to the door and began examining it. Because of the curved sides of the pipe, it wasn't so much a door as a hole cut in the shape of a door, with the cut out piece remounted. A huge biopolycrete drainage pipe like this one had to be manufactured with thick walls, so the hole had been widened enough so the 'door' would swing outward on its one heavy-duty hinge. Still, the crack wasn't quite wide enough for Bryn to fit her fingers into. The pin side of the hinge and the door handle were on the exterior, with no hardware evident on the inside. Bryn could see the door latch in the crack but couldn't reach it.

She remembered reading about biopolycrete in grade school. After the widespread flooding caused by Poppy in 2020, much of New York's older sewage infrastructure had needed to be replaced and the relatively new, eco-friendly compound had come into fashion. While much lighter than concrete, biopolycrete was still very dense, but at the same time tougher and more flexible. Even if she had a sledgehammer, she didn't think she'd be able to break through.

And yet, the door was the only way out.

Chapter Fifty-three

After Esmie left, Lo attempted to call Shasta, but got her holomail. She put her phone away and said to Scott, "Shasta asked you not to leave the hospital, but it wasn't an order, right?"

"She said it like it would be a favor to her if I stayed put."

"So, theoretically," Boardman said, "if you were to, say, take a drive to the beach for some target practice, that wouldn't be a problem, would it?"

"Theoretically," Lo said, "*driving* would be a problem. People are evacuating. The roads in that direction are impassible."

Scott pulled the tape off his IV and slid the needle out of his vein. "We don't have time to pretend to discuss this theoretically. Are you with me?"

Lo's cheek bulged out a little as she pushed on it with her tongue. "We won't have access to the weapons room. What do you guys got at home?"

Boardman shrugged. "Two pistols, a shotgun and a crossbow."

"Mad Eyes got my gun," Scott said. "Besides, we don't have time to run all over town arming ourselves. We need a one-stop shop."

He looked around the room and saw a wide door that looked like a handicap-access bathroom and another, narrower door. "Is that a closet? Are my clothes in there?"

Lo opened the door and said, "Looks like just your pants and shoes. Shirt and jacket's probably in an evidence bag somewhere."

"Toss me the pants," Scott said.

She did, and as soon as he caught them, the weight told him the bag of money had been overlooked. He pulled it out and handed it to Lo. As he put on his pants, ignoring the pain in his back, she unzipped the bag and whistled.

192

"That'll buy us an armory," Boardman said. Scott was gratified that he didn't point out the obvious: the money should have been in an evidence bag somewhere, too.

"You know what else it'll buy?" Lo asked. "A fast way to get us in and out."

Boardman stood and reached for his crutches. "My girlfriend brought me some clothes last night. I think there's an extra shirt I can lend you."

Once the decision had been made, they came up with a plan and moved quickly. Lo drove them in her personal vehicle, a restored 1974 Mustang II. The hazy air smelled like smoke and some areas were so thick with it visibility was limited. Twice on the short drive they had to pull over for fire trucks.

Their first destination was the gun shop, owned by Bernard 'Bud' Greenberg. Boardman and Lo went up to the counter, identified themselves as federal agents and held their hands under the government-issue holoscanner so Bud could verify their identities and permits to carry. He looked at Scott, who held up his hands. "No prints."

Bud frowned, said, "That's too bad," and turned to Boardman and Lo. "What can I help you with?"

As Lo fired off a list of weapons, holsters, vests, jackets and ammo, Bud walked around the store unlocking cabinets and drawers and pulling it all out. It was obvious from Scott's input that some of the items were intended for him, but Bud didn't concern himself - and he didn't even blink when they used the cash to buy everything. He only said, "Getting pretty ugly out there, isn't it?"

Back in the car, they changed into the vests, strapped on the holsters and loaded their new weapons. Lo made one call to her friend Tad Munson, and within a surprisingly short amount of time had finagled them a helicopter. From the gun shop, they didn't have far to drive.

"You're a rock star, did you know that?" Scott asked as they got out of the car at the heliport.

"It's been said," she replied.

Munson met them on the helipad dressed in a blue coverall with a patch over the left breast that said Munson Helicopter Company. He squinted at Boardman's crutches and Scott's eye patch. Scott kept his hands in the pockets of his new jacket and noticed Boardman did, too. In the current climate of xeno paranoia, he figured it would be best to keep his alterations hidden even though as Lo's friend, Munson would know she had one.

Munson walked them to a sleek black aircraft with decorative red pinstripes and a corporate logo Scott didn't recognize.

"Just added her to the inventory last week from a company that went out of business." He patted Lo on the back and exclaimed, "Is that a - are you *packing*? Damn it, Tina, don't even bother bringing her back if she's got even one bullet hole in her. You might as well fly straight on down to Mexico."

Lo offered him a cheeky grin, "You're such a worry-wart, Tad. Have I ever let you down?"

"Multiple times! You know, you only get a limited number of favors for saving a person's life."

Scott heard a definite note of affection under Tad's blustering.

Lo handed him a wad of bills and retorted, "It doesn't count as a favor when it's this lucrative."

"Yeah...just be careful. Don't get killed or anything."

Within ten minutes, Lo had gone through her checklist, warmed up the helicopter, and eased them into the sky.

Chapter Fifty-four

The formerly bright portable light had gotten dim. Any second now Bryn expected its batteries to die completely and leave them in the dark to await their fate. She'd already partially dissected it, breaking off a chunk of its plastic housing and slipping it into the door crack to poke at the latch unsuccessfully.

Since then she'd been pacing the pipe lengthwise until Mia asked her to stop stomping past Jason's head, then she sat for a while before popping back up and pacing the width of the pipe. It only took her four steps to get from one side to the other, but after a few turns, she noticed something.

"The pipe is moving, can you feel it?"

Jason lifted himself up on his elbow, ignoring Mia's protest and said, "Yes."

Bryn looked at his bruised and swollen face and smiled. "Are you thinking what I'm thinking?"

"Only if it involves breaking the hell out of here."

She put her hands on her hips. "It does. Can you walk? Because we'll need your weight."

"Walking won't do it. We'll have to move fast."

"What are you talking about?" Mia asked.

"If we can roll the pipe," Bryn replied, "we might be able to crush the door handle on the outside."

She picked up the portable light. It was heavy. If they did manage to get the pipe to roll, she didn't want it careening around in here. She carried it to the far wall and tried to wedge one of the handles behind the railing Jason and Junk had been handcuffed to.

"No, wait," Jason said. He'd managed to get to his feet but didn't look too steady. "Hang onto that. We need all the weight we can get."

"Okay, and I think we should concentrate on this side." She gestured to the side of the pipe with the railing. "We got to hit it at the same time."

"Synchronized," Mia said. "Got it."

Bryn stood on one side of Jason and Mia on the other. She wrapped her arms around the light. "Ready? Go!"

It took them a while to get a good rhythm going, but soon they had it down, their footsteps clanging on the metal flooring. Bryn could feel the pipe moving each time they hit the wall, but it was slight, and they couldn't seem to get enough momentum going. The cinder blocks that had been pushed up against the outside edges were doing their job.

Jason was tiring rapidly, and Bryn was getting desperate. This *had* to work. If it didn't, they would die. She was scared, hungry, thirsty and had to go to the bathroom, but she mentally pushed all that aside and attacked the wall with renewed energy. "Come on! Let's move this monster!"

After a few more passes she sensed Jason had almost reached his limit. Gritting her teeth, she took three steps back, let out a wordless battle cry and leaped up onto the railing.

The pipe moved with a jerk, just enough to tell them they were on the right track. Grinning wildly, she jumped back down. Jason bent almost double and raised one of his hands. "Break please," he gasped.

He sat on one of the mats, head bent forward while Mia pressed her ear to his back to listen to his labored breathing. Bryn briefly worried that Mia would accidentally touch his xenograft, but she seemed to be avoiding it.

"Has the pain gotten worse?" Mia asked.

"I don't think that's possible," Jason replied.

Mia shot Bryn a troubled look. "I guess your torturer would be proud to hear that."

"I'm alright." He struggled to a standing position, but his head still hung forward. In a weak imitation of his usual self, he said, "Let's roll."

Bryn knew her voice lacked enthusiasm, but she said, "That's the spirit. I think we should try something different. What if we all climbed up on the railing?"

"Will it hold us?" Mia asked.

"If it doesn't, we'll come up with something else."

Jason shook his head. "I don't think I can. I could maybe slump on it."

"I'll help you," Mia said.

"You'll help me slump?"

She made a face at him.

Bryn gripped the portable light, backed off, ran forward and jumped. She lost her balance, but instead of falling, she quickly twisted around on

196

one foot, like a gymnast on a balance beam, and leaned her backside against the wall. Jason rested his right buttock on the rail and Mia helped him lift his leg up. Then Bryn held out her hand and helped Mia climb up next to her. The pipe tilted a bit, so Bryn started rocking her torso back and forth. Mia joined in.

"I think it's working," Bryn said just before she experienced a disorienting fall backwards as the pipe began to roll in earnest. They laughed and shouted, but stopped as the pipe continued to roll, and it became obvious they were about to get tossed around. The 'wall' Bryn had been leaning against soon became the floor. She tried to gain her footing, but only managed two stumbling steps before falling. Before she knew it, she was tumbling around like wet laundry in a clothes dryer. When the metal flooring came full circle, she slammed face-first into it. Then with a crunching sound, the pipe hit something that stopped its momentum. Unfortunately, instead of staying put, it began to roll in the opposite direction.

Bryn caught a glimpse of Mia scrambling for one of the mats and thought, *that's a good idea*. She didn't have time to think anything else as the pipe spun her around some more. It rolled full circle twice and then the bottom-heavy flooring asserted its influence and, after rocking a bit, the pipe settled down.

Bryn had somehow kept hold of the light throughout. She got to her feet and aimed it at Jason and Mia, who lay together in a tangle. Mia quite selflessly had wrapped the mat around Jason's head and torso.

"You guys alright?" Bryn asked.

Jason's muffled voice came from somewhere underneath Mia. "Is the door open?"

Chapter Fifty-five

Above the city, it was a clear, cold day. The westerly winds sent the smoke from multiple fires trailing out over Long Island and The Sound. Lo wore a set of headphones and kept up a steady stream of chatter with other pilots of small aircraft. Scott sat in the co-pilot's seat and stared out towards the ocean, oblivious to the scenic beauty of it. The interior of the helicopter had been well maintained and would seat a total of seven people. He hoped those seats would be full on the way back.

By the time they reached the airspace above the marina where Maddy's yacht was berthed, it was midmorning. Lo had brought them to a much lower altitude, but he couldn't tell from above whether any of the larger vessels in the marina were Maddy's. It was logical to assume she would leave via the yacht, and it would have been nice if he could determine whether she had already done so.

Then, several blocks away he spotted the top of a large, distinctly shaped black vehicle headed towards the Marina. He tapped Lo on the arm and pointed. "That's Maddy's Hummer!"

Lo slowed, dropped altitude and maneuvered the helicopter above the road. When the Hummer rounded the corner, they faced it head on. Boardman had grabbed one of the new high-powered rifles and slid the door partially open.

The Hummer stopped abruptly and sat in the middle of the road for several minutes.

"What are they doing?" Boardman asked.

"Probably discussing their options," Scott replied.

Finally, the Hummer made a wide turn on the narrow road, driving up and over someone's front lawn before speeding back the way they'd come.

"Woo!" Boardman shouted over the noise of the rotors. "That's right! Run from the big, bad helicopter!"

Staying above the telephone poles in the old neighborhood, Lo followed the Hummer back to a huge slab of concrete - the roof of the underground mall that was Edgemere. Scott noted the absence of the sheets of solar fabric that had been strung up between the rusty rebar poles the day before. They were definitely leaving if they'd removed their power source. He also noticed an area to the north of the slab that had been cleared of underbrush. The ground had about a dozen rectangular, evenly spaced mounds that resembled recently dug graves.

Maddy's driver - a man Scott would very much like to meet - swerved the Hummer off the road and headed down the slope towards the drainpipe entrance. He came to a stop and immediately the rear doors on either side opened and two men got out. From the huge shoulders on one of them, Scott knew it was Dillo. He expected them to pull out the big guns and begin shooting, but they merely ran into the drainpipe.

Then the passenger door opened and Maddy herself stepped out. She shut the door and walked away from the Hummer with her empty hands spread wide. The wind from the rotors blew her white-blond hair around her head wildly. Behind her, a smaller figure appeared.

Padme.

Chapter Fifty-six

Bryn shined the light on the door. It wasn't open, but it hung crookedly and had been forced inward. She got up, put her foot against it and shoved. The pipe rocked again.

"Is it loose?" Mia asked.

"Yeah. Can you guys provide counterbalance?"

Mia stood and said, "Ready." Jason took a bit longer to rally. He crawled to the opposite side of the pipe and said, "This is the best I can do."

Five minutes later, the door went crashing down to the ground. Bryn went out first, slowly, so Mia and Jason could stabilize the pipe against rocking. It was a frightening experience climbing over the lip. If her weight made the pipe roll again, she'd be crushed for sure.

As soon as she hit the ground, she noticed that the glowing lines and curves of the bioluminescent tubes lighting Edgemere had changed. Maddy had kept her word and broken them open. Green slime oozed down the walls and puddled everywhere. It smelled terrible.

There was no one left to smell it, however. No one but the prisoners in the dungeon. None of them felt sick, so Bryn suspected the threat of dying from methane had been dramatic posturing on Maddy's part. They probably would have died from dehydration first.

She avoided stepping in the ooze as much as possible as she searched for heavy items to use as blocks to keep the pipe from rolling again. Once Jason and Mia got out, they headed straight for the main entrance. The mushrooms that had lined that pipe were gone, of course. Even the shelves had been dismantled and removed. They had only gotten a few steps when the distinctive *whup-whup-whup* of a helicopter, amplified by the pipe into disorienting surround-sound, came from outside.

Bryn's first thought was that they were going to be rescued, but then, at the far end of the pipe, a dark vehicle suddenly appeared in a cloud of dust, blocking the light of day. Bryn exchanged an alarmed look with Jason and by unspoken agreement, they turned and went back inside, pushing a protesting Mia ahead of them. They'd just gotten themselves hidden behind a stack of abandoned crates when Dillo and one of Maddy's soldiers entered Edgemere and headed straight for the dungeon.

Jason whispered, "As soon as they get close enough to see we're not in there, we run for the exit. Understood?"

Bryn nodded. Running was their only option, even if more soldiers were right outside. She thought about Scott, how he'd been shot in the back. Tears started in her eyes. Was that going to be her end, too, as she ran for her life? She peered out from behind the crate, watching as Dillo and the soldier got further away. Her hands closed into fists as she summoned the last vestiges of her nearly exhausted willpower.

Not if I can help it.

Chapter Fifty-seven

Scott turned to Lo, "Can you set us down?"

She nodded and looked around for a suitable spot. Once they were on the ground, Scott said, "Let me see what Maddy has in mind. Cover me."

Cautiously, he got out and walked towards Maddy and Padme, at least a hundred feet away. He'd seen Dillo and the other soldier go into the drainpipe and suspected they had a bead on him, so he kept his hands where they could see them. He got maybe halfway when Padme suddenly broke away from Maddy and bolted in his direction. He turned to Boardman and Lo, both poised to shoot from inside the helicopter, and waved that it was okay.

"Scott!" Padme cried, flinging herself into his arms. He grimaced in pain, but held her as she babbled, "I thought you were dead. She showed me your bulletproof vest. How did you survive? How are you here?"

He didn't answer her questions. Now was not the time. He did ask by rote, "Are you okay?" But he'd never been worried about her safety. He'd known all along Maddy wouldn't hurt her. She was too valuable.

Unbidden, the image of the grave-like mounds came into his mind. *She's* not *dead*, he told himself.

Padme grabbed his hand and tugged on it, facing in the direction of the helicopter. "Run!"

"What?" He shook his head. "No. I need to talk to Maddy."

"No, you don't. Trust me. It's a trap!"

He pulled his hand free. "I have to."

Padme stamped her foot in the dirt and burst out with a wordless shriek of fury. "You're doing exactly what she wants you to!"

He had no doubt that was true, but it was a chance he would have to take. He walked away, deaf to Padme's continued words of warning and condemnation. When he got close enough to hear her, Maddy said, "Cougar. I'm glad to see you're alive."

"I'm sure you are. Attempted murder looks better on a rap sheet than actual murder any day."

She laughed. "Contrary to what you might think, I had no intention of killing you. My men had orders not to harm you, but to otherwise do whatever necessary to rescue Padme."

"Rescue? Seriously, that's your story?" He glanced over his shoulder. Padme was standing several feet behind him, looking crestfallen.

"Yes. Rescue. From Fournier or anyone else who wanted to use her," Maddy said, tilting her head and giving him a sober look. "She's very fragile after all she's been through."

"That we can agree on. But don't bother trying to convince me you had noble motives for 'rescuing' her. Now where's Bryn?"

She ignored his question. "From what Padme tells me, you were planning on running away together before you were shot. Her instinct was to blame me for your death, and I accepted responsibility for it. I told her I would somehow make up for it. Take care of her. Give her back her freedom."

It was obvious Maddy's words weren't directed at him. Padme was listening.

"Her freedom? In exchange for?" Scott asked.

"This is real life, Cougar. Everything comes with a price. She knows that. When we saw you in that helicopter, very much alive, she was...quite upset...thought I'd lied to her, but I honestly thought you'd been killed. So did she, having witnessed it. So I told her we'd come back here, and she could go to you." Maddy paused. "You had your chance to take her just now but chose not to. Why?"

Through gritted teeth, he snarled, "*Where's...Bryn?*"

"Bryn. For a man who's supposed to be in love with another woman, you have an uncommon concern for her. Perhaps Padme's trust in you was misplaced. A handsome, dangerous man trained in the art of deception. Hard to resist, even for someone as smart as she is."

Maddy seemed determined to provoke him into confirming he'd duped Padme, but she had to know he would never admit it. No, she was up to something else. He looked over at the entrance pipe to Edgemere. He'd assumed Dillo and the other soldier had gone inside to find better coverage than the Hummer offered them. All along he'd figured they were lying in wait for Maddy's signal. Now he realized they'd gone to get the one thing that would force his hand and turn Padme against him.

Just as he put two and two together, Bryn appeared in the opening.

Chapter Fifty-eight

As it turned out, they decided to run for it before Dillo realized they'd broken out of the dungeon. That way, if they managed to sneak out, they might get a head start on any pursuit attempt. Bryn and Mia supported Jason from either side as they quietly advanced on the exit. Jason stumbled over the lip, sending a muffled thump echoing through the pipe. Bryn threw a quick look over her shoulder, but Dillo and the other man hadn't been alerted. Inside the pipe, Jason's labored breathing sounded as loud as thunder. She found herself holding her own breath in an attempt to make up for it. Just before they reached the end, she stepped into the sunshine slanting into the pipe, squinting in the brightness. As they'd suspected, there were people just outside. She blinked and tried to focus. Were her eyes were playing tricks on her, or was that a ghost standing with Maddy and Padme on the far side of the Hummer?

She sucked in a quick breath and whispered, "*Scott,*" as a tumult of emotions overwhelmed her. Confusion, disbelief, joy.

He had a black patch over one eye, but she was certain he looked right at her before deliberately shifting his gaze back to Maddy and Padme, whose backs were to the entrance. She didn't let his apparent snub sting. Her intuition said this was his way of telling her not to call out to him.

Off in the distance, a black helicopter waited, its rotors still slowly spinning. It had to be how Scott got here. "Let's circle around to the helicopter," she whispered.

Jason only grunted. He was leaning very heavily on her now. She'd had to keep her head tilted away from him to avoid poking him with her quills, and her neck and shoulder were beginning to cramp up. It would be a challenge to get him past Maddy without alerting her, but they had to try.

She and Mia had just eased him past the lip of the pipe onto the sandy dirt when Dillo's voice came from behind. "That's far enough!"

Rumbling footfalls told her he and the other soldier were running through the pipe. Maddy spun around. Their escape was officially foiled.

"Leave me," Jason said. "Run."

Bryn swallowed back a sob. "There's no point. They'll just shoot us."

He surprised her by rousing himself enough to pull away and stand on his own. With one hand on her back and one on Mia's, he shoved them forward. "Go!"

Bryn took one hesitant step as he turned to face Dillo, but Mia said, "No," and went back to put her arms around his waist. A quick glance told Bryn Scott hadn't moved. She wondered briefly about that; *what was he waiting for*? But Dillo and the soldier had appeared in the entrance, both holding guns.

With no warning, two shots rang out, so close together they were almost simultaneous. The soldier dropped like a stone. The same ray of sunshine that had blinded her earlier highlighted a puff of fine, red mist that sprayed up from Dillo's shoulder, He, too, fell back. Shocked, Bryn spared a glance at the helicopter and for the first time noticed the gunmen.

She took a moment to close her eyes in relief. The cavalry had arrived. Then she took up her former position at Jason's side, urging him to run. It seemed as if they were going to get away, but after only a few faltering steps his legs collapsed, and she and Mia couldn't prevent him from falling.

Mia dropped to her knees and barked, "Help me turn him over!"

Between them, they rolled him onto his back. He was wheezing now; his lips tinged with blue.

"If we don't get him to a hospital *right now*," Mia said, "he's going to die."

Chapter Fifty-nine

A few seconds after Mia spoke, Dillo's voice followed. "I'm not out of the game yet, Your Majesty," he called. "I've got her in my sights. Just give the word."

Maddy sighed heavily. "Well, Cougar, it would seem we are at an impasse. Meanwhile, Dragila is apparently running out of time. We can turn this into a bloodbath if you like: your people kill me, Dillo kills Bryn. Messy. Or you can tell Padme the truth and we go our separate ways."

Scott ground his teeth together. Maddy had gone to a tremendous amount of trouble to gain Padme's complete loyalty, even risking her own safety. Her plans for the nanoneuron program must be grandiose indeed.

She'd couched it in terms of his having options, but there was only one logical course to take. Before he could respond, however, Padme spoke.

"You don't have to say it. I don't want you to say it." She looked up at him, eyes mournful. "I already know...I think I've always known who you would choose."

Part of him would never forgive her for the things she'd done, but for now, compassion won out. "I'm sorry. I wish things had been different."

She smiled tremulously at Maddy. "Things *will* be different."

Maddy smiled back. "That's my girl." Then she shouted, "Stand down, Dillo!"

"Understood," he shouted back.

"Get your people to the helicopter." Maddy was all business now. "I'll wait right here until you're gone. I trust you won't shoot me out of spite?"

"Scott would never do such a thing," Padme said. "That's why I love him."

Chapter Sixty

Mia's face was pinched with worry until she found the helicopter's medical kit. It was a large, soft-sided, zippered blue bag, and she muttered to herself as she dug through it, finally saying, "Ah-ha!" and pulling out a small green oxygen cylinder. She attached a clear plastic facemask to it and gently placed it over Jason's mouth and nose.

"Is that better?" she asked.

He took a few shallow breaths and nodded, but Bryn had the feeling he was just trying to calm her down. He was clearly in a tremendous amount of pain.

Mia turned to the pilot and asked curtly, "Where's the nearest hospital?"

"Course already laid, ETA three minutes," the slim woman replied. "But only official medical aircraft are allowed to land on the roof. I'll see if I can get emergency permission to put us down nearby and have an ambulance meet us."

"You do that," Mia said. She dug around in the medical kit some more. This time, she found a bottle of water, uncapped it and removed the oxygen mask to hold the bottle to Jason's lips.

Bryn licked her own lips, wishing there was another bottle in the bag. Scott reached into the medical kit and took out a gauze pad. He tore open the wrapper and turned to her with it, firmly wiping her cheeks and under her eyes. She thought about the black makeup she'd put on prior to her arrival at Edgemere. It must have smeared something awful the way Scott was going at it.

He looked into her eyes. "It's almost over."

She nodded. She wanted to talk, but the noise of the rotors made it difficult. Not to mention, she was having difficulty thinking straight. Thirst, hunger, exhaustion and stress hadn't exactly nourished her brain.

When Mia had coaxed Jason into drinking as much water as he would take, the bottle was still three-quarters full. She held it up to Bryn and said, "You want the rest?"

"I'll split it with you."

"No," Mia said. "I'll wait."

Bryn guzzled it down, thinking that now they were on their way back to civilization, Mia's tendency towards germophobia was reasserting itself. Although she did notice Mia hadn't bothered to search the medical kit for latex gloves and in fact, kept a comforting hand on Jason's naked arm at all times. She'd definitely formed a bond with her patient. Maybe it had something to do with attending the deathbeds of so many of Maddy's people last night. She couldn't save them but seemed determined Jason would be another story.

The pilot kept her word and got them to a field adjacent to the nearest hospital in three minutes, faster than the ambulance, as it turned out. The rotors had almost stopped spinning by the time it showed up.

"'Bout time you got here!" Mia said as the paramedics wheeled the stretcher up to the doorway.

"Lady," one of them replied, "do you have any idea how busy we are? It's a nightmare out there. Damned xenofreaks."

Scott stepped forward and said deliberately, "Here. Let me give you a hand with that."

The paramedic who'd spoken caught sight of Scott's xenoalterations and recoiled. "Jeez, you guys are everywhere."

"Mister," Mia spat, "the injured man is a federal agent. If he dies because you hesitated to treat him, I will personally see to it you never work in the medical field again. Got that?"

"Yes, ma'am," the paramedic muttered. He wisely kept his opinions to himself after that.

Mia insisted on riding in the ambulance with Jason, claiming to be his personal physician, which Bryn figured was technically true enough.

There was no fanfare for the rest of them. They had to walk. It was cold out, and the air in this part of Brooklyn was hazy and smelled of smoke. Scott introduced Boardman, who said, "Hey," and Lo, who said, "I had no idea you were *that* Bryn."

Once they entered the hospital and got in line at the front desk, Bryn asked meekly, "Do any of you have any change? I haven't eaten in...I can't remember how long."

Scott patted himself down and grimaced apologetically. "I think all I have is, um, really big bills."

Lo held out a twenty and Bryn excused herself to hit up the snack machine down the hall, but the oddest thing happened when she tried to choose something: nothing looked good. The thought of eating anything at all made her mouth water like she was going to throw up. She stared at the selection, suddenly conscious that half an hour ago she'd thought she was going to die. Had seen a man die. The soldier with Dillo had never gotten back up. Had Maddy left him there, or had they taken the time to bury him next to the graves she'd spotted when the helicopter first lifted off?

She shook herself out of her reverie when she realized she was staring at the snacks, but not seeing anything at all. Her gaze focused on the glass front, at her own reflection. It was no mirror, but she could tell she looked like hell despite Scott's ministrations. Behind her, a dark shape with looming shoulders materialized. She froze in fright and then when a hand reached out for her, uttered a little shriek and flinched away.

"Bryn! Hey."

It was Scott, of course. Not Dillo, as her imagination had conjured.

"You okay?" he asked.

She shook her head. "No. No, not really."

Chapter Sixty-one

Scott took the twenty-dollar bill out of Bryn's limp hand and put it into the machine. She had such a brittle look about her that he didn't ask what she wanted; just chose his favorites. When he opened the package of coconut cream Nom-Nom cakes and held one under her nose, a spark of interest appeared. She reached up and stuffed it into her mouth.

"Good, huh?" he asked. "My mom used to put those in my lunch every day. The preservatives keep 'em fresh for like a hundred years, but I think they add something special, don't you?"

He got her a carton of vanilla biomilk to go along with it and watched as she lustily drank half of it and then consumed the other cake.

"I like a girl who's not afraid to eat," he said, grinning.

"They starved me!" She socked him in the shoulder, and when he winced, said, "Oh, I'm sorry! You...they...was it a lie? Padme said...*did* you get shot?"

"Reports of my death have been greatly-"

He didn't finish. Couldn't, because Bryn was kissing him. He wrapped his arms around her and pulled her close, ignoring the pain in his back. She tasted like coconut and he didn't even care that her quills were poking him in the forehead. After a few minutes, she pulled away and said, "Don't ever die again, okay?"

"I'll try not to."

He was about to go in for another kiss but heard someone behind him clear their throat. Without looking, he said, "What?"

Lo responded, "Shasta's on her way."

With a deep sigh, he dropped his arms, but took Bryn's hand. "Better go pay the piper."

Chapter Sixty-two

When Shasta arrived, Bryn expected to be left alone while she debriefed her agents, but that didn't happen. Shasta commandeered an isolated section of the waiting room and included both Bryn and Mia in the conversation. Everyone was seated except Shasta, who stood in front of the five of them like she was conducting an orchestra, firing off questions and pointing at the person who should answer.

Only when a chronological depiction of events had been thoroughly laid out for her did she sit in a chair across from them, shaking her head.

"I would love to take the time to analyze every nuance here, but I can't. Not to downplay the significance of," she waved her hand in a wide, all-encompassing gesture, "everything that's happened, but there is a *major* crisis going on. I just spent the last several hours with Deputy Director Unger and the mayor in a holo conference with the Secretary of Defense. The biggest factor influencing the riots at the moment is, of course, social media. It's been flooded with inflammatory speculation about the typhoid, which we need to counter with facts as soon as possible."

Her laser gaze pinned Mia to her chair. "First and foremost, Dr. Padilla, how does this thing spread? Is it or is it not air-borne?"

"Oddly enough, my experience at Edgemere has shaken my confidence in my previous conclusions about that. However, I can't make the call with any certainty at this point. If we had the body of the carrier, I'm sure we could confirm or debunk it once and for all."

Bryn and Scott spoke at the same time. "I saw something-" and "There were mounds-"

He deferred to her, saying, "You go ahead."

"You saw it, too, didn't you? The graves?"

He nodded. "It sure looked like graves to me."

He told Shasta about spotting the disturbed earth from the helicopter.

"I saw it," Lo said. "Almost put the helicopter down there because the ground had been cleared."

"That's great news," Mia said. "I mean, not about - not because they all died, but it would be great if we can exhume Robert Cruise's body." She looked at Shasta. "How fast can I get a team out there?"

"Immediately," Shasta said, springing up out of her chair. "In fact, sooner if I have anything to say about it.

"As for you," she indicated everyone but Mia. "Go home and get some rest. That's not a suggestion. It's hitting the fan today, and tomorrow I predict we'll all be knee deep and armed with teaspoons."

"Even me?" Bryn asked.

Shasta made a faintly sardonic face. "Well, I'm not going to deputize you or anything, but yes, it would be nice if the XIA could count on your cooperation."

Bryn wasn't sure how to feel about that but nodded.

"Dr. Padilla, shall we?" Shasta asked.

"I need to check on Jason, I mean Agent Alton, first."

Shasta dipped her head in agreement. "Of course."

With Shasta gone from the vicinity, Bryn felt a distinct lightening of the atmosphere.

Boardman let out a relieved exhale, like he'd been holding his breath the entire time. "Why do I have the feeling we did exactly what she wanted us to do?"

"I know," Lo said. "I expected her to yell at us. Or at least *mention* that we went over to the rogue side."

Scott stood. "That could still happen once things settle down. In fact, you might as well just count on it. Shasta never forgets."

Chapter Sixty-three

If Scott were a writer, he'd put together a treatise on the restorative powers of a hot shower. Bryn had gone first, and while she was using up most of the hot water, he changed the sheets on his bed. Not because he anticipated using it for anything but sleeping, but because he wanted her to feel as clean as possible after all she'd been through.

It had been a simple matter of asking to get her to agree to stay with him. Getting to his apartment had been a chore all unto itself, though. First, they'd checked on Alton. His lung, as Mia had suspected, had collapsed, but his doctor said he'd be fine.

Lo had then flown them back to the helipad before driving them to the parking structure where he'd left the old truck. That polluting eyesore had turned out to belong to Alton, not to his surprise. He'd had to drop it off at headquarters to retrieve his motorcycle. Luckily, he always carried Bryn's helmet with him. They would have stopped to pick up fast food, but everything was closed as the city braced itself for more violence.

After he made the bed, he called Carla and gave her a brief, highly censored account of events. She wasn't able to bring over Bryn's car or any of her things because she didn't have a driver's license and city bus services had been temporarily suspended due to the unrest.

When Bryn, cheeks pink either from the shower or embarrassment or both, appeared in the doorway of the bathroom wrapped in a towel, he told her to help herself to anything in his dresser that fit.

He went into the bathroom and saw her dirty clothes in a pile on the floor. Her shoes were in the metal basket he used as a trash can. They had faintly glowing greenish residue on the soles and smelled like rotten eggs.

Thanks to the lukewarm, but still refreshing water, he was forced to shower quickly. He reached back and used his claws to peel off the dressings from the shallow, stitched-up gunshot wounds and rinsed away the unpleasant scent of antiseptic.

After he dressed in loose cotton pants and a t-shirt, he went out into the living room. It smelled like food.

He found her in the kitchen, wearing a baggy t-shirt and his oldest, most threadbare pair of sweatpants, devouring a bowl of ramen.

"I don't know how long that's been in the cupboard," he said.

"Well, it was the only thing *in* the cupboard, so I helped myself. I hope you don't mind."

"You can have anything you want."

She took a breath and laughed a little. "A week's worth of sleep?"

Outside, an emergency vehicle went by with siren blaring. "You can try."

Later, he lay down with her. Her quills made snuggling a challenge, but they made do.

He had something on his mind, but didn't know how to broach it; wasn't, in fact, sure he even *should* broach it. But it felt like an invisible barrier between them.

"I, um...I did something pretty lousy," he finally said, thinking about how he'd led Padme on.

She blinked at him, her green eyes sleepy. "I doubt that."

"No, really. It's about Padme."

"I heard her say she loved you. Did you sleep with her?"

"No! Did you sleep with Alton?"

"What?"

She didn't deny it, and worse; she looked away, a reflex that only made her look guilty. He suffered through a rising tide of jealousy, fighting to maintain common sense. If Bryn had slept with Alton, he told himself, it was just another sin to lay at Padme's door.

Bryn put her hand to his cheek and said, "I didn't. I wouldn't. I'm not interested in him. Please believe me."

He turned his head and kissed her palm. "Didn't Padme...?" he started to ask about the pleasure, but left it hanging.

Her eyes closed tightly for a moment. "She did, but...it ended before anything too bad could happen."

He almost pushed it, almost asked her to clarify what she meant by 'too bad,' but he realized it didn't matter.

"I'm glad."

She nodded, the movement of her head scratching her quills across the fabric of the pillowcase.

"Sorry in advance about your pillow," she said, her eyelids drooping.

"Don't you worry about no stinkin' pillow."

214

Her lips curved in a faint smile that faded as she slipped into slumber.

Very quietly, so he wouldn't disturb her, he said, "I love you."

The end.